Jake Lawrence, Third Base

(Bottom of the Ninth, Book 3)

Jean C. Joachim
Moonlight Books

ABOUT THE E-BOOK YOU HAVE PURCHASED: Your non-refundable purchase of this e-book allows you to only ONE LEGAL copy for your own personal reading on your own personal computer or device. **You do not have resell or distribution rights without the prior written permission of both the publisher and the copyright owner of this book.** This book cannot be copied in any format, sold, or otherwise transferred from your computer to another through upload to a file sharing peer to peer program, for free or for a fee, or as a prize in any contest. Such action is illegal and in violation of the U.S. Copyright Law. Distribution of this e-book, in whole or in part, online, offline, in print or in any way or any other method currently known or yet to be invented, is forbidden. If you do not want this book anymore, you must delete it from your computer.

WARNING: The unauthorized reproduction or distribution of this copyrighted work is illegal. Criminal copyright infringement, including infringement without monetary gain, is investigated by the FBI and is punishable by up to 5 years in federal prison and a fine of $250,000.

A Moonlight Books Novel
Sensual Romance
Jake Lawrence, Third Base
Bottom of the Ninth series
Copyright © 2017 Jean C. Joachim
Cover design by Dawné Dominique
Cover Photographer: Kristi Hosier - Photography
Cover Model: Eric Emerick
Edited by Sherri Good
Proofread by Renee Waring
All cover art and logo copyright © 2017 by Moonlight Books
ALL RIGHTS RESERVED: This literary work may not be reproduced or transmitted in any form or by any means, including electronic or photographic reproduction, in whole or in part, without express written permission. All characters and events in this book are fictitious. Any resemblance to actual persons living or dead is strictly coincidental.
PUBLISHER
Moonlight Books

Dedication

To great baseball players, from the Little League to the Major Leagues, who made me fall in love with the game.

Special Dedication
To the late Marilyn Reisse Lee,
my dearest friend.

Acknowledgment
Thank you for your support:
Sherri Good, my editor, Renee Waring, my proofreader, Kathleen Ball, Vicki Locey, Diana Finegold, David Joachim, Steve Joachim, and Larry Joachim.

Books by Jean C. Joachim

BOTTOM OF THE NINTH
DAN ALEXANDER, PITCHER
MATT JACKSON, CATCHER
JAKE LAWRENCE, THIRD BASEMAN
NAT OWEN, FIRST BASE (Coming)
BOBBY HERNANDEZ, SECOND BASE (Coming)
SKIP QUINCY, SHORTSTOP (Coming)

FIRST & TEN SERIES
GRIFF MONTGOMERY, QUARTERBACK
GRIFF MONTGOMERY, QUARTERBACK (EDIZIONE ITALIANA)
BUDDY CARRUTHERS, WIDE RECEIVER
PETE SEBASTIAN, COACH
DEVON DRAKE, CORNERBACK
SLY "BULLHORN" BRODSKY, OFFENSIVE LINE
AL "TRUNK" MAHONEY, DEFENSIVE LINE
HARLEY BRENNAN, RUNNING BACK
OVERTIME, THE FINAL TOUCHDOWN
A KING'S CHRISTMAS

TUFFER'S CHRISTMAS WISH (Short Story)

THE MANHATTAN DINNER CLUB
RESCUE MY HEART
SEDUCING HIS HEART
SHINE YOUR LOVE ON ME
TO LOVE OR NOT TO LOVE

HOLLYWOOD HEARTS SERIES
IF I LOVED YOU
RED CARPET ROMANCE
MEMORIES OF LOVE
MOVIE LOVERS
LOVE'S LAST CHANCE
LOVERS & LIARS
HIS LEADING LADY (Series Starter)

NOW AND FOREVER SERIES
NOW AND FOREVER 1, A LOVE STORY
NOW AND FOREVER 2, THE BOOK OF DANNY
NOW AND FOREVER 3, BLIND LOVE
NOW AND FOREVER 4, THE RENOVATED HEART
NOW AND FOREVER 5, LOVE'S JOURNEY
NOW AND FOREVER, CALLIE'S STORY (prequel)

MOONLIGHT SERIES
SUNNY DAYS, MOONLIT NIGHTS
APRIL'S KISS IN THE MOONLIGHT
UNDER THE MIDNIGHT MOON
MOONLIGHT & ROSES (prequel)

LOST & FOUND SERIES

LOVE, LOST AND FOUND
DANGEROUS LOVE, LOST AND FOUND

NEW YORK NIGHTS NOVELS

THE MARRIAGE LIST
THE LOVE LIST

THE DATING LIST
SHORT STORIES
SWEET LOVE REMEMBERED
THE SECOND-PLACE HEART (Coming)
THE HOUSE-SITTER'S CHRISTMAS

Chapter One

With a breeze ruffling his hair, and Dolly Parton blasting from the CD player, Jake Lawrence eased his foot down on the gas until his brand-new, platinum Lexus GS F sedan hit eighty. Leaving California behind, he zoomed down the Arizona highway seeking adventure.

Resurrecting a lifelong dream of driving across the country, he jumped at the chance to take delivery of his new car in Los Angeles instead of New York. He'd begged the manager of the New York Nighthawks, Cal Crawley, to let him out of spring training early for the trip.

Singing along with his favorite country music singer, he raised his voice full blast to the tune of *Here You Come Again*. The lyrics heated his blood. The third baseman's rich girlfriend, Angela Carpenter, was off to Europe for three months and he didn't give a damn. He was ready to trade her in for a newer, hotter model.

It was time he got what he needed when he needed it in the bedroom. Nope, his high society chick had made headlines in the papers but fell short on passion. And Jake Lawrence, slugger extraordinaire, was definitely a passionate man. Her society gossip and endless dress-up charity events bored him to tears. She never came to a game, either, a serious strike against her.

He stretched his shoulders, feeling unfettered. Freedom! Excitement churned in his belly as the vast road heading East would take him places he'd never been. Hell, he'd be traveling twenty-eight hundred miles and was sure to see new sites and meet some new chicks. Road trip sex? Why not? With his looks and build, he'd never had trouble picking up women.

He grinned, up for anything that came along. As long as he got home in time for practice before opening day, he was good. He and his father had mapped out a route the night before. All he needed to do was about two hundred miles a day to make it on time.

In his new car, driving for three hours each day would be a pleasure. He admired the dark red interior and ran his palm over the dashboard. He'd have to figure out all the dials and gizmos. But hey, that's what nights without a woman warming his bed were for, reading the manual.

Thinking back on the last season, he didn't mind losing out on Nighthawks MVP to Matt Jackson. After all, Jake had won it two years ago. Matt deserved it. He'd had a hell of a year and pulled it together for the team during the series.

Jake still owned the fourth slot in the batting lineup, and that's all he cared about. His dad had nicknamed him "slugger" when Jake was ten and played in Little League. He'd been a star from the get-go. Now, at twenty-nine, he was in his prime, his bat ruining the ERA's of some of the best pitchers in the league. Jake had never met the pitch he couldn't hit.

He loved the tune *Nine to Five* and when it came on, he raised his voice again. Along with baseball, Jake had studied music. His mom had wanted him to be a concert pianist. He had the hands for it but not the discipline.

When it was time to practice piano, Jake would be out swinging his bat with his father. But his mother had instilled a love of music in him. They'd go caroling at Christmas time and Jake sang in the choir until he got to high school. His tomcatting ways made his participation in church activities a bit embarrassing.

He loved to sing. Sang in the shower at home and in the locker room. The guys liked his voice and most encouraged him, when they weren't ragging on him, calling him "Opera Man", even though he didn't fancy opera.

Dan Alexander, the star pitcher, said it saved buying a radio. The third baseman loved classic country music best, The Oak Ridge Boys, Johnny Cash, Willie Nelson, and was good at imitating some of them. One year at Christmas, he found a cowboy hat hanging on his locker. No one claimed the prank, but Matt Jackson had laughed the loudest when Jake discovered it.

When the album finished, he punched up his speakerphone and dialed his father.

"How's it going?" His old man asked.

"Like a dream. Wish you were with me, Dad. This baby rides like nothing. Amazing."

"Wish I was, too, son. You've worked hard for it. Enjoy yourself, but drive careful. Not over seventy."

Jake glanced at the speedometer which read eighty-two. "I hear ya, Pop. I'll be careful."

"Good."

"Give Mom a hug for me."

"Will do. Call if you need us. Otherwise, we'll be watching you hit it out of the park on opening day."

"Love you."

"Love you, too, son."

In the tiny town of Santa Juana, right off the highway in New Mexico, Kate Mackenzie searched her laptop computer.

"It has to be here. Mom, you said you'd send it." Kate wrapped her sweater tighter around her body against the early morning chill. The heat wasn't working properly in her dumpy motel room. Giving up, she closed the machine and paced. She had to ante up another fifty bucks to stay the night in this fleabag joint. It was all she could afford, but now she didn't even have that.

She left the room and walked down the way to a large chain restaurant, Max's. She needed food. Looking left and right, she saw nothing but highway, chain restaurants, and stores. The sky was huge and blue without a cloud, but the temperature hovered at about forty-five degrees.

She rummaged through her purse until she located her wallet. No matter how many times she looked through it, she couldn't scrounge up more than three dollars and fifty-six cents. She prayed it would be enough to buy breakfast. As to her next meal, well, she'd have to figure that out. She stepped up to their front door and looked at the menu. One item under four dollars. She went in and sat at the counter.

"Coffee?" The waitress asked as she turned the cup in front of Kate right side up. The young woman put her hand over it.

"No!" She didn't have enough money for coffee. "I mean. Thank you, but just water, please."

The woman gave her a quizzical stare. Kate sensed heat in her cheeks. She'd never been this broke before and this far from home.

"What'll ya have?" The woman clicked the point down on her pen.

"Uh, these little pancake rolls?"

"How many? Six? Nine?"

Kate licked her lips. Hunger gnawed at her belly. "Only three today. That's two-fifty, right?"

"Yep. Two-fifty for three."

"Coming right up," the waitress said, scooping up the menu and looking hard at Kate.

She wondered if poverty showed, like a tattoo or a stamp on your hand when you went to a dance club. She lowered her gaze to her fingers shredding the napkin.

When the woman walked by, she stopped to pour a cup of coffee before Kate could protest.

"Comes with the pancakes," the waitress said, clearly lying.

Kate was grateful. "Thank you." She added milk and sugar, then took a sip. It tasted like heaven. Within a couple of minutes, the woman reappeared with her pancakes.

Tears stung at the backs of her eyes when she saw how small they were.

"Oh, I almost forgot. Comes with a side of rye toast, too," the waitress winked and shot her a sympathetic smile.

The server's generosity touched Kate's heart. The tears she'd been holding back burst forth. She buried her face in a napkin. The waitress put down two tiny containers of jam and patted Kate's arm.

"It's okay, honey. We've all been there." Then she went away.

Hunger trumped humiliation. She wiped her face then wolfed down the meal, including every crumb of the toast with jam. She needed all the sustenance she could get. The waitress put the check in front of her and Kate picked it up. Three dollars on the nose. She fingered the two quarters in her pocket.

She might need one to make a phone call when her cell was cut off because she hadn't paid the bill. She shrugged. Where could she find a pay phone, anyway? She dropped both quarters on the counter and took the bill to the register. The waitress smiled at her and pocketed the change. Kate smiled back.

After hitting the restroom to repair her face, she returned to the motel where she wrote out a check that most probably would bounce—if her suspicions were correct about what her mother had done with the money. Kate stuffed her few belongings in her backpack and snuck out. She'd left the check on the dresser, hoping the money her mother promised to deposit in her account would clear before it hit the bank.

Writing bad checks was against the law. The last thing she needed was to get arrested. That'd fix her career on the Broadway stage. She'd be over. The highway stretched out before her, empty and cold. She'd have to find a job waitressing for a day or two to eat. Then it would be hitchhiking to New York City, hoping she didn't get picked up by a serial killer.

It didn't take long for the desk clerk to come racing out of the motel, hollering. She looked at him and took off. But where could she go?

Next to driving his new car and sex, food placed high on Jake's list of pleasurable necessities. When he hit Santa Juana, Jake's stomach rumbled. He'd hoped he could find a little mom and pop restaurant, like there were in New York City, along his route. But he couldn't even find a downtown area.

The big sign of a popular steak house franchise caught his eye. A steak sandwich with fries would go down great right about now. He glanced at the clock on the dash. Only eleven. He wondered if they'd be serving lunch yet.

His mouth started to water as the image of a huge Philly Cheese Steak flashed through his mind. Hitting the turn signal, he stepped on the brake and pulled off the highway. His eye was snagged by a pair of perfect legs and a mighty cute butt hightailing it down the service road.

She was running at full speed not jogging, and he couldn't figure out why. After pulling into the parking lot, he got out of the car and spied a man in hot pursuit of the cute chick. He had to know what was going on. He parked the car and followed the action.

Sure enough, the man caught up to her. He was yelling. It appeared she was crying, but he couldn't tell, so he moved closer. A damsel in distress, what could be more appealing? His stomach would have to wait because he needed to make sure the girl was okay.

Sure enough, the man hit her. He slapped her across the face, then punched her in the shoulder, knocking her to the ground. Curiosity turned to anger as Jake ran over and grabbed the man's fist.

"What the hell? What are you doing?" His brows knit as he jerked the man's arm behind his back and held it there.

"This bitch owes me fifty bucks. She ran out on her bill," he said, then spat on the ground at her feet.

"Whoa! Wait a minute. You can't just go hitting people, especially not women. Look what you did. She's bleeding."

"Where? My face? Oh my God. My face. It's swelling. I can't believe this is happening."

"Your face, what do you care? You a hooker? Probably," the desk clerk said.

"No, you idiot. I'm a Broadway actress. My face is everything." She broke down in tears.

"Hey, hey, don't cry. Can't you just pay the man?"

"I would, but I don't have any money. My mother was supposed to transfer money I made doing a show, but it's not in my account."

"Why don't you call her? Maybe the transfer's going through today."

"That's what I hoped. I left a check in the motel room."

"Check. Pfui! What's that worth? Fucking piece of paper," the man said.

Jake tightened his grip until the man squirmed. "Apologize to the lady."

"Okay, okay. Sorry I hit you. Cough up what you owe me," the clerk said, grimacing in pain as Jake twisted the man's arm.

She opened her phone but didn't dial. "Phone's dead."

"Use mine," Jake said, tossing her his phone with his free hand. "And you. I should punch your lights out, but I don't want to injure my hand for an asshole like you. Here's your money.

Don't ever hit a woman again. And next time I see you do that, I will take you out. Count on it."

Jake peeled off fifty bucks and threw it on the ground. The man scooped up every dollar then shot a hostile look at Jake, who raised a fist at him. The coward jerked away, then ran back to the motel. The ballplayer turned to the young woman and handed her his handkerchief. She hit speaker on the phone so she could wipe the blood from her face.

"Ma?"

"That you, Kate?"

"Yeah. Where's the money? You were supposed to put my check for twenty-five hundred bucks in my account. Did it arrive?"

"It did. I cashed it, just like you said."

"So? Where is it? Ma, I gotta eat, buy a bus ticket and stuff."

"Well, I thought that twenty-five hundred wasn't very much. Since you're going to New York City and all..."

The woman buried her face in her hands. "You didn't, Ma. Say you didn't."

"I was only trying to help. I thought if I could double that at the track, well five grand would go a lot farther in the Big Apple."

"Ma, I needed that money."

"Hey, I was doin' great. Got it up to thirty-five hundred. Then my luck broke."

"Lost it all?"

"Sorry, babe. Hey, I gotta go. Harry's waitin' for me. We're takin' the free bus to the new casino. Wish me luck. I'll call you if I win your money back."

"You do that, Ma."

The woman clicked off the phone and handed it back to Jake, who stood staring wide-eyed.

"I'm sorry, Mister. I'm not gonna have your fifty bucks for you." She opened a side pocket in her backpack and rummaged around for something.

Jake had never heard a conversation like that before. "Your mother gambled away your money?"

The woman plucked a compact out and opened it. She nodded before gasping as she viewed her face. Fresh tears started.

"I have an audition in two weeks. Look at my face!"

He couldn't take his eyes off her. Topping off one smokin' hot body was the darkest hair he'd ever seen. Long and silky, framing peaches-and-cream skin with eyes a mixture of green and blue. Those eyes were troubled now, glancing up at him.

"Uh, yeah. She did. It's not the first time. Damn it!" She swiped at the tears on her cheeks and stood up. "I have to get to New York in two weeks. I have an audition."

"You're a Broadway actress?" Jake couldn't keep the awe out of his voice.

"No. Not yet. Regional theater. Summer stock. Crap, look at my face. How can I audition looking like this?" She shoved the things she'd removed to get to her mirror back in the satchel. "I had bus fare only as far as Santa Juana. Now I'm stuck."

"You'll never make your audition," Jake said.

"Gotta be a place along this road that needs an experienced waitress. That's me. I'll get a job. Work a couple of days..." She brushed off her beige jeans and dark turquoise T-shirt before sticking out her hand.

"Kate MacKenzie. Thank you so much for paying off that asshole. If you give me your name and address, I'll mail you a check for the money. I'm good for it. Really. I've got this job in the bag. I just know it."

"Jake Lawrence. Don't worry about the money. I can swing it. You're really gonna do that? Look for a job, then hop a bus?"

"Of course. What other option do I have? Oh, wait. I could hitchhike. But that might be risky."

"Might? Might?" His voice rose. "You'll get jumped by the first guy who stops for you."

"Me? Why?"

"Just look at you."

"Yeah. So? I'm a little dusty, but..."

"Dusty? You're beautiful."

She stopped and blushed. "Think so?"

"I don't think. I know. Come on. I can't leave you out here. I'm gonna get lunch in Smokey's. Join me, and I'll take you to New York."

"What?"

"Yeah. I'm headed that way."

She backed up. "No, thanks, Mister. I'm not that hard up. I'd rather walk."

"No, no. I'm safe. Honestly. I'm a professional baseball player."

"Yeah? And I'm the Tooth Fairy."

"Really. Look," he said, pulling his wallet from his back pocket and flashing his identification.

"Well, son of a bitch, you are! Jake Lawrence and you play for the..." she leaned over to read it, giving him a nice view of her cleavage. "New York Nighthawks. Well then, I guess you are heading to New York."

"Opening day in a little over two weeks. Come, let's eat. I'm starved."

Kate followed him into the restaurant. It was dark, and they were shown to a booth with a round table. Always the gentleman, Jake let Kate slide in first. He made sure not to get too close. The woman had been assaulted and was skittish. He got that.

The hostess left menus after seating them.

He snuck a sidelong look at his lunch companion. She looked thin, even for an actress. He wondered if she had eaten that day.

"I'm not hungry," she said, closing the menu after looking at every single page.

"I am. I'm gonna have a Philly cheesesteak, even though we're in New Mexico, fries, and a milkshake."

"If I ate like that, I'd gain thirty pounds."

"I work it off on the field and in the gym. Come on. You gotta be hungry after that idiot smacked you around."

She licked her lips, enticing him with the sensuous swipe. Unconsciously, she gently rubbed her sore cheek and met his gaze with wary eyes.

"Come on. You gotta eat something. It's on me. Don't worry, I'm not going to jump you or anything."

"A freebie? There's no such thing."

"Yes, there is. Such an optimist one minute, and now you think I'm Jack the Ripper."

"Well, are you?"

He laughed. "That guy died a long time ago."

The waitress came by to take their orders.

"Nothing for me. Wait. Water. A big glass, please."

"Water? You're joking?" He placed his food order, "And a root beer float."

He watched her eyes grow large. "A root beer float. Wow."

"And she'll have one, too. Bring her a burger, too. With fries."

"How do you like it cooked, miss?"

Kate glanced at him. "Medium, please."

Jake grinned. "I knew you were hungry."

"Be right back with your drinks," the server said.

Jake looked her over. She flipped her long hair over her shoulder and avoided his gaze. *Could she be afraid of me?*

"Are you scared of me?" he asked, never being a shy guy.

"Well, I don't know you and you offered to buy me lunch. Lotta guys would expect something in return, if you get my meaning?"

"I get it. I'm not one of them. I'm not that kinda guy. Look, Kate, to be blunt, I don't have a hard time getting laid. And even if I did, I'd never buy sex or take advantage of a woman down on her luck. That's not how I roll."

"A gentleman? Been a long time since I've seen one of those."

Jake grinned. "Take a good look, 'cause you're seeing one now."

The beverages arrived. After her first sip, Kate's eyes widened. She clapped her hand over her mouth. He grinned.

"Damn this is good," she said, scooping up some ice cream.

He watched her devour the sweet. Must have been a long time since she'd had anything like that. Or maybe since anyone bought her a meal. When the food arrived, she tucked into it with the same enthusiasm. Watching her eat, his heart melted. It made him feel good to make her happy. Times like these, being financially secure paid off.

His cheesesteak tasted great, juicy and tender. But nothing was as good as the performance she gave, savoring every fry, every pickle—hell, she even ate the lettuce.

"Guess you were hungrier than you thought," he said.

"Guess so." She wiped her mouth and faced him. "That's the best meal I've had in a month. Thank you."

"You're welcome. Mine was pretty good, too."

"You gonna eat that pickle?" She pointed.

"Be my guest."

"I hate to waste food."

He laughed, watching her devour it along with his tomato and lettuce, too.

He paid the bill and opened the door for her.

"Where's your car?"

He pointed around back. Using the remote, he unlocked his gorgeous vehicle.

"Oh my God. Look at this! It's beautiful!"

He opened the door for her. "Hop in. We need to get on the road."

She bumped her shoulder on the doorframe and hissed in pain.

"Let me take a look at that." Jake pushed up her sleeve to expose the darkening bruise on her shoulder. Instinctively, he leaned down and kissed it. He saw a tear splash on her skin.

"No one's done that for me in a long time," she whispered, her voice hoarse.

"Sorry. Just knee-jerk. I used to do that for my little sister when we were kids. Always worked back then."

"You've still got the magic touch. It feels better already."

Obviously, she was lying, but he smiled at her and took her backpack.

"Okay if I put this in the trunk?"

She nodded, fastening her seatbelt.

Jake slid behind the wheel and put the magnificent machine in gear. He turned right onto U.S. 70 and hit the gas. The smooth ride lulled Kate to sleep. Her head lolled over to rest on his shoulder. Although he'd been looking forward to taking the trip alone, he relished sharing his luxurious vehicle with such an interesting companion. He had to laugh to himself. Her misfortune was his good luck.

Without much effort, he leaned down and kissed her head. His nose picked up a faint scent of lilacs. He wondered what the guys would say as he rode into New York in his silver carriage with a princess tucked inside. His teammates would shake their heads and swear he had all the luck. Perhaps this time, they were right.

Chapter Two

Kate shifted in her seat, nuzzling a firm shoulder under her cheek. Jerking awake, she shrank back against the passenger door.

"I'm sorry. I don't usually do that with people I don't know." She took a long side look at him. The man was gorgeous. Blond hair, blue eyes, and a body that wouldn't quit.

"No problem," Jake shot a grin at her then turned his eyes back to the road. "We're just about to cross over into the great state of Texas, I think."

"Do you have a route planned?" Fighting a yawn, she fished in her purse for a mint.

"My dad and I roughed out something. Wouldn't hurt to have a navigator. You interested?"

"Sure." She offered one to him, but he shook his head.

"In the glove compartment."

She looked around for a minute or two before figuring out how to open it. "This is some car. Do you know how to use everything?"

"Nope. Figured I'd learn on the way home."

She nodded, retrieving a folded paper. "A list?"

He nodded. "It's a list of roads my dad and I got from the road atlas. If we follow each of these to the next one, it should take us to New York."

After unfolding it, she studied the words as she sucked on the candy. "Got a map?"

"Road atlas under the seat."

She pulled it out. "We can stay on this road and pass through Texas quickly. It goes across the Panhandle."

"Sounds like a plan."

"It's the fastest route." Glancing at him, she did a brief study of his profile. Straight nose, strong jaw, definitely a handsome guy. Biceps bulged a bit as he gripped the wheel. Strong forearms, too. *Hell, he's a slugger. Can't do that and be a weakling, can you?* Turning her gaze out the window, she wondered what it would feel like to be in his arms. Would he be safe? Would he protect her? He did already, so, yeah, he probably would. If he liked her.

What guy takes on a woman whose mom was a gambling addict? He had to wonder if the apple hadn't fallen far from the tree. Besides, she didn't have time for a relationship. She was going to be a Broadway star or die trying. That would take all the energy she had. Still, with a nice hunk like Jake, it might be fun to take a detour for a month or two.

"That works," he replied.

She eyed the fancy sound system. "Do you like music?"

"Love it."

"I need to rehearse for my audition. Would you mind if I sing?"

"You're doing a musical?"

"Yes, it's kind of a revival, sort of. New show old music. From the 1930's."

"Interesting."

"Some great music was written back then."

"Cole Porter. Can't do better than him, except maybe Johnny Cash."

"You like Cole Porter and Johnny Cash?"

"Weird, I know. I like Mozart, too. My mom's a music teacher."

"Do you play an instrument?"

"Nah. Too busy with baseball practice."

"Can you sing?"

"A little."

She clapped her hands. "Fantastic! The number I'm doing, *Friendship,* is a duet. I'm meeting my partner in the City. We won't have time to practice together, so would you sing with me?"

"Partner?" He frowned. Kate stifled a smile. *Maybe he is interested.*

"Performing partner. He's gay."

"Got it." One side of Jake's sexy mouth curved up.

"So will you?"

"Sorry, I don't know the song."

"I'll feed you the lyrics. Let me go through it a couple of times."

As they drove through the flat plains of the Texas Panhandle, Kate sang the song over and over again. Since there wasn't much traffic, she didn't worry about distracting Jake while teaching him the song. He caught on fast and had a remarkably good voice.

Kate relaxed as she did what she loved most. Jake cast an admiring look her way. No one had appreciated her in a very long time. Show business was a struggle to get parts, then a shitload of hard work to stand out. She wasn't afraid of the challenge of making it on Broadway.

Nothing in her life had come easy, why should this be any different? That wasn't exactly true. Her naturally stunning voice and looks had opened a few doors for her. But once she hit New York, that wouldn't matter anymore. She'd be one of hundreds with talent and looks, competing for a handful of spots.

By the time they got back on the highway, it was three. The sun shifted in the sky. Night was coming on fast.

"Let's stop outside of Amarillo. I don't want to get mixed up in city traffic. I need to stretch my legs and it's almost dinner time," Jake said, stifling a yawn.

Kate checked her watch. It read six o'clock, Texas time.

"Okay. Where do you want to stop?"

"I'm up for some Texas steak. Look for a steakhouse. And not a chain. See if you can find a local place."

He slowed the car, making it easier for her to check the signs. As they neared Amarillo, the barren plains had become dotted with stores, restaurants, and motels. *Shit! Motel.* Panic welled up in her for a moment. *I'll sleep in the car.*

"I see Cowboy John's. Looks like a restaurant. Has a big picture of a steak."

"Sounds good. Let's try it," he said, pulling off the highway.

Jake picked up on the worried expression in her eyes. *Must be scary to be a woman, traveling alone, no money, with a strange guy.*

"Come. I'm buyin'. Don't worry about money. I do real well. I can afford to take you along with me so relax."

She had appeared to be in her element in the car. When she sang, her whole face lit up, tripling her energy and beauty. Jake almost drove off the road, staring at her and listening to her. Her voice was the sweetest, clearest he'd ever heard. Even so, he knew that setting her sights on Broadway was about the toughest choice she could make.

Hell, pro baseball hadn't exactly been easy. He'd practiced his balls off to get there. And still worked like crazy to stay sharp. But, at least in baseball, there are a lotta teams and they scout you. Broadway shows weren't exactly employing a thousand leading ladies, were they?

Recalling her phone call, he concluded she had at least one other strike against her. His heart melted at her determination, despite the odds. He had to help her. Helping people is what he was raised to do, along with play baseball. It was his mom's influence, and he had prided himself on being a gentleman and helpful to all. Besides, if she got grateful enough, a guy might get lucky.

He'd stolen enough looks at her chest to make his mouth water. Her body was fine, about the finest he'd ever see. What he wouldn't give to see it all. Fat chance, but he could dream. Nope, he couldn't make a move on her. Wouldn't be right. He sighed as he put the car in park.

"Something wrong?"

"Just a little tired, I guess."

"How long you been driving today?"

"About five hours."

"You're ahead of schedule," she said, unfastening her seatbelt.

"Yeah. Thought I might want to stop for a day or two along the way. See some stuff. That okay with you?"

"Honey, this is a free ride for me. I'll go along with anything you want to do." She picked up her purse.

"Anything?" He cocked an eyebrow.

She gave his shoulder a playful slap.

"Just kiddin', Kate. Just kiddin'."

"You'd better be.

They entered the restaurant. Jake ordered a thick steak, baked potato, and salad. Kate had a steak salad. She had wine, and Jake slugged down a beer. When he reached the car, exhaustion took over.

"Can't do it."

"Can't do what?"

"Can't drive much anymore tonight. Hell, it's eight already. I'm usually in bed by ten. I need to find a motel."

"I can sleep in the car," she piped up.

"Don't be silly. We'll get a room with two beds."

Jake took the next exit off route 40 and pulled into the parking lot of a motel chain he was familiar with, Carruthers Inn.

"I have points at this place. It's pretty nice."

Kate hung back. "What if they don't have two beds?"

"We'll cross that bridge if we come to it. Come on. I'm beat."

Taking her time, Kate got out of the car. Jake retrieved her backpack along with his small suitcase and headed for the front desk. When the desk clerk said they had a room with two doubles, she let out a breath. He chuckled to himself to see how relieved she was to be able to put some physical distance between them for the night.

This would be a first for him. He laughed.

"What's so funny?"

"I don't usually spend the night with a beautiful woman just sleeping."

"There's a first time for everything."

"I guess so."

He handed her the key, and she unlocked the door. "Pick your bed," he said, setting down the luggage.

She jumped on the one nearest the bathroom and bounced, giggling like a little kid. The few times she dropped the wariness and fear, her sense of fun shone through. She intrigued him. How did she get to where she was and who, exactly, was she? Did she gamble like her mom? His head buzzed with a zillion questions.

"I sleep in boxers. I hope that won't offend you," he said, pulling a toilet kit out of his bag.

"Nope. Just like a bathing suit, right?"

"Right."

She bit her lip as she rummaged through her stuff. "Hmm. I only have something that's not appropriate to sleep in."

"Really?" He looked over at her.

"Yeah." She blushed. "I usually sleep nude."

A thump in his dick set his whole body on high alert. His mouth went dry, and he lost the ability to speak for a moment or two. An idea popped into his head.

"I've got a jersey. Would that do?"

"Oh, yeah. That'd be great. Thank you."

He opened the case and pulled out his number twenty-two pinstriped top and tossed it on her bed. She held it up.

"A little big, but it'll do just fine." With that, she disappeared into the bathroom.

Jake let out a breath and sank down on the bed. How the hell was he going to hold it together if she kept saying things like that? He took off his shirt and pants, folded them and put them on a chair. Sweat gathered on his forehead. He needed a shower but would have to wait until morning. Nothing would keep him awake tonight and since he was sleeping alone, he didn't have to worry about being stinky up close. Too bad.

Doubt crept into Kate's mind as she undressed in the bathroom. She'd never met a man like Jake Lawrence. Didn't think there was a man on Earth who wouldn't take advantage of her in this situation—or try to. Nope, she wasn't going to have sex to put a roof over her head. No way.

She unbuttoned the jersey, then held it to her nose. It smelled fresh and clean, with a hint of Jake in it. The amazing new car smell had mixed with the rich leather and Jake's scent. Now some of that was on the shirt he'd lent her. She put it on, looked in the mirror, and laughed. If ever there was something that wasn't sexy, this was it.

The huge jersey fell along her slim frame like a giant bag. Everything was covered up, as it fell to her knees. *Like sleeping in a dress.* She took a deep breath. This was the perfect outfit. Hell, what man would want to sleep with a woman who was drowning in a baseball jersey?

Confident she'd cool down whatever desire Jake might have for her, she opened the door and waltzed into the bedroom.

"A perfect fit," she started until she laid eyes on his almost naked body. Her breath hitched as her gaze drew down his wide, muscular shoulders and chest. Some blond hair curled on his pecs, inviting her to touch him. She swallowed some saliva and sensed heat in her neck.

As her gaze dropped down to his tight abs and narrow hips, desire flared in her loins. Mentally kicking herself, she shouldn't have been surprised. The guy filled out a T-shirt and a pair of jeans like she hadn't seen before. She should have expected, once he took his clothes off, that he'd be just as gorgeous underneath.

"I see," he said in a raspy voice.

Color seeped into his chest, like a sex flush, and she got the message. Her nipples hardened under his scrutiny. Looking away before she betrayed her own feelings any further, she pulled down the covers and slid into bed. He did the same. Facing him, she glimpsed the quick flash of fire in his eyes, before it died. Being in a motel room with Jake Lawrence and keeping her distance proved to be a daunting challenge.

She fluffed up her pillow, raised the bedclothes to cover her chest, hiding her reaction to him. She turned on her side and curled up, facing his bed. Jake extinguished the light.

"Good night," he said.

"Night," she responded.

The air hung heavy with unspoken need. They were quiet for a few moments.

"Does your mom do that to you often?"

"Do what?"

"Gamble away your money?"

Humiliation clutched her heart, robbing her of words.

"I'm sorry. I shouldn't have asked that. It's none of my business. You don't have to answer."

"She's been doing that all my life."

Silence.

"I'm sorry," he said.

Words tumbled from her mouth before she could stop them.

"My mom's been addicted to gambling ever since I can remember. My dad couldn't take it and left when I was ten. He paid our rent until I was eighteen."

"I'm so sorry. Hey, you don't have to talk about it. Forget I asked."

"Sometimes it feels better to talk about it, instead of keeping it secret." She blew out a breath.

"Not like it's your fault or anything," he said.

"No, it isn't."

"Has she tried to stop? Or get help?"

"Sure. Plenty of times. Her life with my dad was one of broken promises, gambling in secret, and missing money," she confessed.

"That must have been hard on you," he replied.

"I became self-sufficient at an early age."

"I'd guess you'd have to."

"Right. I worked after school, dog walking, babysitting, whatever I could get. Started when I was ten and daddy left. I kept my money hidden."

He was quiet. Emotion built inside her as old memories flooded back. Her voice quavered.

"But she always found it. She was like a bloodhound. I thought I was so clever, finding places she'd never look. But it never worked. She'd find it and it would be gone."

He was quiet. Tears slipped from her eyes. An urge to crawl into his bed and cuddle up with him seized her heart. She figured she'd find comfort in those strong arms of his. She might be able to lose herself in his embrace, but she'd be giving him the green light to make love, and she wasn't ready for that. Though the idea tempted her.

She wiped the wetness off her cheeks with her palm, then bunched up the extra pillow, hugging it to her chest, the way she had when she was little. She curled her legs up around the squishy thing and rested her cheek on it. A position she'd used to fall asleep after her father had moved on.

When she closed her eyes, she could pretend the pillow was Jake's chest. The image soothed her. She sighed, recalling his pleasing scent and his sweetness.

Jake didn't know what to say. The urge to go to her, take her in his arms, and hug her to death almost overwhelmed him. He'd swung one leg over the side of the bed before he caught himself. His going over there would simply scare the shit out of her.

Her story touched his heart. So beautiful and talented, yet so alone all her life—one parent gone, the other an adversary. Words escaped him, though he wanted to say something, anything to soothe her.

"Did you get to spend any of it on yourself before she found it?"

He heard her sigh.

"I did. Wasn't long before I got wise. If I spent it on myself, then she couldn't gamble it away. So I'd buy a burger or a new skirt with it. I knew she was mad that she couldn't count on that money, but I didn't care."

"Do you support her now?"

"Yeah, sort of. But I'm still paying off college loans. She gets social security now. That pays her rent and food, if she's careful."

"So you send her money?"

"I buy gift certificates for the grocery store for her. She's tried to turn them in for cash, but they got wise and don't do it. I need to know she's eating. Ya know?"

"I get it."

"She's not a bad person. Never hit me or anything. She's just got this problem and it's taken over her life."

There was silence.

"You're very brave," he said.

"Thank you."

Lying on his back, Jake laced his fingers behind his head. The minute he'd seen her wearing his jersey, he'd wanted to jump her bones. Blood had pumped to his dick, forcing him to turn his back to her. The huge garment made her look small, delicate, and vulnerable. He'd wanted to grab her, hold her, kiss her, and make love to her.

His reaction surprised him. The bulky uniform hid her charms, but it gave her a waifish quality he found irresistible. Chatting with her in the dark, he realized she was no poor, defenseless woman, but a strong one, who had already weathered a whole lot of shit storms.

His new knowledge about her fanned the flames of his desire. Underneath that frightened demeanor lay the heart of a tiger. He bet she was amazing in bed and ached to find out. *Hands off, buster.* He knew he couldn't be putting any moves on her. She was trapped, like a cornered mongoose, and she'd fight like hell to survive.

He wondered if he'd ever see her again after he dropped her off in New York. Maybe that would be the right time to ask her out. He decided it would and resolved to form a plan, a special date, and spring it on her just before they parted.

A question interrupted his thoughts.

"What was your childhood like?"

"Pretty normal. My parents are still married, still living together."

"Nice."

"Baseball became my life when I was about ten. Dad devoted much of his time away from work teaching me. Training me."

"What does he do for a living?"

"He's an engineer. Packaging engineer. He tried to explain what he does once, but I never really got it. Mom's a music teacher."

"Yeah, so you said. Any siblings?"

"One younger sister. You?"

"No."

"She was kind of a pain when she was little. But when I went off to college, she'd bake cookies and send 'em to me. We became friends."

"Where is she now?"

"Married. No kids yet. Living near my parents in California."

"You don't get to see them much, do you?"

"No. But it's okay. I've got my teammates. We hang together. My family flies in for one game every season. Especially if we're in the playoffs."

"Sounds nice."

"I guess it was boring. I'm probably boring, too."

"I would have loved to have lived a boring life."

Silence.

"I'm sorry. I shouldn't have said that. Yeah. I was a lucky kid," he said.

"You were. You should appreciate that."

"I do."

"Good," she replied.

"I'd better get some sleep. Long drive tomorrow."

"Where're we going next?"

"Oklahoma."

"I'll look for stuff to see there tomorrow," she said.

"Great."

"Good night, Jake. Thanks for being such a great friend."

"You're welcome. Good night."

The one word no man ever wants to hear from a beautiful woman is "friend". He didn't want to be her friend. He wanted to be her lover. Guess he'd have to settle for friend. Did that mean she wasn't afraid of him anymore? Maybe, maybe not—he still needed to watch his step.

At second thought, coming from Kate, "friend" was a compliment. He guessed she didn't have many male friends, except maybe gay ones. What man could keep his hands off her? His chested puffed up a bit, as he realized it was an honor to be considered her buddy. Was it possible to turn a friend into a lover? He'd have to figure out how tomorrow.

He rolled over and sleep claimed him.

Chapter Three

Jake slept like a dead man. When a small stream of sunlight snuck between the curtains, he opened his eyes. A glance at the clock showed it was seven and he didn't need to get up yet. A subtle swish of movement captured his gaze.

Kate was up and dancing or stretching or something. She stood facing away from him. She'd shed his jersey in favor of leggings and a sports bra. One hand rested on the back of a chair. The other stretched gracefully out to the side. She'd lifted her right leg and stretched it high up.

Even in the dim light, he made out the outline of her leg muscles. She repeated her action on the right, then switched to the other side. Her legs were beautiful, strong, slim, and well formed. He longed to touch her but lay completely still so as not to interrupt.

Her lifts were rhythmic, as if she moved to music, though there was no music playing. Had she been singing softly, humming, or even imagining the music? She'd talked about being a singer, then demonstrated her silvery pipes, but dancing? Of course, she couldn't dance in the car. He guessed actors had to dance to be on Broadway.

Her graceful movements captivated him. He watched until she put her leg down and turned around. He prayed he'd closed his eyes before she saw him staring at her. Embarrassment flooded his body. To be caught watching her would be the next best thing to being a stalker.

He'd never met a girl like her. While her talents and beauty fascinated him, her sad history tugged at his heart. The combination was lethal. Had he finally met the girl he couldn't date casually and leave when the mood struck him? Her voice broke the silence.

"You can stop faking. I know you're awake."

Caught! He cracked one eye open. "Who me?"

She laughed. "Good try. I could feel you watching me."

"Okay, okay. Guilty as charged." He threw down the covers. "I'm going to get a shower. Do you need the bathroom?"

"You go ahead."

He turned on the water and while he waited for it to heat up, he looked at the little bottles by the sink. These were her secret potions to help her look so amazing. *Bah, she didn't need a thing.* Obviously, she was born that way. Dropping his boxers, he stepped under the hot spray and wished she'd join him. But wishing wouldn't make it so. He picked up a washcloth and gave voice to his favorite shower song, *Take Me Out to the Ballgame.*

After his shower, he dressed in the bathroom, then turned it over to her.

"And they say women take forever to get dressed," she harrumphed.

"Sorry. I'm not used to sharing a room with a woman I don't share the shower with."

He laughed at her blush as she scurried into the bathroom and slammed the door. He repacked his few belongings and stood at the window, watching the sun grow in the sky.

When she ambled into the room, she wore a pair of navy blue leggings and a long, thin white sweater. She toweled her hair as she joined him at the window.

"Why don't you keep the jersey, for now?" he said, watching her blue-black hair, tousled and damp, falling lower than her shoulders. The urge to run his fingers through it forced him to clamp his hands together.

"You sure?"

"You'll need it every night, right?"

"Guess so."

"As long as I get it back when we get to New York."

"Of course. Thanks."

At the front desk, they got the recommendation of a diner a mile down the road for breakfast.

Once they'd placed their orders, Kate reached across the table.

"Gimme."

He cocked his head. "What?"

"Your phone. You want me to look up someplace to go in Oklahoma, don't you?"

"Oh. Yeah! Oh, yeah. Right. Here." He handed it to her.

She punched in letters while he drank coffee.

"What kind of things do you like?"

"I don't know. Surprise me."

There was silence as she worked the cell. Their food arrived.

"Got it," she said.

"What?" He took a forkful of eggs.

"Animals."

"Animals?"

"Yep. Woolaroc Museum and Wildlife Preserve. In Bartlesville."

"Where the hell is that?"

"North of Tulsa. Where are we now?" she asked.

"Outside of Amarillo. About fifty or sixty miles."

"Okay. So it's about, hmm, three hundred twenty-five miles."

"Not for today, then."

"Maybe early tomorrow?"

"Perfect," he agreed.

She smiled and handed him back his phone.

They finished eating and got back in the car.

"Today, I expect you to sing along with me. You've heard the song enough to know the lyrics."

"I'll give it a try."

"I'll correct you when you need it."

"I'm sure you will." He grinned.

"What's that supposed to mean?" She shot him a pointed stare.

"Just that you're sure not shy about speaking up."

"If I waited for others to speak up for me, I'd still be waitin'."

"I get it. Sorry."

"Nothing to be sorry about. My life was my life. I've survived. I'm doing pretty well. Got my degree, going for a great job. I think things are gonna get better for me. Hell, they can't get much worse!" She gave a short laugh.

They sure are going to get better for you if I have anything to say about it. He patted her hand. "You have a great attitude. I'm sure you'll be a big success. I hope you'll give me an autograph when you're rich and famous, so I can say I knew you."

"You're funny," she said, laughing. "Let's go. Time's a wasting."

She started it and cued him when to come in. He tried a few times and messed up. But they kept at it and, finally, he got it. Her patience impressed him. He relaxed and stopped feeling silly as his voice rose in song with hers.

They sang their way across the Texas Panhandle and into Oklahoma. At six, Kate spotted a well-known Italian food chain restaurant and they stopped to eat. There was a motel with a flashing vacancy sign a mile from the restaurant. They lucked out getting a room with two double beds.

Jake turned on the television to check on the hockey game while Kate did vocal exercises and leg stretches. He tried to keep his focus on the game, but her lithe body drew his eye time after time. After the Rangers were ahead by five goals, he was about to switch it off, when his cell rang. He muted the tube and answered. It was Skip Quincy, Nighthawks' shortstop.

"Hey, Jake! How's the car?"

The third baseman filled his buddy in on the glorious experience of driving his new Lexus. Then Kate piped up.

"And tell him it's not a total gas guzzler," she said.

In a moment of silence, his stomach clenched.

"Did I hear a woman's voice?" Skip asked.

"The TV," Jake lied.

"Bullshit."

"I think the other team just scored," Kate said.

Jake covered his eyes with his hand. No hiding her now.

"That was a woman! I know a live woman's voice when I hear it. So, you've picked up someone, already?"

"No, no. Nothing like that." But, in fact, that's literally what he did—picked her up.

"Don't lie. I know you. Is she hot? Stupid question. Of course, she's hot. Blond or Brunette?"

Not usually a shy man, Jake got too flustered to respond.

"Oh, a redhead? I see," Skip continued.

"No, really. You got it all wrong."

"Am I interrupting?" Skip sniggered.

Jake heard the others in the background. Then it sounded like Skip had dropped the phone. A different voice spoke.

"Hey, asshole, you busy?" It was the catcher, Matt Jackson.

"Yeah. I'm watching the Rangers game. What do you want?"

"You're watching the game with a hot chick in your room? Right," Matt said, chuckling.

"You want something?"

"Nope. Not a thing."

"Good. I'm hanging up now."

"Don't want to keep you from your, uh, date."

"Are you saying she's a hooker?"

"Only you would know," Matt teased.

"Fuck you, Jackson."

"So you admit you've got a girl there?"

"It's a long story."

"I'll bet. Wait. Nat wants to talk to you."

Jake made an impatient sound, drawing Kate's attention.

"What? Your teammates?"

"Yeah, annoying pains in the ass," Jake mumbled.

"So how's the car?" Nat asked.

"Fine. Look, I gotta go," Jake said.

"Got a girl there?"

"So?"

"Don't let me stop you," he snickered, laughing.

"I won't. There's nothing happening here. It's not like that, for the millionth time. So fuck off!" Jake clicked his phone off, mumbling more obscenities.

"Pleasant conversation?"

"How'd you guess?" He looked up. Kate had slipped on his jersey and was headed for her bed. Looking at her, waif-like in the giant garment, never got old. He wanted to hug her and hold her all night long. *Never gonna happen.* He sighed.

"Lights out?" she said, slipping between the sheets.

"Don't think that isn't sexy on you." He rolled on his side.

"I bet it's sexier on you," she countered.

He laughed. "Not from where I'm sitting." *She thinks I'm sexy?* Hope rose anew in his chest.

She propped her head up on her hand. "I doubt I'll ever be able to repay you."

"For what? A couple of meals? I'd get the motel room anyway."

"It's more than a couple of meals."

"Don't worry about it. I've been there."

"Liar. No you haven't. If I get the part, then I'll have the money to pay you back."

"Forget about it, will you? It's chump change."

"Not to me. You're my hero."

There was no comeback to that. No one had ever called him a hero before. Emotion swirled through him.

"Thanks," he coughed out.

"Welcome. Come on. Douse the lights. We've got an early day tomorrow if we're going to see the bison in Bartlesville."

"Yep." He reached out a long arm and flicked off the light, but stayed facing her. Again she took the spare pillow and hugged it to her, circling it with her body. He wished he could trade places with that bundle of fluff.

They sang together through Oklahoma until they got to Tulsa and headed north.

"You're pretty good, you know," she said, punching the address of Woolaroc into the GPS.

"Good at what? Driving?"

"Singing."

"Me?" He laughed. "My mother would disagree."

"You're good. With some lessons, you could do it professionally, if you ever leave baseball."

"I love baseball. Singing is for fun."

"I get it," she checked the website. "It says not to use the GPS."

"That's weird."

"They give directions. We're not that far."

"Good. I need to stretch my legs."

The image of him dressed only in boxers flashed through her brain. His legs were something else. Strong thighs and calves, shaped perfectly. Nothing bulgy or out of proportion about Jake Lawrence. When he turned his back to her, she had wanted to touch his shoulders. Watching the muscles work as he got dressed, or undressed—even better—turned her on.

They had been traveling for five days. Kate managed to hold out, but she didn't know for how much longer. Every night she got into bed, wishing a fairy godmother would change the pillow clutched to her chest to Jake. She chuckled to herself. She didn't need a fairy godmother. She could do it herself. With one look, one gesture, he'd be in her bed in a heartbeat. He'd sure made that clear enough.

The thought of his desiring her made her mouth water, then go dry. Giving it up to Jake might be what she needed. Loneliness had been her constant companion for so long, she'd become used to it. Obviously, he was smitten with her, or was he only interested in sleeping with her? She doubted that. A man only looking for sex wouldn't have been such a gentleman for so long. He'd have put the moves on her by now.

Maybe there was something there for them. They sure got along great, traveled together seamlessly, and had fun singing together. She knew the song so well by now, it's as if she'd written it herself. A doff of the hat to Jake for that, for his patience listening to her sing it a hundred million times, then joining her in song.

She liked him. He was a nice guy with talent. Nice to her, which she wasn't used to. He brought out her softer side, which she was sure had evaporated long ago. He took care of her. No one had since she was ten. She'd lived without it for so long, it no longer mattered. But Jake had unearthed an overwhelming desire to be cared for, even a little bit. A desire she thought long dead had turned out to be alive and well.

How could she trust him so fast? It wasn't like her, but he hadn't done anything to frighten or hurt her. She'd needed to believe in someone for so long and maybe Jake Lawrence was the answer. The thought scared the shit out of her.

They pulled up to the parking lot. Jake forked over the twelve dollars, and they went in. The museum was an eclectic mix of artifacts, Indian blankets, and art set inside a large log building with a stone facade.

"Come on. Outside," he said, taking her hand.

They walked the trail, looking for animals.

"I want to see some bison. Up close and personal."

They found the creatures and Jake hopped over the pen.

"Be careful!"

"I'm fine."

One of the huge creatures didn't fancy Jake in his space and made chase. The ballplayer took off, vaulting over the fence and ripping the skin of his hand open on a piece of metal. He whipped out a handkerchief and wrapped it around his left hand.

"Oh my God. What did you do?"

He frowned. "I know. You told me not to go in there."

"Come on. Let's get you fixed up." She tugged on his sleeve and found someone in charge. They had a first aid kit. The woman gave Jake a hard stare.

"Did you see the sign?"

"What sign?"

"The one that said keep out?"

"Nope. Sorry."

The cut didn't need stitches. The woman bandaged him up and refunded his money.

"I think maybe we'd better leave, ya know?" Kate said. Jake agreed. While the woman wasn't mad, he was noticeably embarrassed. He hadn't even glanced at the sign, but they saw it on their way out. How could he have been such an idiot? Relieved to get back in the car, Kate navigated them back to Tulsa.

"We need to stop and get supplies for that hand."

"It's nothing."

"It's not nothing."

He kept going, heading for Tulsa.

"If you don't stop, I'm going to yell and scream that you're holding me against my will when we stop to eat."

Jake grumbled but pulled into the lot of the next big pharmacy they came across. Kate hit the first aid center. She noticed Jake wander over to the counter.

She found antiseptic cream, bandages in various sizes, and pain killer before she joined him. He was stuffing something in his back pocket.

"Gimme that stuff," he said, grabbing the basket. They went to the cashier, a middle-aged man. He looked at Jake, then at Kate. A slow, salacious grin spread over his face as he rang up the items. The man's eyes rested on her chest a moment too long. He looked up at Jake and winked. Something was going on, and she didn't like it. Folding her arms across her breasts, she moved back, almost behind Jake. He paid for the stuff and took the bag.

As they walked out, she glanced back at the man, who was still smirking at her, and closed her fingers around Jake's biceps.

"What the hell was that about?"

"Sorry. I bought some condoms from the guy first. Guess he put two and two together."

"Well, he's sure added wrong, didn't he?" She stepped away from him.

"I'm sorry, honey. Honest. They're cheaper here than in New York. I was only buying them to take home."

"Yeah, right." She shot him a suspicious glance.

"If I should get lucky—remember I said IF. I'm prepared. That's all."

"And you were a boy scout, too, weren't you?"

"An Eagle Scout, to be exact."

"That clerk thinks we're getting it on," she piped up.

"Who cares what he thinks? He's a rude asshole. Come on, it's time for lunch. Get us to Tulsa. Let's find a mom-and-pop place to eat," he said, opening the car door for her.

"I'm on it."

She watched him get in the car. He flinched when he tightened his left hand on the wheel, but he didn't say a word. If she changed her mind about sharing his bed, at least she'd be safe. She chuckled to herself. *Maybe getting those was a good idea.*

"What's so funny?" he asked, putting the car in reverse and backing out of the space.

"Nothing. Let's go. I'm hungry."

"Yeah? Me, too." He turned the wheel and sped out of the lot and onto the road heading for Tulsa.

I'm hungry. Hungry for you Jake Lawrence, baseball player, gentleman and hottie.

Kate found a little café. There was parking right out in front, which made Jake happy. He would be leaving his luxurious car where he could keep an eye on it. The waitress recognized him and gave them a table in the window.

"Jake Lawrence, New York Nighthawks?" Her brown eyes got wide.

"Yep."

"Can I have your autograph? You're lucky, honey, to be with this guy."

Jake signed something for her, and they placed their order. Kate knew she was lucky to be with him, but it was strange to hear the woman say so. Maybe someday she'd be famous, too, as a Broadway star. Then someone might say he was lucky to be with her. A rueful smile played on her lips. She was so far away from that day, it was silly to even think about it.

She had ham and waffles, Jake had a burger deluxe. He left a big tip and they climbed into the car. The GPS showed them the way and before long, they were back on Route 40 heading east.

Jake played Dolly Parton as they whizzed along the highway, heading for Arkansas. Kate went to sleep, resting her head against his shoulder. When she awoke, they'd reached Fort Smith.

Tight little lines around his mouth and a slightly paler complexion bothered her. He was driving mostly with his right hand.

"Why don't we stop and find a motel early? I need to change the dressing on your hand."

"It's okay."

"Are we going to go through this again?"
"What?"
"Me threatening you to get you to do the right thing?"
"Okay, okay. Where do you want to stop?"
"Next sign that says motel and vacancy."

They pulled into another Carruthers Motel. Jake checked them in. Kate carried her own backpack so he wouldn't use his left hand. He flopped down on the bed by the window, understanding she preferred the one by the bathroom.

Once they were settled, she took the bag with the first aid supplies and approached his bed, where he was stretched out.

She took his hand and ripped the bandage off fast. He jumped but covered up the pain. It was as she had suspected, getting red and possibly infected

"This doesn't look good. You need to soak it." His hand rested lightly in her palm.

"It's fine."

"Shut up! I'm in charge here, and I say it doesn't look good. I'm going to get a bowl."

Chapter Four

When the door clicked shut behind Kate, Jake closed his eyes. His left hand had been throbbing for a while. It hurt more than he let on. He refused to appear weak in front of her. But, damn, it was sore and driving had been difficult. Gripping the wheel only aggravated the cut, increasing the pain. The constant pulsing ache, hour after hour, wore him down. Although he wouldn't admit it, he was tired. When she had wanted to stop, he was relieved.

The third baseman was about to doze off when she entered, chattering away and carrying a stainless steel bowl. She approached him.

"Don't fall asleep! Let me fix this up first."

"It's fine. Really." He tried to sound convincing but didn't even impress himself. Still, he needed to sleep and her insistence annoyed him.

"Would you shut the fuck up and let me take care of you?" His eyes widened, and he faced her. Anger and concern flashed in her eyes.

"But I don't—" he started, sitting up.

She placed her small palm on his chest and pushed him back down. He collapsed like a deflated balloon.

"Let me do my thing. You've been taking care of me, now it's my turn. It won't hurt. I promise."

"I've heard promises like that before," he mumbled through tired lips.

The fight went out of him. The pain refused to go away, alarming him. Whether he'd admit it or not, he needed help. He did as he was told, secretly glad to have her in charge. She ran water in the sink, then returned with a steaming bowl, and placed it on the nightstand.

"Let's get this cleaned up." She took out gauze and dipped it in the water, then added soap. Holding his hand, she gently cleaned his cut. Even with her soft touch, it hurt like hell. He flinched, then cursed himself for looking like a sissy.

"Now soak it," she instructed, slowly easing his hand into the hot water.

"Damn! It's hot!" He yanked it out.

"That's the point. Get used to it a little at a time." Holding his hand, she eased it into the water. Within a few minutes, he was able to stand the heat. After he soaked it, she applied antibiotic ointment, cleaned up the mess, and returned to his bedside.

"How does that feel?" Her thumb stroked his wrist. Her tender touch made him smile, despite the ache. For such a brash woman, she had a sweet, softer side that surprised him.

"Pretty good." Her fingers soothed his nerves.

"Too hot?"

"Nope. Just right."

"Okay. I'll change the water in five minutes and make it hot again."

When the time was up, she examined his hand, cleaned the wound again and refilled the bowl. She repeated the process every five minutes for half an hour. Her nursing skills reminded him of the care he got from his mother whenever he'd hurt himself as a child. It pleased him to be under Kate's sharp eye.

"Looks like your body is taking care of this now. I see the red is getting lighter." She cleaned it up and bandaged it. She bent down and placed a kiss on the gauze, then handed him a glass and two ibuprofen.

"Here, take these. Then it's nap time."

He did as he was told. Kate grabbed the extra blanket from the closet and spread it over him. She tugged on his shoulder. When he sat straight up, she put the second pillow behind him, punched it a few times and urged him back. She leaned down and brushed her lips against his forehead.

"Gotta rest to heal."

"You know what you're doing. Ever been a nurse?"

"I used to take care of my mom when she got hurt. Sometimes she'd find an abusive boyfriend at the track. I'd patch her up."

"You have a healing touch."

"Thank you," she said, her gaze dropping to her hands, her blush heightened her coloring.

Exhaustion and her kiss had relaxed him. He'd never expected such intimacy or sweetness. She kissed his hand again.

"My dad used, to do that. And it always helped. I don't know if I have his magic touch, just thought I'd try," she said, the deepening blush shading her cheeks.

"It does help," he said, cupping her cheek for a second with his good hand.

She fished a book out of her backpack and stretched out on her bed. His eyelids weighed a ton, so he closed them. Soon he was asleep, dreaming of being enveloped by her gentle love and spending a glorious night in her bed.

She lay there, staring at Jake while he slept. Her gaze roamed slowly over every inch of him. He looked cherubic, his face relaxed, the pain lines eased away. He slept on his side, facing her. She studied the slope of his nose, his blond lashes—which she bet were longer than hers—fanned out on his cheek. His lips, decidedly masculine were so kissable, she had to hold herself back from climbing on the bed and ravishing his mouth.

Such a perfect specimen, she wondered where his cracks were. No one was perfect, and that included slugger, Jake Lawrence. She wondered why such a hot guy was single. Not met the right girl yet or was he a womanizer? Recalling his conversation with his teammates the other night, she guessed the latter.

Well, there it was. A master seducer and leaver of women. Jake fit the part perfectly. Take 'em in with his charm and good looks, sleep with 'em, then on to the next. The idea sent a cold chill up her spine.

Would he do that to her? An easy friendship had grown up between them. Gentle teasing in the car, singing together and critiquing each other's performances. Sharing food, a bathroom, and a motel room without sex sure didn't sound like a womanizer's scenario. What if he didn't see her that way? It's not like he didn't want to sleep with her. She'd seen the sparks in his eyes when she paraded around in that floppy, baggy jersey of his.

She shrugged. Who knew what went on in his mind? The more he resisted her, the more she wanted him. It didn't make sense to her at all. But there it was. Regardless of what she said, she'd flop into his bed in a heartbeat. Doctoring his hand, touching the calloused palms, the sensitive skin on the back of his hand, lit her fire.

He was warm, strong, and protective. Safety existed in his arms, only a bed away, didn't it? Safety, something she'd longed for all her life and never found. The only safe person in her life had been herself. Self-reliance, the backbone of the United States, and the existence of Kate MacKenzie. She'd contemplated giving it up a few times before when enormously attractive men made plays for her. But it had never turned out well. She'd either been hurt or wounded him and had to move on. What made her think she could expect this to be different?

But she wanted him and denying herself was getting her nowhere. The feelings hadn't gone away, in fact, they had only intensified. Not staring at him when he undressed, or dressed, or walked to the bathroom in his boxers, wasn't an option. She knew he noticed, too, and it had embarrassed her, but she couldn't look away. Who knew when she'd get another view of such fine male flesh again?

When she did her warm up exercises in the morning, his gaze behind her enveloped her like warm hands. She teased him with her leg lifts, and he loved it, smiling at her with heat in his eyes. When would the two forces stop dancing around each other and come together in a meteor shower of passion that would burn the motel down? She didn't know, but it had to happen as they inched closer and closer to each other. Kate's mouth felt dry.

She tried reading but lost interest in her book almost immediately. She drifted off, imagining if things were different if they were stranded on an island together. Would they be so reluctant to couple up then?

"Hey, lady. Time to get up." Soft words buzzed her ear. Was she dreaming? "Come on, honey. Time for dinner."

She opened her eyes. Jake sat on the corner of her bed, dressed and ready. The pain lines in his face were gone. He looked good.

"How's the hand?"

"Doesn't hurt. Looks like the swelling's gone down. You did good, lady."

She sat up, quickly turning her attention to his bandage. "We should change this before we go out."

'I'm hungry. Can't it wait?"

"I want to take a look. If we have to soak it, we can do that after dinner."

"Okay, okay. Ever been in the military? You're a drill sergeant."

She glared at him before gently removing the bandage. The cut had begun to knit together. It was still an angry red line, but the edges were clean, and the swelling was gone. It appeared to be mending well. "Looks good." She popped up and poked around in the first aid bag for the cream and bandages. After fixing him up with a fresh covering, she slipped on her shoes, combed her hair, grabbed her purse, and marched to the door. "Ready."

"Where do you want to eat?"

"Hmm. I don't eat it often, but how about pasta?"

"Fine. Did you see a place?"

"Let's ask at the front desk," she suggested, moving ahead as he held the door for her.

Jake's hand was well enough the next day for him to take the wheel. He drove all day, stopping for a quick lunch in Little Rock, then making tracks to Memphis. Halfway from Memphis to Nashville, Jake spied a billboard for a mom-and-pop steak joint in Garfield Glen.

"How about dinner at Mrs. Mansfield's Steak House?"

"I could use a good steak."

"Settled then. Getting off in Garfield Glen. Find it," he said as the Lexus roared down Route 40. Kate located it and directed him off the proper exit. They pulled into the parking lot, which was half full.

Jake stretched his legs and yawned before taking her hand and heading to the restaurant. He was surprised to find that Mr. Mansfield, who was seating people, recognized him. He shot a silly grin at the couple as he showed them to a romantic table with two candles on it.

"She's quite a looker, Jake."

"She is, isn't she?" The ball player smiled while Kate blushed.

"You jocks get all the prettiest gals, I swear," he said, handing them menus.

Both ordered steaks and baked potatoes. Kate ordered salad while Jake selected the green beans, instead.

When the waiter brought their food, Jake asked him about a motel.

"We're tired and need to break for the night. Know anyplace nice to stay around here?"

"Hmm. Let me see. There's the Dew Drop Inn. But that's more for transients. Not for famous folk like you, Mr. Lawrence."

"Jake."

"Jake. Let's see. Oh, yes. There's the Colonel's Inn. It's like a bed and breakfast, but it's a big mansion. Got a great suite on the top floor, too."

"Sounds perfect," he said, taking a knife to his meat. "Thank you."

"You're most welcome. Enjoy your meal." The waiter returned to the kitchen.

"I'll call and make a reservation," Kate said, her hand out for his phone.

"I don't know why I don't just give this to you."

"You might get another call from your teammates, checking up on your sex life."

He chuckled. "Then it'd be perfect for you to answer, wouldn't it?"

She dialed the B and B but couldn't hear well.

"I don't know what I reserved, but we have a room there."

"Great! How about dessert?"

"You've got to be kidding," she said patting her stomach. His gaze followed her hand.

"Come on. Share one with me. Look, strawberry cheesecake or molten lava chocolate cake? Says they're both made here."

She paused, gazing at him. "Okay, okay. I'll have a little."

He ordered the chocolate confection and two spoons. When it arrived, he scooped up some and fed it to her. When she opened her mouth, he watched her eat. A jolt in his groin almost knocked him off his chair when she licked chocolate off her bottom lip.

The heat between them escalated with every bite of the sexy dessert. When they finished, Kate sat back and stared at him.

"What? Did I get something on my shirt?" He looked down.

"A little chocolate, here," she said, leaning in and licking a smidgeon from the corner of his mouth. His intake of breath made her smile. He folded his fingers around her waist to steady her, then turned his head so his lips met hers.

This time, she gasped. He lingered for a second or two before easing her away from him. Yep, she tasted every bit as delicious as he had imagined. The waiter bumped Jake's hand with the bill, breaking the mood.

Kate blushed, her eyes wide, and smoldering. He knew then, that she wanted him, too. They only had a few days left. Could he make it happen before he dropped her at Keith's place?

He paid the server and they headed for the car.

"I'll put the address in the GPS. The guy said it wasn't far."

They pulled up in front of a large log home. At the front desk, Jake checked in.

"We have a reservation for a room with two double beds," he said, removing his wallet from his back pocket.

"Nope. Says here, the Apache room."

"The Apache room?"

"Yep. One king bed," the desk clerk said.

"Kate! Wait a minute."

He strode over to her. "Didn't you reserve a room with two doubles?"

"I couldn't hear the guy real well. That's what I said and he said something and I said 'okay'. I assume he had a room with two doubles. Is there a problem?"

"You might say that." Jake returned to the desk. "Do you have anything else?"

"The Cherokee room. But it has only one queen. Rest are booked for tonight."

Jake looked at his watch—already nine-thirty. "We'll take the one with one king."

Kate wandered over. He explained the situation and shrugged.

To his surprise, she said, "We'll manage."

"Sign here, please. And your credit card."

His hand was a little sore from driving all day, so Kate schlepped her own backpack up the stairs to their room. The western theme in the B and B continued into the guest quarters. A Native American blanket hung on the wall. There was a fireplace across from the bed, but it didn't look used much.

The king size bed dominated the room. A fluffy white comforter covered it. A homemade quilt, folded, rested at the foot of the bed. The low lighting gave the room a romantic air. Jake's heartbeat sped up. A nightstand, a small dresser, a wing chair by the fireplace, and a small desk with chair were the only other furnishings in the room. No place for either of them to sleep except in the bed. He swallowed saliva and avoided her gaze.

"It's big enough for each of us to have our own corner."

"A corner for me? I'm a little big for that. But I'll stay on my side. Unless you say otherwise."

She didn't respond, simply took her backpack and headed for the bathroom. Jake toed off his shoes and removed his clothes. He made sure he had a fresh condom in his wallet and placed it on the stand next to the bed.

The room was charming, decorated in red, green and white. The old West and Native American flavors blended well. He stretched out on the mattress and laced his fingers behind his head. His gaze scanned the room, taking in the little details that gave it an authentic feel.

The opening of the bathroom door drew his eye. Brushing her hair and clad only in his jersey, Kate stood in the doorway. The light behind her outlined her silhouette. His mouth dried.

"Your turn." She walked over to the bed.

Jake washed up quickly. When he returned to the room, the only light was the one next to his side of the bed. Kate was in bed, covers pulled up tight with her back to him. He sighed, disappointment turning his smile to a frown. This might be his only chance to get close to her and it had evaporated before his eyes.

He climbed into bed, switched off the light, and turned his back to her.

"Good night," he said, his voice low.

"'Night," she replied.

Even after a long day of driving, Jake wasn't sleepy. He lay on his side, thinking. He had an incredible woman a few feet away from him and in a few days, he'd probably lose her forever. But he was paralyzed. If he made a move, he'd scare her. He'd given his word that he wasn't there to jump her bones. He had to stick to it, no matter how difficult. Her even breathing indicated she was asleep. Tomorrow would be another long day of driving, he'd better get some shut-eye. He let out a breath and closed his eyes.

Kate lay still, hoping her even breathing would fool Jake into thinking she was asleep. Every nerve in her body tingled. Heat from him so close traveled under the covers. Time slipped through her fingers as she searched her heart. There he was, only inches away. She wanted him, more with each passing minute. There'd be no ignoring Jake Lawrence tonight. And no sleep.

He shifted position twice. *Does he feel it, too?* The pull to him drew her like a magnet draws iron. Afraid to roll over where she could see him, she struggled to keep her body still. His male scent, faint but distinguishable, teased her nose. She rolled over. Her gaze fastened on his muscular back, naked and visible.

Should she hold out or not? As her brain fought with her libido, she slipped into slumber. Visions of Santa Juana and the long, empty road stretched in front of her. She was hungry but didn't even have a quarter. As she walked, stores and restaurants vanished like mirages in the desert. The road emptied and the sun beat down on her back.

Thirst tore at her throat making it dry and raspy. She tried to sing, but couldn't. Not one car drove by. Totally alone, she panicked, desperation growing in her belly. She'd starve, die of thirst, or bake to death in the sun, alone, with no one to help.

Tears pricked behind her eyes. She willed herself not to cry, not to waste precious water in her body. Then she saw a car in the distance. She ran toward it, crying out, "Help! Help me!"

Something shook her shoulder. Kate's eyes popped open.

"Kate, Kate! Wake up. Wake up."

It was Jake. Her breathing ragged, she stared up at him. Moonlight through the window outlined his large form looming over her.

"Oh my God," she said, fear receding, tears of relief dampening her eyes.

"Did you have a nightmare?" His palm caressed her cheek.

She nodded. "It was awful. I was alone. Had nothing. No water." Then the tears burst forth. Jake scooped her into his arms, hugging her to him as she cried on his chest. The warmth of his skin, the firmness of his muscles, and the protection of his arms soothed her.

"It's okay, honey. You're safe now. You're with me. Nothing bad'll happen."

She melted to his form, listening to his words, spoken in a low, even tone. He stroked her hair, his lips rested on her forehead. Kate raised her leg and slid it around his waist. This was it. There was no parting from him now. Wide awake, desire thrumming in her core, she'd made up her mind to have him.

She pressed her hips against his and he responded.

"Do you want this?"

"Oh, yes. Yes."

"Are you sure?"

"Yes."

"Really? No regrets?"

"None. Stop talking. Do it. Make love to me."

His low chuckle fanned her flames. "My pleasure, honey," he said, tackling the buttons on the jersey. She helped and within a minute, it was open. He wasted no time sliding his hand down her chest to cup her breast.

"These are great," he said, lowering his head in the dark to kiss them.

She flattened her palms against his pecs and caressed her way up to cup his shoulders. His touch spread heat across her body. He pinched her peak gently, telegraphing lust right between her legs. She massaged his shoulders, pressing the pads of her fingers into his muscles. Sensing his strength added fuel to a growing fire.

He eased her down on her back, then sucked one nipple, while his free hand glided down her smooth side then back to her rear. He squeezed it.

"I've wanted to do that for the longest time," he whispered.

He continued to explore, his palm resting on the back of her thigh. He eased his hand up slowly, driving her wild with desire. Why was he taking so long? His fingers dove between her legs, and she let out a sharp cry.

"Did that hurt?"

"No, no. Just surprised me. It's great. God, it's great," she said, her eyes drifting shut.

His fingers skimmed along her slippery flesh before easing inside her. She groaned and reached down for his shaft. He was hard as steel. She moved her hand down to cup him and smiled as he grunted.

Jake removed his fingers to explore her fully. Searching for her sweet spot, when he hit pay dirt, she gasped. He chuckled once and zeroed in, stroking her. As her breathing became ragged, he slipped his fingers inside her again and pumped in and out, raising her heat to a raging fire.

"Stop. I'm gonna come."

"Ladies first," he chuckled.

She squeezed him and drew her knees to her chest. "Please. Do it. Do it."

"You got it," he replied, rising to his knees. He retrieved the condom from his wallet and applied it with lightning speed. Kate lay waiting, her breathing uneven, aching to have him quench her fire. He fumbled in the semi-dark until he was positioned perfectly.

"Sure now?"

"Oh, God! Stop torturing me! Yes!"

He chuckled, then thrust in, hard. She moaned as he filled her. He pushed up, his hand on her hip to steady her. He started slow, leaning down to kiss her, gently, then more savagely, his mouth possessing hers. She wanted to belong to him, to be taken, marked as his.

He picked up speed, moving faster. Heat mixed with passion in her blood, coiling tighter and tighter. Then it took off, commanding her totally as a huge orgasm ripped through her, clenching each muscle, then releasing pure pleasure to every nerve in her body.

She cried out his name as she arched her back and clutched his shoulders. Balancing his weight on his hands, he buried his face against her neck, his hips moving in a steady rhythm.

It had been so long since she'd slept with anyone, she'd forgotten how wonderful sex was. Then again, maybe she'd never had truly great sex before. As he worked toward his climax, her body continue to respond, tingling at the touch of his lips on her skin. Through her hands on his chest, she felt him stiffen. He grunted once, muttered something that sounded like her name and stopped for a moment, before collapsing on top of her.

"Ooph," she said as his weight squeezed the air from her lungs.

"Oh, sorry, sorry," he panted, shifting to his arms. He sat up and padded to the bathroom. When he returned, he slid over to her.

"You okay?"

"Are you kidding? That was amazing," she said, cuddling up to him.

Jake wound his long arm around her shoulders and pulled her against him.

"Was for me. God, it's been so hard not to touch you."

She pushed up to stare into his eyes. "I know! Me, too."

"Why didn't you say something?"

"Didn't want to rush it."

He laughed. "We've known each other for ten days."

"That's my point. It's only been ten days."

"Funny how different our perspectives are."

She rested her head on his chest and listened to the steady beat of his heart. He kissed her head and stroked her back. The sex part was great, but the cuddling part after was to die for. Not all guys liked to cuddle. She'd had some encounters where the man got dressed and left right after. Always made her feel cheap and alone. Jake had nowhere to go. Would he stay with her if he did? She didn't know the answer, but she didn't care. They were together.

She focused on the warmth of his fingers caressing her back, and the happiness flowing through her.

Jake couldn't stop smiling. Best sex he'd ever had. Maybe when his heart was involved, it took a different road? Or was it that he'd waited so long to have her? Whatever it was, satisfaction flowed through his veins as he held her close. Kate was not a girl you'd want to cut and run from. No, sir, the after-sex stuff was almost as awesome as the sex. Well, not really. Still, he couldn't take his hands off her.

Her skin was soft, warm, and smooth under his fingers. Her hair smelled like pears and lilacs. He combed his fingers through it like he'd wanted to do from the get-go. She eased her leg over his, hugging his thigh between hers.

Her fingers stroked his chest, brushing through the hair there. He kissed the top of her head.

"You okay?"

"I'm great," she muttered.

"You feel safe and stuff? I didn't force you."

"Shut up," she said, giving his pecs a playful slap. "You're ruining the mood. Stop worrying. I've been wanting this for a while, too."

He pulled the covers up over them and closed his other arm over her. Holding her seemed right, she fit perfectly against him. He yawned, then rested his head on hers.

"I hope you can sleep okay now."

"Are you kidding? Nothing could keep me awake."

He grinned. He loved a satisfied woman and so did his dick. A twinge from his hand reminded him that the cut hadn't healed completely yet. He placed it out of harm's way as his breathing settled down and he drifted off.

Rolling over in the dark, he bumped into Kate. The encounter woke him up. Nope, he hadn't been dreaming, Kate lay next to him, stark naked and almost purring. He touched her breast and she stirred, opening her eyes.

"Hey, handsome," she said, stretching, pushing herself into his hand as she arched.

"Hi, gorgeous."

"You up for more?" Her voice was lazy, sleepy.

Could you have morning wood in the middle of the night? He smiled. He grazed her cheek with his thumb, then followed with his lips. She purred, facing him, her eyes closing again.

He cupped her shoulder, pushing it back against the mattress. After pulling the covers down, he opened her knees and knelt between them. Jake Lawrence knew how to get a woman where he wanted her, fast. He lowered his head and tongued her flesh.

Kate flinched. Her hips rose and she moaned. Pleased with himself, he kept it up. Turning her on spiked more blood flow between his legs. Need grew until he didn't know how much longer he could wait. Then it happened, her hips bucked, and she cried out. He rode it out until she collapsed, panting.

At the point of bursting himself, he leaped off the bed and sprinted across the room, cursing himself for not putting a second condom in his wallet. He returned to the soft giggles of his satisfied woman. Covering himself with the speed of light, he was inside her before she could blink.

"Oh, God. Kate," he moaned.

She reached up to cup his cheek and draw his lips to hers. After one peck, he lost control, pumping into her hard and staring into her shadowed eyes. He bit back words of love that begged to be spoken. Turning his head, he kissed her palm, then thrust one final time before his balls tightened and he shot against the rubber.

His body stiffened, jerked, then relaxed. He blew air out and settled down on his elbows. The release was so powerful it robbed him of words. Even with steady girlfriends, he'd never had an experience like this. The emotional had blended with the physical for the perfect sexual experience—a first for him. He grinned to himself at the irony.

Jake had slept with plenty of women, some he had cared for, some not, some one-night stands, some longer term, but he'd never had overwhelming feelings for his partner before. As the rising sun shot beams of red and orange into the sky, her face came into focus.

The look of vulnerability melted his resistance. Fear mixed with what he could only term shyness to give her a vulnerable aura. Love grew in his heart. He wanted to protect her forever, to wipe away the loneliness, the sadness, the hardness, and the want from her life. Could he wrap her in his arms forever and keep her safe?

He spread his legs to either side of hers and sat back on his haunches. His gaze traveled down to her breasts. He couldn't wait to see them. He'd been envisioning them while he drove, stealing a glance here and there and imagining how round they were, how they sloped or didn't.

He cupped one and stared to his heart's content.

"If your eyes were lasers, my boobs would be burnt to a crisp."

"They're beautiful. Do you mind if I look?"

She smiled. "Not really."

"You embarrassed?"

"A little."

He nuzzled her neck.

"Don't be shy.

"Would you hold me?"

He rolled off her and onto his back. The sunlight grew stronger. He scooped her into his arms, tucked her head to his shoulder, and hugged her.

"We don't have much time," she said, nestling into his embrace.

He glanced at the clock. It read six-thirty.

"Check out is eleven. We have plenty of time."

"Oh. Good," she said, snaking her arm around his waist. Peace flowed through Jake. Baseball had taught him to be in the moment. He inhaled her scent, sweetened with a bit of lilac and her musky sexiness. He had no idea what tomorrow had in store, and he didn't care. At that moment, he had the girl of his dreams in his bed, in his arms. Nothing else mattered.

Chapter Five

The sun shone bright as Kate slipped her hand into Jake's. She took a deep breath and grinned at him. After a night of love and a hearty breakfast, the day looked bright and cheery. When they got in the car, he leaned over to kiss her, then revved the motor.

"Can you get us back to Route 40?"

"Yep. Hang on." She consulted a map, then gave him instructions to get back to the Garfield Glen entrance to the highway. They were about a hundred miles from Nashville.

"We'll be in Nashville soon. Wanna stop?"

"It's only about a hundred 'n fifty more to Knoxville. Let's keep going."

"A hundred and thirty-nine, to be precise," she replied.

"Perfect place to stop for lunch," he said.

"Oh yeah? You know a place?"

"I do. Dempsey's, the sweetest little barbecue joint in the world."

"Oh?"

"Yeah. It's run by Connor and Jilly Dempsey. Con used to play shortstop for the Cincinnati Coyotes. He lost an eye to a pitched ball, so he went home and started a restaurant."

"Wow. You know him?"

"Used to play ball with him in college."

"Really? Cool."

"That okay with you?" He glanced over at her.

She smiled and rested her hand on his thigh. "Sounds great! I'm pulling it up on the GPS now."

Once she got the address situated, she sank back into the luxurious seat and gazed out the window at the Appalachian Mountains in the distance. Spring had come earlier to Nashville than it did to New York City. She enjoyed the greening of the fields, farms, and foothills on the way to Knoxville.

Jake hadn't appeared this relaxed at the wheel before. Could it have been the sex? She giggled to herself—probably. The cuddling didn't hurt either. She hadn't slept that well in years. The warmth of his body surrounded her like a cocoon, protecting her from the world.

"You're looking relaxed."

"Might say that. Haven't passed a night like that in a long time." He gave her a lusty look.

"Me, neither."

A look in his eyes she'd never seen before mixed with desire. Could it be love? Not in ten days, what a ridiculous thought! She corralled her heart and put it safely away. Whatever she had with Jake was vibrant and wonderful. That's it. She should let it alone, not try to make it a forever thing, simply enjoy it while it lasted. She made up her mind not to mess up what they had by making unrealistic demands.

"You're quiet today. No singing?"

"Gosh, yeah. I almost forgot about the audition. Let's sing something else. Do you like folk songs?"

"Don't know any."

"Really? How about *Michael, Row The Boat Ashore*?"

"Think I've heard that one. How does it go?"

They sang folk songs all the way to Knoxville. At the appropriate exit, Jake turned the car toward Dempsey's.

They dined on barbecue, homemade cornbread, kale, and finished it off with mint chip ice cream. Hand in hand, they headed for the parking lot and the next leg of their adventure.

"I'm going to be twenty pounds heavier when we hit New York," Kate said, licking the last taste of ice cream off her lower lip.

"You look great. Don't worry."

"If I don't get the part because my butt's too big, it'll be your fault."

He reached behind her and squeezed her rear end. "Feels fine to me. Feels great, actually."

She laughed as he opened the car door for her. After another fifty miles, in the direction of Charlotte, Jake pulled off the highway.

"King's Suites. Nice place to stay. Ready to bunk in for the night?"

The twinkling headlights of other cars lit up the twilight.

"Sure."

They got out of the car, and Jake retrieved their bags from the trunk. Kate put a hand on his forearm.

"Wait. Let's get a room with one bed tonight. Okay?"

He grinned. "You kidding me? Fantastic!" He slung his free arm around her shoulders as they made their way to the front desk.

"Not THE Jake Lawrence? Of the New York Nighthawks?" The desk clerk asked.

"That's me. Got a room with a king?"

"For you and the missus? Sure do."

Kate opened her mouth to correct the man, but Jake winked and signaled her to stay still. Why bother? What did either of them care what a desk clerk in Randville thought, anyway?

"Sign here, please. And could I have your autograph?"

"Sure thing," Jake said, after filling out the hotel form. The man presented a piece of paper and Jake signed it. Then he got the key.

"Second door on the left after you get off the elevator."

Jake led the way. The room was big and so was the bed. Kate threw herself on it and bounced a few times.

"Looks great," she said, turning a hot stare on her companion.

"Looks even better with you on it."

"And even better with you in it. Take those off," she commanded, gesturing at his clothes.

"Don't have to ask me twice," he said, ripping his T-shirt over his head.

Jake awoke first. Kate had curled up next to him with her head resting on his arm. Her face, relaxed and natural, looked more beautiful than ever. He watched her sleep. He'd have a few more mornings like this, but then they'd reach New York and part company. Without her, waking up would never be the same.

His mind wandered back to the lovemaking of the night before and he grinned. Going to bed would never be the same, either. They had a hunger for each other that translated into the perfect rhythm. It didn't take long for Jake to discover what pleased her. Each night trust between them grew and little-by-little Kate loosened up, threw off her caution, and loved him with abandon.

The more they made love, the more he wanted her. Geez, sometimes he'd get hard while driving, simply remembering their hot coupling of the night before. How was he going to let her go? Why should he? Why shouldn't they keep seeing each other? Once she got the part, then she'd be in New York. Sure their schedules might be a little tricky, but at least they'd be in the same city—when he wasn't on the road. Hmm. Maybe he'd better tell her about that.

"Thinking about something?" she muttered, stretching and pulling away from him. A rush of cool air replaced the warmth of her body.

"Yeah. I want to see you when we get to New York."

"I'm going to be staying with Keith."

"Are you going to be sleeping with him?" Jake's heartbeat quickened.

"Keith is gay. He's got an extra bed in his room. I'll be sleeping there."

"Oh. Okay. Or you could stay with me."

"He's my partner in this audition. We have the same agent and she's arranged it. If we both get hired, and that's a big 'if', then it'll be more convenient for me to bunk in there."

Jake stroked her shoulder with his thumb. "Convenient, maybe. But not as much fun."

She grinned. "Probably not. Where do you live?"

"Uptown. Near the stadium. I live in the same building as Dan Alexander and his fiancée."

She nodded.

"It's a luxury apartment. Lots of big windows. Roomy. Plenty of space for two."

"Thanks. I'll think about it." She kissed his cheek, then faced the clock. "It's eight. Don't you want to get on the road?"

"We have to be in New York in three days, so, yeah. I guess we'd better get going."

They grabbed breakfast at a local diner, then piled into his car. He noticed her jotting something down in a little notebook.

"What's that?" he asked, starting the car.

"Nothing. Just a little record I'm keeping."

He nodded, threw the car in gear and hit the highway. "Where am I going?"

"Straight on Route 40. Just past Raleigh we hit 95. We'll hang a left there to head north. Then it's 95 all the way to Manhattan."

"Sounds easy enough. How far to Raleigh?"

"About one seventy-five. Should be there in time for lunch."

"What are you singing today?"

"I thought we'd get to your country stuff today."

"Country? Now you're talkin'!" He smiled as she sorted through his pile of country CD's.

She put in Willie Nelson and sat back, taking a sip of water.

"We don't have to stop seeing each other when we hit New York," he said, his pulse climbing.

"I suppose not. If I get the part, I'm going to be very busy with rehearsals."

"I know. I hope you do. Uh, I travel. We go on the road to play games out of town."

"Oh? How often?"

"Every couple of weeks. The team goes on the road for maybe two weeks, sometimes."

"Hmm," she said, nodding, training her gaze out the window.

"I know that can be lonely if you're the one staying behind."

"Yep. Wouldn't bother me, though. Running my own life takes time. Auditions, haircuts, manicures and stuff. Always have to look my best."

"I hear regular sex is good for the complexion," he said.

She burst out laughing. "If that's true, then my skin should be glowing."

He glanced over at her. "It is."

"That's why you want me to move in?"

Her tone turned icy, her stare hard.

"No, no. Well, of course, that's part of it, but not all."

"Oh?" She cocked an eyebrow at him.

He swallowed some saliva and checked the gas gauge. "I think we'd better stop for gas. Then we can go straight through to Raleigh."

She was out of the car in a flash and headed inside without looking at him. Did he do the wrong thing, trying to dodge her question? He wondered if he should tell her he was falling in love with her. He swiped his credit card and pulled off the gas cap. His heartbeat pumped in his ears. He'd not said those words for a long time. Did she feel the same?

Kate splashed water on her face to cool it down. She was pissed. Was Jake asking her to move in for convenient sex? Not that sex wasn't to the moon with him, but she was more than that. *Am I being defensive? He's been so nice, so respectful. Why am I so angry?*

She stopped to buy some mints and spied Jake washing the windshield and talking to an attendant. Next, he'd be signing an autograph. As she gazed at him, warmth crept through her. Then it hit her, like a tornado. She was falling for the guy and fear had reared its ugly head.

Being afraid of getting hurt had kept her alone most of her life. Not that it wasn't well-founded, it was. But, Hell, it didn't get her anywhere, did it? Protecting herself had eliminated some pain, but also love. Jake hadn't done anything to hurt her, but his offhanded remark about traveling set off alarm bells.

She'd read and heard about pro athletes on the road, screwing every willing female they met. A shudder zinged through her. The idea of him doing that punched her in the gut. Why did she care who Jake Lawrence slept with? Once they got to New York, he'd go his way and she'd go hers, right? Nope. Not right. Not anymore. How could she leave the kindest man she'd ever known, next to her dad?

"Can you make that out to Timmy?" the attendant asked.

"Sure thing," Jake said, writing his name. He looked up. "Ready?"

She nodded. He opened the door for her, then got behind the wheel. They drove for an hour with nothing but Willie Nelson's voice to break the silence. While Jake kept his eyes on the road, she watched the scenery whiz by. When the song finished, he spoke.

"Look, Kate. Maybe I got off on the wrong foot. I didn't mean that I want you to stay with me just for sex. I mean, of course, we'd be sleeping together. Shit. I'm not doing this very well."

"Maybe we could see each other. I mean date, from time to time."

"Okay. I'll take that. Yeah. Dating is good."

"It's better for me to live with Keith, for now. I have a lot of work to do if I'm going to make it to Broadway."

He nodded.

"And maybe this isn't a good time for a commitment. I mean, if you're traveling and all."

"Me? I'm not the problem."

"You'll be meeting lots of groupies, women probably throw themselves at you all the time."

He laughed. "Not exactly."

"Really?" She raised an eyebrow. "You want me to believe that if you go into a bar on the road, women in there don't come up to you and flirt?"

"Lots of women flirt." He glanced at her.

"And you don't flirt back? You don't proposition them and take them to bed?"

He trained his gaze on the highway while his face colored.

"Right. I knew it."

"Not all of 'em."

"Oh, I see. So only three-quarters? Maybe half?"

The color in his cheeks deepened.

"So maybe I'm no boy scout. But you're different."

"I am? Why? I'm just a woman, like all the rest." She leaned away from him.

"No, you're not. You're different."

"Because you took the time to get to know me instead of evaluating me on my breast size?"

"Shit."

"Yeah. Shit is about right. Committing to anyone who's running around wouldn't be good for me. Maybe we should agree to part in New York, Jake." *What am I doing?* Her heart squeezed.

"I did get to know you. I like you. A lot. It's not all about sex."

"I like you, too," she said, her voice softening.

"So what's the problem? Okay, maybe I do size up a chick by her boobs. What guy doesn't?"

"And?"

"And that's not true in this case."

"You didn't do that when you offered me a ride?"

The blush reappeared. "Okay, maybe I did. But I didn't do it because I wanted to sleep with you."

"You mean you didn't want to sleep with me?"

"You're getting this all mixed up. Of course, I did. What man in his right mind wouldn't want to sleep with a beautiful woman like you?"

His compliment stopped her.

"I did. To be honest. Of course, I did. But that's not why I offered you a ride. You were in trouble, and I wanted to help."

"And you put your sex drive aside?"

"Yeah. I know you won't believe that. I mean, guys can't help it. You know? That's how we're wired."

"You all think with your dicks."

"Yep. But then, sometimes, our brains actually kick in."

"For some of you."

"For me. It wasn't about wanting to get you into bed. Hell if it had been, I wouldn't have waited so long."

"Oh, really? You think you could have seduced me sooner?" She sat up straight.

"I didn't seduce you at all. You came to me willingly."

She crumbled in her seat, like a deflated balloon. "True."

"Thank God. At least you're honest. So what are we talking about here?"

"New York."

"Yeah. I want to see you. If I'm dating you, I won't be running around on the road. I promise. But what about you?"

"Maybe we could date with no commitment?"

"So you want to run around while I'm away?"

"I didn't say that."

"Might as well have. Good to know where I stand."

She covered her face with her hands. "Arrrggh!"

"Maybe we should stay on the road, Kate, we do fine here." He shot her a warm grin.

"Maybe." She leaned toward him and rested her hand on his thigh. Losing Jake would be a big mistake.

"How much longer to Raleigh?" he asked.

"Not long. Maybe twenty-five miles?"

"Good. I'm hungry. Can you find a place with steak?"

"I'll look." She got busy with her phone. "By the way, thanks for the loan to get my phone back up."

"No problem."

"I need it in case my agent calls."

"And to make dates with me."

"That, too," she said, shooting him a smile.

She found a restaurant called *Cattle Call*.

"Sounds like they'd serve beef," he said.

She agreed and gave him directions. Jake exited the highway and pulled into the parking lot. When he got out of the car, he and Kate did a few stretches.

"I'm going to the ladies room," she said, walking ahead of him. He nodded as his cell rang. It was Nat.

"You fucker! Why didn't you tell us?"

"Tell you what?"

"Come on. Don't play dumb."

"I don't know what you're talking about."

"It's all over the papers, Jake. Congratulations, buddy."

"What the fuck are you talking about?"

"Your marriage. Eloping with that chick. You surprised all of us."

"What?"

"It's all over the Internet, Jake. Congratulations, man. Chicks everywhere are gonna be cryin'."

"Nat, believe me. I didn't get married."

"I guess you'd better contact the media, then. Because it's everywhere that you did," Nat said.

Skip came on. "We're planning a bachelor party for you, buddy."

"Why didn't you tell us?" Matt Jackson, catcher, had grabbed the phone.

"Oh, man. There is some mistake. Some huge mistake, guys."

"Good luck. See ya in a couple of days," Matt said.

Kate waited at the door of the restaurant. She raised her eyebrows. "Bad news?"

He shook his head. "Remember that desk clerk at the Colonel's Inn?"

"Yeah?"

The maître d' showed them to a table.

"Seems he's well connected with Internet news sources."

"What do you mean?"

"Sit down. You might want to order a drink."

They placed their orders for steak sandwiches and beer. Jake searched his name. Sure enough, up popped headlines, *Baseball Slugger Elopes. Dark-haired Beauty Tags Jake Lawrence at the Altar.* Jake shared the results with Kate.

Although they didn't have her name, her picture was plastered right next to Jake's.

"Married? Us? Married?" she repeated, her eyes wide.

"Yeah. I don't know how, what, why..."

She burst out laughing. "This isn't gonna help your rep on the road, Jake."

"You're not mad?"

She shook her head. "Why should I be? They don't have my name. It's free publicity. Besides, being coupled with a sexy, famous guy like you can only help me."

"Gee, I thought you'd be pissed.

"I could do a lot worse than be married to you," she said.

The power of her words drew color to her face. Jake snapped to attention. *Did I hear right?*

"I mean, if they're gonna hook me up with someone, you're a good bet."

"I am?"

"I mean. It could be worse."

"Thanks a lot!"

She put her hand on his arm. "I didn't mean it like that."

"How did you mean it?"

She gazed at her food. "A girl would be happy with a guy like you."

"Really?"

She nodded, still not raising her gaze. He put a large finger under her chin and tilted her head up. "Same goes for you. Someday, some guy is gonna be damn lucky to call you his wife."

The waiter arrived. "Can I take these plates away?"

Annoyed at the interruption, Jake showed his palm. "We're not finished."

"Sorry, sir."

Once he was gone, the ballplayer took Kate's hand. He raised the back to his lips.

"You'll be a big Broadway star and won't have five minutes for a slugger like me."

She cupped his cheek. "So long as you're not mad to be paired off with a nobody."

"You're not a nobody to me."

They finished eating in silence, exchanging hot looks from time to time. Jake wanted her more than he wanted his food. He finished eating quickly.

"I'm feeling a little tired. Let's find a place for the night."

She nodded and pushed to her feet. Jake paid the cashier, dropped a few bills on the table, and they headed for the car.

Jake's cell rang. It was his manager, Cal Crawley.

"What's up, Cal?"

"Need a favor."

"Shoot."

"There's a farm team in Durham. Guy there named Gary Nevers. Could you stop and take a look at him?"

Jake raised his eyebrows in question at Kate.

"Maybe for a few hours tomorrow? That okay?"

"Perfect. Tell them you're my scout and report back to me when you get here. Thanks."

The phone went dead.

"It'll only be a few hours. Do you mind?"

"Nope. I've got a couple of days before the audition."

"Good. Now let's find a place to crash."

He put the car in gear.

Chapter Six

They headed for downtown Greensboro.

"Let's try the Jackson Arms Hotel," Kate said, punching the information into the GPS.

The downtown area was charming with some tall office buildings and quaint brick alleyways and shops. They pulled up to the hotel and a valet took their luggage, then parked their car. Kate was impressed.

They strolled up to the front desk. The clerk greeted Jake by name. Kate frowned. This might prove to be embarrassing.

"How long you and the missus staying, Mr. Lawrence?"

Jake shot her a look and cleared his throat. Kate covered her mouth with her hand.

"Just the night. Need to move on in the morning."

"That's right. Opening day's coming real soon. Here you go. I happen to have a suite available. I can give it to you for the cost of a king room."

"That's awesome! Thank you so much."

"Just sign here and give me your credit card."

While Jake took care of business, a tingle ran up Kate's spine. A suite and the third baseman—did life get any better than that? She licked her lower lip and stared at Jake's back. His shoulders pulled a little at the T-shirt, straining to cover his muscular frame. Soon he'd be ripping that off and making love to her.

He held out his hand, but she took his arm, instead, and they took the elevator to the top floor. The room was splendid, with floor-to-ceiling windows overlooking the city. Jake closed the door and faced her.

"The missus. Guess that bit of gossip has traveled the world."

"I could do a lot worse, slugger." She put her hands on his shoulders. His mouth descended to capture hers almost before he closed his arms around her. He backed her to the bed. When he let her up for air, she spoke.

"I had a feeling when you wanted to stop early that you had something in mind."

"Got me figured out already? We must be married."

He slid his fingers under the back of her T-shirt. They were warm on her skin and excited her in anticipation of the delights yet to come. The bed hit the back of her knees and she went down, taking him with her.

"Look out!" he said, laughing as he fell on top of her.

"Ooph."

As quickly as he landed on her, he pushed up on his elbows, and spread his legs with knees on either side of hers. Kate looked up at him. Something about the position, or Jake, his smile, lusty and loving, spread a sensation of safety alongside desire through her.

"Do it, do it, Jake," she breathed in his ear.

He laughed. "Nope. Takin' my time."

She squirmed under him.

"You can do that all you want, but I'm not rushing."

"But, I..."

"Nope. We've only got a couple of days left. Tomorrow, we head to Durham, then it's Virginia, and home in a day, maybe a day and a half."

"So?"

"I don't know what'll happen then. I need as much of you as I can get. Now. So I'm takin' my time, pretty lady. Not rushin'."

"But we can see each other in New York."

"Who knows how that'll play out? This is now. You're here. Now. I'm gonna take my time."

She sighed. After traveling across country with him, she knew that when Jake dug his heels in like this, there was no shaking him. She lay back, raised her arms, and combed her fingers through his hair. Their eyes met. Behind the lust, she saw a softness, questioning. Was that love? Couldn't be—not so fast.

She pushed up and yanked her shirt off. His hand stopped her unhooking her bra.

"Let me."

She dropped her hands and let him undress her, watching him. He cupped her chin and lifted her mouth to his. She met his passion with her own. Choking back the word *love*, she arched her back, pressing her breasts to his chest. Her nipples hardened, awaiting attention. His tongue snaked past her lips to caress hers. His warmth ratcheted up as his hands met her breasts.

Kate committed every sensation to memory. She figured making love with Jake in this beautiful suite would be a one-time thing, something she'd never want to forget. Her future was uncertain, and romantic ties now didn't make sense. Today had to be everything as tomorrow wasn't guaranteed.

But Jake Lawrence wasn't about sense, he was about feeling. Kate shut off her mind and let her body take control. Passion coiled inside, winding tight. She tugged on his pants.

"Off."

"Take it easy, woman! We have all afternoon. No reason to hurry."

"I want you. Isn't that reason enough?"

His grin warmed her. "I want you, too, honey. But I want to make it last. Like a box of fine chocolates, you don't eat them all in one sitting."

He shucked his shirt and pants and joined her on the big bed.

After tossing a couple of condoms on the nightstand, he asked, "Where were we?"

"Right here," she said, pushing him down on his back and straddling him. She leaned down to kiss him.

He hugged her to him, then rolled them over. Kate opened her heart as well as her body and let him in.

Heavy blinds kept the sun out of their room, so Kate and Jake slept until ten. She opened her eyes first. He was spooning her, his muscular arm wrapped around her chest. She sighed and snuggled into him another inch.

The hair on his chest tickled her back. She eased the covers over her bare shoulder as her mind roamed over their marathon lovemaking session of the night before. A slight tenderness between her legs reminded her of his incredible stamina and expertise. She'd never had a lover like Jake and probably wouldn't again, so she savored the experience.

She kissed his arm and settled into the warmth generated by him that was trapped under the blankets.

"Hey, gorgeous," came a deep-voiced, sleepy greeting from behind her.

"Hey, yourself."

"You were incredible last night," he whispered in her ear, bestowing a kiss on her hair.

"You were amazing. Totally new for me."

"Who've you been sleeping with?" he asked.

"No one like you, big guy."

He chuckled. "Good. Let's keep it that way."

One glance at the clock and she gasped. "Crap! It's ten-thirty!"

"Shit! We need to check out by eleven and hit the road. I promised to be in Durham by one."

"Last one in the shower's a rotten egg," she said, throwing off the covers and sprinting to the bathroom.

Jake leapt over the bed and chased her to the stall.

"If we go in there together, we'll be here until next week," he said.

"But there's no time to shower separately," she argued.

"Okay. But no touching," he replied.

She laughed and turned on the hot water.

They washed in record time and jumped into their clothes. Hitting the front desk at eleven on the nose, they asked for a recommendation for lunch.

"Do you like barbecue?"

They nodded.

"Stamey's has got the best in all of North Carolina. Maybe even the world!"

"Great! Directions?"

While the clerk printed out Jake's receipt and gave Kate directions to the eatery, Jake toted their bags to the car and packed up. As soon as she closed the door, he put the car in drive, and roared out of the lot.

After wolfing down Stamey's pork barbecue sandwiches with barbecue slaw, they got in the car. Kate jotted something down in a small notebook.

"What is that? You keep doin' that. What are you writing?" he asked, maneuvering the car onto the shoulder.

"Nothing. Never mind. I'll tell you later."

When she turned her head, he snatched the notebook. She grabbed for it, but he held it away from her grasp. He read a series of numbers. "What the hell?"

"It's what I owe you. For all the meals and stuff."

"You don't owe me anything," he said, tossing the book from the window before pulling back onto the highway. "Don't you dare even think about paying me."

"But I..."

"But nothing. This is insulting. I'm taking care of you because I want to. It makes me happy. And don't you turn it to shit dollars and cents." He clamped his lips together and stared at the road.

"I'm sorry, Jake. Please. I'm sorry. It's just that I don't like to owe anyone."

"You don't!" He hit the gas harder.

"Okay, okay," she said, raising her palms.

"That's settled," he said.

"Thank you," she said and leaned in to kiss his cheek.

"You're welcome," he said as they sped toward Durham.

"How about a song?" he asked.

"How about rehearsing our number again?"

"Shoot, babe," he said.

"Tonight we'll go over the steps," she said before breaking into song.

"Steps? Like dancing?"

"Yep."

"Thank God, I don't have to do this audition. I have two left feet. I'm no dancer."

"It's okay. You take Keith's part. I need to practice."

"Fine. Let's go," he said, passing an SUV.

She started the song and he chimed in on his cue. They sang all the way to Durham. Kate punched in Durham Devils' stadium and the GPS showed them the way.

When they got out of the car, he motioned for her to join him. He slung an arm casually around her shoulders. She snaked hers around his waist as they headed for the ballfield.

Jake introduced himself to the manager.

"I'm here to take a look at the team for Cal Crawley."

"Great. We're practicing now. By the way, congratulations on your marriage."

"We're not married. That was someone making a big mistake."

"Oh. Sorry."

"No worries."

The manager glanced at Kate.

"With a filly like that, I'm surprised you're not." He chuckled.

Heat suffused her face. This marriage thing was getting out of hand. Would she like to be married to Jake Lawrence? Hell, she didn't even know if she believed in marriage, after watching her parents' disintegrate. But if she did believe, then, Jake was the type of man she'd marry. At least what she knew of him, so far.

They spent the next two hours watching the Durham Devils play each other. Jake chatted with the team and the manager. At three, they bid farewell to Route 40 and headed north on Route 85 to Virginia. Two hours later, they cut across Route 58, heading for Euphoria, where they picked up Route 95. Kate sat back. That highway went all the way to Maine, so she didn't need the GPS unless they decided to get off.

It wouldn't be long now before they'd be in New York.

At five, Kate said, "It's only an hour more to Richmond. Do you want to stop there for dinner?"

"Sure."

"You're not tired?"

"Not too tired to take you to the moon tonight, sweetheart."

They stopped for a quick meal just off the highway, a few miles north of Richmond. Determined to spend the night in Washington, D. C., Jake hit the gas. They rolled into town about nine-fifteen. Kate navigated them to the Washington Arms hotel on Dupont Circle. The small, elegant building had one room left. It was on the top floor with a view of the city. Jake checked in and rode in the elevator, holding Kate's hand.

This would be their last night on the road. The last time they'd be together without the outside world poking its nose in their business. Emotion gripped his throat. Would he see her again? Would a Broadway star want to have anything to do with him? He swallowed. And if she didn't make it? Then what? He'd be there to pick up the pieces. Either way, he didn't want to say goodbye to the best woman he'd ever known.

He stood at the window while Kate took over the bathroom. He heard the water running in the tub. His cell dinged. He checked the screen, it was Angela calling. This was her third call in two days. He'd ignored the others but figured he could take this one since Kate was occupied in the bath.

"Hi," he said, not anxious to give a lengthy, warm greeting he didn't feel.

"Hi, yourself. What's this I hear about you being married?" That's Angela, straight to the point with no beating around the bush, or warm hello, either.

"It's a mistake. I'm not married."

"That's not what the Internet says."

"And you've never known the Internet to be wrong? Where are you?"

"France."

He breathed a sigh of relief.

"But I'm thinking about coming home early."

"Don't bother on my account. I'll be going on the road soon, anyway."

"That's not very welcoming," she responded.

"We agreed to see other people while you were gone."

"And?"

"I think we should keep it that way." He shifted his weight.

"Are you breaking up with me? Long distance? On the phone?"

"Didn't think we really had anything to break up." He tilted his gaze up to look for the Big Dipper.

"I've been gone two months. I thought we'd agreed to put it on hold."

"We did. But now, well…"

"Have you met someone else?"

He picked up on the note of jealousy in her voice. "The point is, we're kinda done."

"So you have. Hmm. I see. Not very loyal."

"Call it what you will. We were heading this way anyway."

"I didn't think so. Can you keep an open mind? I'm coming back in a couple of weeks."

"Whatever. We had fun, Angie. Let's leave it at that."

"Whoever she is can't hold a candle to me."

"I've gotta go. Hitting the road early tomorrow. Goodbye."

He clicked the phone off. God, he hated women who didn't let go. There hadn't been anything there with Angela for at least a month before she left. He'd been counting the days until her ship sailed. Jake had never liked breaking up. He hated to hurt anyone. But in this case, he knew damn well Angela didn't give a shit about him.

But she was competitive. Once she sensed another female was involved, she'd come roaring back into the picture, determined to win him back. He frowned. Not this time. There'd be no reconciliation. He realized what he'd been missing and had found it in Kate. No one was going to mess with that—not as long as he had a say about it.

"Who rained on your parade?" she asked, wearing a towel fastened around her chest and drying her hair with another one as she headed toward the window.

"Can't believe it's our last night on the road," he said, ignoring her question. Let her think his bad mood was due to the end of the trip. She stood next to him. He draped his arm around her shoulders.

"Me, neither. The audition is two days away. I'd better call Keith. Make sure everything's okay. Better tell him I'll be bunking in with him tomorrow." She wandered over to the luggage and retrieved her phone.

Jake stood where he was. He heaved a sigh—just his luck to have Kate moving on and Angela coming back. He gave his head one shake. Nope, Angela would not be returning, not to his bed or to his life. They were done. When he thought of his time with Kate compared to days he'd spent with Angela, he wondered why it had taken him so long to shake loose from the society babe. After a deep breath, he forgave himself. Steady, ho-hum sex was better than none at all, wasn't it?

Of course, now he was ruined for any other woman. Who could stand up to the Earth-shattering lovemaking he'd had with Kate? He doubted there was another woman on the planet who could arouse him like she had. And where would he ever find one as responsive? The slightest touch from him got her motor running. He grinned.

There had to be a way to keep her in his life. He needed to continue to wake up smiling every day.

"What? What?"

Kate's anxiety-filled voice cut through his private thoughts. She slumped down on the bed, the phone to her ear. Her brows were knit and her blue-green eyes clouded. He joined her.

"Okay, okay. I'll be there tomorrow. If you're sick you're sick. I know. Love you, too."

"What happened?"

"Keith could hardly talk. He's got strep throat. He's really sick. I'm not sure he can do the audition with me."

"Oh no!"

"Yes. And he says I can't stay there 'cause I could get it, too."

"I can fix that."

She turned full eyes to him. "You can?"

"Stay with me."

"Thank you." She put her hand on his arm. "Maybe he'll at least be well enough to sing in two days. If he rests and doesn't talk."

"Maybe. We can hope."

She exhaled.

"I don't like to be negative. I'm just curious. What happens if you don't get the part?" he asked.

"I don't know. Haven't thought that far ahead."

"This guy I know owns a bar called Freddie's. It's near the stadium. We hang out there after a game sometimes. Have dinner there. He's always saying he should hire a singer. He's already got one of those little pianos."

"If I spend time trying to figure out a what-if scenario, it takes away from my positive energy. I need to be completely focused on getting this in order to ace the audition. I know myself. If I'm distracted, I'll stumble and fail."

"I shouldn't distract you, then," he said, pulling away from her.

'Get back here! You're not a distraction. Well, maybe you are, but a positive one."

"I am?"

"You boost my confidence."

"Scoot over here. I feel like boosting you," he said, sliding her onto his lap. The towel came undone. Jake feasted his eyes on her breasts.

"These are so perfect."

"Nothing about me's perfect."

"Everything about you is perfect. Perfect for me," he said, lowering his head to capture her peak between his lips.

Chapter Seven

They roared into New York City at four in the afternoon. Kate had called Keith, and he could barely talk. She went back to Jake's place. He lived in a posh high-rise, with a doorman and a valet—and a view of the Hudson and New Jersey.

The attendant took the car, after a warning from Jake about taking care with the expensive vehicle. Then the third baseman escorted his lady upstairs. They were on the tenth floor, not the highest, but not the lowest, either. After they settled in, Jake popped open two beers and they lounged on the couch, watching the sun set.

The red sky foretold a beautiful day coming the next day. Jake had practice at the stadium, and Kate had planned to rehearse her audition piece.

"How about doing the dancing part with me again. Just to keep me loose," she said.

"Sure. Though I stink. Good thing you're not auditioning with me. The producers would be laughing their asses off."

"Come on. Let's get those feet moving."

They sang and danced for an hour.

"Dancing made me tense. I need to be relaxed tomorrow when I start swinging the bat."

"Sorry about that."

"There's something you can do to help."

A sly grin stole across her lovely face. "I thought so. Come on, sexy. Let's get naked."

"Ladies, first," he said, following her into the bedroom.

"Not this time." She reached for the snap on his jeans. She had them unzipped and dropped to his thighs before he could stop her. Kate fell to her knees, ripped his boxers down, and thrust his hardening shaft into her mouth.

"Holy Hell," he muttered, tripping backward until he fell on the bed. Kate stayed with him, kneeling beside him on the mattress. He ran his fingers through her hair, trying to look at her but unable to tear his mind, his senses away from the ecstasy her mouth created. His hand wandered to her breast. He found her nipple and gave it a little pinch. Then he slipped his fingers under her T-shirt and snapped open her bra.

"Your turn."

He had her undressed and bending over the bed. He held her hips, then slipped inside her, savoring the grip of her muscles. Bending over, he managed to cup a breast when she pushed up. A moan from her lips brought a smile to his. He loved pleasing her as much as himself.

Steadying her hips, he pounded into her.

"Oh, God!" She moved up and down.

He felt a gush of wetness inside her and knew she had climaxed. He loosened his control and release shook him to his ankles. He groaned and eased down on her back, absorbing his weight with his hands on either side of her, his sweaty chest resting lightly on her back.

Again the three little words were on her tongue. She swallowed. This was no time to be saying that to Jake or anyone else. She had a career to take to the next level and now was her time. Jake's sweet sexiness tugged at her heart. How easy it would be to give it all up and settle in with him, if he'd have her. That was a big IF. Best to continue on her own and create her own security. Then, she'd come back to him, when she had something to offer.

"I have practice at nine tomorrow. Let's go to bed."

She nodded. "Works for me. I've got to get limber and practice tomorrow. My audition is Tuesday afternoon."

They cuddled up together. They were asleep before the clock struck ten. At six, they were awakened by her cell. She rubbed the sleep from her eyes and glanced at the screen. Her agent?

"Lacy? What's up?" She pushed up on an elbow. Jake sat up, yawning.

"Keith went to the emergency room last night."

"What? What happened?"

"His fever spiked to a hundred and six. He's really sick, babe, might have pneumonia. No way he's auditioning with you tomorrow. You go on, as scheduled."

"But I need a partner."

"One of the assistant producers will do it with you."

"Oh, shit," she moaned.

"You'll be fine. Kill it."

"How's Keith?"

"They brought his fever down and sent him home this morning. He just called. He'll be okay. Be at the Porter Theater by four. Break a leg, babe."

The phone went dead.

Panic grabbed her, tightening her chest. Tears stung her eyes. She struggled to wake up and take in what Lacy had said. Keith was out. What was she going to do now?

"What's the matter, honey?" Jake's warm hand on her bare back released her emotions.

"Keith's real sick. I have to audition by myself," she cried, burying her face in her hands.

"You'll be fine. You know it cold. You're great."

"But it's for two people. Now I have to do it with some assistant producer who doesn't give a shit about me."

"Really? A stranger? Can't you just do it by yourself?"

She shook her head. "It's a duet."

He drew her into his embrace. She wiped her eyes with her hand. His hug helped, but wouldn't fix this situation.

"There is someone who knows this as well as I do."

"Really? Great. Call him," Jake said, rubbing her back.

"I don't have to. He's right here."

"What? He lives in this building?"

"Yeah. He's you, Jake."

"Me? Me?" His voice rose an octave. "Me audition with you for Broadway? Are you joking?"

"I couldn't be more serious. Please, Jake. If you're there, I'll be okay. I'll do my best."

"I couldn't. I'm not. Kate, I'm a ball player, not a singer and definitely not a dancer."

"Don't worry. You don't have to be a good dancer. You're a great singer. Our voices blend perfectly." She sat up.

He was silent, watching her.

"It's not until four on Tuesday."

"That's opening day. I have a game at noon."

"Noon? When would it be over?"

"I don't know. If we tie, then it could go into extra innings."

"Shit." She sank down, like a deflating tire. "I'm finished."

She lowered her gaze, then peeked at him through her lashes. He appeared to soften.

"I can't guarantee when I can be there."

"You'll do it?" She straightened up immediately.

"I can't promise. But if we're done on time, then, yes. I'll be there."

"Oh, Jake! I love you, I love you. Thank you, thank you!!" She jumped on him, hugging him, smothering him with kisses.

"I'll do my best."

"I know you'll be there. How can I ever thank you?"

"I'll think of something," he said, his eyes twinkling. Then he frowned. "Look, don't count on me. The game has to come first."

"I know. But I'm praying you beat their butts and then come on down to me."

"Baby, if I can be there, I will. I promise I'll do everything I can."

"I know you will. Thank you."

"Did you mean it?"

"What?"

"The *I love you* stuff?" he asked, his expression shy.

Caught. The words gave her away, and she couldn't lie now. She could never lie to Jake.

"Yes. I did. I do. I'm sorry. I'm sure you're not interested. But I couldn't help it."

"Oh, baby. Music to my ears. I love you, too," he said, grabbing her upper arms.

The alarm went off before he could kiss her.

"Time to get ready to go."

"Okay. I'll be here. I'll make something nice for dinner."

"Great. I'll see you at six." He pushed up from the bed and padded, naked, to the bathroom. Kate watched the muscles in his back and buttocks as he moved. She loved watching him, especially when he was unaware. His body was like a panther's, taut, strong, and ready to pounce. She shivered at the thought that he loved her back.

Now she had to get moving, practice, and rustle up a dinner fit for a king. How many ways could Jake bail her out? Perhaps he was a sign that her luck had changed. While he showered, she explored the kitchen, discovering thick steaks in the freezer.

Dressed, Jake ambled into the kitchen. Kate had coffee, fried eggs, and toast ready.

"Didn't know you could cook," he said, tucking into the perfectly prepared food.

"You never asked. Besides, this is nothing. Tonight'll be great."

He finished, dropped his dishes in the sink. Then he kissed her, dropped three twenties, and a spare key on the table and headed for the door. Kate finished her coffee and called her agent.

"It's okay, Lacy. I've got a partner. He's great. Yep. We'll be there." When she hung up, she uttered a little prayer that Jake could make it on time.

Pocketing the bills, she stuffed the key in her pocket and made tracks to the grocery store. Tonight she'd concoct a meal to remember.

Jake rolled into the parking lot and turned off the motor. After his trip, he was looking forward to seeing his teammates again. He couldn't stop smiling. She'd told him she loved him. He'd won the best girl in the world, and now he'd push his body into shape and whoop ass on the baseball diamond.

He whistled the song *Friendship* as he strolled to the locker room. His closest buddy, Skip Quincy, the shortstop, was already there, rummaging through his locker for something.

"Jake!" Quincy hollered. He grabbed his friend's left hand. "No wedding ring!"

Jake snatched his hand from his friend's grip. "I told you. I'm not married."

"But there's a girl?"

"Yeah. An actress. Singer. Gorgeous."

"And you two traveled together?"

"Some asshole desk clerk assumed we were married, just because we were checking into the same room."

Skip wiggled his eyebrows. "Not married, but enjoying the honeymoon?"

Jake felt color in his face. "None of your business."

"How did you meet her? At a bar?" Nat Owen asked.

"That's a long story."

Before Jake could launch into his tale, Cal Crawley, the manager, entered the locker room.

"Hey, Jake. Good trip?"

"The best."

"Did you manage to see that guy in Durham?"

"Gary Nevers?"

Crawley nodded.

"Yes," Jake said.

"Come, fill me in." Cal motioned for Jake to follow him. His teammates gestured behind the manager's back, but Jake simply shrugged. When Cal Crawley beckoned, you followed.

An hour later, he joined his buddies in the workout room. He set the treadmill and jogged. Matt Jackson, Dan Alexander, Nat, Skip, and Bobby Hernandez gathered around.

"Okay, buddy. What happened on the road?" Matt asked.

"Let's go! Get out there. Jake, batting. Quincy, fielding. Owen, first base. Matt, behind the plate. Come on. Tomorrow is opening day."

The guys dispersed before Jake had a chance to clue them in. He put on his batting glove and hit the field. Time to tap into his amazing focus and hit a few out of the park.

At noon, the players hit the meeting room. There was a buffet of sandwiches, salads, and iced tea, milk, and juice. Accompanied by the rest of the starting infielders, Jake sat at a long table. He dug into a plate piled high with a hero sandwich, macaroni salad, potato salad, and pickles.

"Okay. We've waited long enough," Skip said. "Give."

Jake took a couple of bites, then a swig of his drink.

"You're not going to believe my luck," he started.

As he talked he heard footsteps behind him.

"All that time and you weren't doing the deed?" Dan Alexander asked.

"Nope. That's what was so funny about the clerk thinking we were married."

"And now?" Skip raised his eyebrows.

"That's none of your business," Jake said, casting his gaze at his hands.

"Let's go. Back outside," Cal called, bailing his third baseman out of an embarrassing situation.

As they headed for the field, Matt asked, "So you're going to be auditioning for Broadway?"

"No, not me, you moron. Her. I'm just along for the ride. She needs someone who knows the song."

"But you're going to sing back, right?" Matt continued.

"Yeah. But it's not about me. They'll be watching her. No one gives a shit if I sing on key."

"At least you've got a pretty good voice," Nat said.

"For singing in the shower. I'm not a professional or anything. Not even close."

"Coulda fooled me," Nat mumbled as he slipped on his glove.

Jake patted his friend on the back. "Thanks, Nat. Just hope they feel that way about Kate."

He stepped up to the plate while Moose Macafee headed to the mound. It was the relief pitcher's turn to go head-to-head with the Nighthawks' biggest hitter. Jake went into the zone, marshaling his impressive ability to focus on the ball. He didn't expect to be able to get back into the game so fast, having spent two weeks falling in love. But he did. His head was on the field, his eyes narrowed as the ball was released.

He knocked it into centerfield, sending Chet Candelaria back to the warning track. But the ball was out of the park. Jake chuckled and insisted on loping from base to base. His body hummed, performing at a high level as Jake whacked pitch after pitch into the stands.

After a dozen, Moose took off his glove. "I give up, man. What've you been eating?" The pitcher shook his head and made tracks toward the bullpen.

Kate showered and slipped on Jake's jersey and nothing else. Potatoes were baking in the oven. Steak sizzled in the cast iron grill pan while sautéed mushrooms and onions rested in a skillet, keeping warm on the stove. A crisp salad hid in the fridge.

A hint of chocolate in the air gave away her secret dessert, warm brownies with vanilla ice cream. As she rubbed more garlic on the steak, her stomach growled. Her mouth watered at the tantalizing aromas swirling through the apartment.

Kate wanted to give her lover the meal of his life before opening day. There was so much she owed him for everything he'd done. She was so far in debt, she'd never be able to repay him. Tomorrow he'd be stepping in for Keith. Maybe she'd have to marry him and spend the rest of her life making it up to him. Her hand flew to her mouth. Who mentioned marriage? No. No way. She had lots to do before she could even consider that. But, if she'd accomplished everything on her mental list, Jake would be in the running for her hand. Although she hadn't known him long, she had a feeling he was husband material.

"Honey, I'm home!" Jake's voice boomed through the apartment. Kate jumped, then laughed.

"Oh, it's my big, handsome, strong man!" She fluttered her eyelids at him and joined her hands in front of her chest.

He snickered, then stopped to stare, his gaze sweeping over her slowly. "Wearing that again?"

"I thought you'd like it."

"I love it. Now take it off."

"Uh, uh, uh," she said, wagging her finger at him. "Dinner first."

"What's cooking? Something smells great," he said brushing his lips over hers before removing his jacket and hanging it in the front closet.

"Come on," she said, taking his hand, leading him into the living room. She had set the table by the big windows.

"Do you want to open the wine?" she asked as she lit two candles.

"No wine for me. Opening day tomorrow. Noon. I need to be sharp."

"None for me. Bad for the vocal chords before an audition."

"I guess that's for me, too. Though nobody's going to be listening to me."

"You never know. What if they wanted to hire you *and* me?"

He laughed. "Fat chance."

"Would you leave baseball for Broadway?"

"Nope."

"Aww. It would be such fun to be kissing on stage as well as off."

He gave her rear a pat. "Never happen. Dinner ready yet?"

"Hungry?"

"Starved."

"Coming right up." She swung her hips a little more than usual as she headed for the kitchen.

Jake followed. "Can I help?"

She gave him the salad and then the water pitcher. She prepared plates with steak smothered in onions and mushrooms, and the creamy potatoes with butter in the kitchen and carried them to the living room.

His eyes lit up when she placed the plate in front of him. "Amazing! Did you make this?"

She nodded. He sliced off a piece of meat and popped it into his mouth. As he chewed, he closed his eyes and moaned. "Delicious."

She grinned, then took a taste herself. "Not bad."

"Not bad? This is gourmet, baby."

Jake dug into the tempting meal with enthusiasm. Kate asked him questions about practice and the opening day game happening the next day.

"We're playing the Philadelphia Bucks. They should be easy as shit to beat. We wiped them out again and again last year."

"Then the game will be quick?"

"You never know in baseball. But it should be over in about three hours, tops."

"Then you'll come down to the theater, right?"

"Right. I'm taking the car. You know how fast I can go."

She took his hand between hers. "You're the best, Jake."

"And that meal belonged in a four-star restaurant. Or my belly. Thank you." She palmed his cheek. He turned and kissed her hand.

When they finished, he cleared the dishes away and loaded the dishwasher.

"Leave the rest. Blanche will get them tomorrow," he said, taking her hand. "Come to bed."

"So early?"

"We need to be rested for tomorrow. And relaxed." He wiggled his eyebrows at her.

Her eyes widened. She grinned. "Oh, yes. Relaxed. Absolutely."

He picked her up over his shoulder, rear end to the sky. With a playful, gentle slap on her butt, he headed toward the bedroom.

Kate giggled as she clung to his neck and shoulder to keep from falling.

"My caveman!" She shrieked, laughing.

"I want my woman," he said, giving a low growl and grinning.

After they made love, Jake turned off the light. Her body relaxed, but her mind worried. Tossing, she found it difficult to find a comfortable position.

"Restless?" he whispered.

"Yeah. Nervous. Tomorrow," she replied.

"Come here. I've got you," he said, drawing her into his embrace, then rolling her on her side. He spooned her, wrapping his arms around her. He lowered his head to kiss her neck.

"You're the best. Really talented. Now you have to believe you can do it. If you do believe, you'll succeed. I believe in you."

"You do?"

"I do. If it were up to me, you'd be hired."

"But that's because you're sleeping with me."

"No. Objectively, if I can be objective. I'd hire you."

"Thanks."

"Remember to focus on what you're doing and forget everything else."

"Is that what you do?"

"Yep. And it works."

"Okay. I'll try. Thank you." She kissed his forearm.

"I love you, Kate. You can do it. You can do anything."

The warmth of his love surrounded her, protecting her, cocooning her with a veil of affection. His strong arms would keep the bogeyman and the nightmares away. For now, she was a winner, she had Jake's love. And that would have to be enough. Tomorrow was a crapshoot, with the outcome unpredictable. She let it go and closed her eyes.

Chapter Eight

Tuesday morning, Jake and Kate rose quietly and went about getting ready for their day without much conversation. She made bacon and eggs for him, which he wolfed down with two mugs of coffee.

"Aren't you eating?" he asked.

She munched on a piece of bacon. "I'm too nervous to eat a lot. I do better without a big, full stomach anyway."

"I always chow down before a game."

"Different styles," she said, smiling.

"I run it off, believe me."

"I do." She refilled her mug and poured him a glass of juice.

Jake threw on his sweats and headed for the door. As he kissed her, she slipped a piece of paper into his palm.

"The address of the theater."

"Thanks. I'll see you at four."

She smiled. "Good luck. Hope you win."

"Winning the opener gives us momentum."

"Then I hope you do."

He put his car in gear and drove to the stadium. On the way, he focused his mind on the game and what he remembered about the players on the Bucks. Time to get in the zone and go out there and beat the shit out of the Philadelphia team.

There was the usual buzz in the locker room. Married teammates talked about their plans for Easter with their kids. Single guys related a few hot moments from recent dates or asked for advice as they got dressed.

Jake was silent. The sound of locker doors shutting broke his concentration.

"Ready?" Skip asked, slipping his glove on.

Before Jake could speak, Cal Crawley entered.

"Gather around," he said. "Okay. We didn't make it last year. This year, we're gonna get to the series and win it. Win it. Yep. This is our year. You're in top condition, practiced your balls off. You should be ready. Let's go out there and show the Bucks what the Nighthawks are made of."

The team let out a yell and followed their manager to the field. Jake stood next to Skip Quincy and Matt Jackson for the national anthem. He sang out loud and clear. Figured he was simply exercising his voice for the audition later that day.

The Bucks were the visiting team, so they were up to bat first. Jake and Skip loped out to their positions at third base and shortstop. They nodded to each other and waited for Dan Alexander to take the mound. Matt put his face mask on and went into his crouch. The game was on. First pitch—a strike. Jake smiled, things were going his way.

Three up, three down—Dan struck out the first three batters. The Nighthawks headed for the dugout. Nat Owen was up first. Then Skip, then Bobby Hernandez, the second baseman. Jake sat back, watching Nat loosen up. Matt approached Jake holding a baseball cap upside down.

"You in?" he asked.

"Nah. Too much on my mind today."

Matt nodded and smiled. He understood. Almost every game, the Nighthawks collected a pool. Every guy put in five bucks. The money went to the player who spotted the hottest chick in the stands first. Gave them something to do while they waited to bat.

The catcher sat down next to Jake.

"Same old, same old with this team?" Jake asked.

"I don't know. They've got a couple of new players."

"They stunk really bad last year," Jake said.

"We'll see about these new guys," Matt replied. "Might be different this year."

Nat struck out, Skip drew a walk. Bobby moved him to second with a sacrifice fly to left field. After waiting in the on-deck circle, Jake strode to the plate as Bobby hit the dugout. He took a deep breath and narrowed his eyes at the pitcher.

This guy was new. Jake was taking until he could get a handle on the man on the mound. After two balls and a strike, Jake was primed and ready to do serious damage to the ball. The pitcher let fly and it was straight down the middle. Jake swung and connected. He pulled it foul. But the next pitch was high and outside, Jake's home run territory. And kill it, he did. The ball soared into the stands. Jake brought Skip home for a two-run lead.

After the congratulations from his buddies, the third baseman took a seat.

"Looks like getting laid regularly agrees with you," Skip said.

"Don't give Kate all the credit. I had something to do with that."

"I'm shooting her a thank-you email," Bobby said.

Jake laughed.

Matt Jackson walked and Chet Candelaria hit into a double play. The left fielder struck out and the Bucks were coming to bat.

The game went on without much action. The Bucks were held to two hits but no runs. Their pitcher managed to shut down the Hawks, too, much to Jake's surprise. He checked his watch. At two, they were in the top of the sixth inning. He let out a breath. Looks like everything was going along perfectly. Until that son-of-a-bitch, Newsome Edwards came to bat.

Jake bent over, hands resting on his knees, chewing gum, eyes focused on the ball. Dan hurled the ball and that asshole Buck swung. He nicked a piece of it and it flew, like a bolt of lightning, into Dan's shin. The pitcher went down. The batter took off, high-tailing it to first.

Shit! Dan was rolling around on the ground, grabbing his leg. The umpire called time and two Hawks' trainers raced out to the mound. Skip and Jake huddled together, watching. After a few minutes, Dan stood up. With an arm around one of the trainers, he limped off the field. The crowd gave him a round of applause.

Crawley had to call in another pitcher. Dan was due to leave in the seventh anyway, but he'd been doing great and Cal might have wanted to leave him in. Now his pitching status would be put on hold until they could heal his leg. Jake said a prayer that it wasn't broken. A ball that hard, could easily have shattered the bone.

Woody Franklin, a Hawk's relief pitcher, loped out to the mound. He started warming up with Matt. The next batter was a new guy. He was reputed to be a long ball hitter, but Jake hadn't seen anything but a string of foul balls and then a strikeout from the guy.

The game resumed. *Long Balls*, the nickname the team gave to Harvey Rutch, Bucks hitter, took two pitches. One strike and one ball. Jake tensed his muscles, focused his gaze on the pitch, ready to move. Crack! There it was. *Long Balls* lived up to his name. Jake whirled around, watching it take flight. Chet ran his ass off, heading toward the warning track. The ball made it about a foot above the wall into the first tier stands just as Candelaria crashed into the wall. The outfielder stood up, rubbing his shoulder as the Jumbotron registered HOME RUN!

Shit, fuck, ass wipe. *Long Balls* had just tied the game and lived up to his new name. Jake threw his glove down in disgust. He needed this game to be over. He glanced at his watch again. The minute hand was inching toward two thirty. A tie would mean extra innings. They needed to get this last out, score, and keep the Bucks at two.

He couldn't let Kate down. He was all she had. A quick prayer and fingers crossed while Franklin went into his wind up. The batter was not their best and the reliever struck him out on three consecutive pitches.

Jake let out the breath he was holding. He hit the dugout.

"Come on guys. We've gotta win. I gotta get out of here by three-thirty."

"Keep your pants on," Chet said.

"It's true love," Skip said, patting his chest over his heart.

"Shut the fuck up and get a hit, asshole," Jake growled.

Bobby was at the plate, so Skip trotted out to the on-deck circle. He shot his teammate a nasty look and swung the bat to warm up.

Jake started to pace. Bobby walked. Skip hit into a double play. Now it was Jake's turn. He tried to focus, but Kate kept creeping into his head. He struck out swinging, that was the end of the sixth.

In the seventh, Woody hit his stride. He got one strikeout, walked one, and the third hit a line drive straight to Skip, who caught it, then fired it to first base, doubling the runner off. Jake patted his friend on the shoulder as they ran off the field.

In the dugout, Jake paced. While the other players joked to relieve the tension, Jake's sense of humor had evaporated. Matt Jackson, their clutch hitter, got on base on a single up the middle. The next batter walked. Hope sprang up in Jake's chest. But the next batter popped one to third and into a double play. Their number seven man in the lineup got tagged out on a rotten bunt attempt.

The Nighthawks took the field in the top of the eighth. Woody Franklin was hot. He rifled curve balls, fastballs, and change-ups past Buck after Buck. Two more strikeouts and a pop foul that Jake plucked from the stands on the fly, meant the Hawks' were at bat again.

Afraid to look, the third baseman couldn't resist checking his watch. Three o'clock. And they still had six outs and maybe overtime to go. The Bucks sent in a relief pitcher. The fresh reliever struck out the Nighthawks' eighth man in the lineup. Woody came up to bat. After two failed bunt attempts, he fouled out to the first baseman. Then it was Nat Owen's turn. Jake was chewing nails, hoping his friend, who wasn't a long ball hitter, would break out of his mold and hit a home run.

No such luck. He struck out looking.

'Fucking asshole! Why didn't he swing?" Sweat poured off Jake's forehead.

Skip put his hand on Jake's forearm. "Hey, buddy. I know you're stressed but back off, okay?"

Jake shook off his buddy's hand, but not his advice. He knew he was out of line, but he couldn't help it. He'd promised to be at the theater by four. Well, no, he hadn't actually promised, but Kate needed him. He had to come through.

The top of the ninth the tension was so high you could almost cut it with a knife. Out in the field, Jake prayed Woody still had his stuff. The first pitch looked good—a swing and a miss.

Jake hardly remembered to breathe, watching Woody winding up and tossing in winning pitches. Bobby Hernandez caught a line drive that was rifled at him like a bullet. Jake muttered a "thank you" under his breath. Woody added another strikeout to his belt. Another foul out to Nat Owen and Jake forgave him for striking out in the bottom of the eighth.

The bottom of the ninth. The lineup was Skip, Bobby, and Jake. The third baseman corralled his two teammates.

"Just get on base. I don't give a fuck how you get there. Just do. I'll connect and bring you home. Not a home run, a base hit. So get on base, and run your balls off to get home." Jake checked his watch—three ten. "Time's running out, guys. I need you to do this for me."

Skip got a base on balls. Then Bobby came up. He hit a bouncer to deep short. Skip and Bobby were running full out. The shortstop elected to pick off Skip, but Bobby beat out the throw to first.

"I'm sorry, man. Sorry," Skip said as he passed Jake heading for the plate.

"No worries. It's okay." Jake nodded, rubbing dirt between his hands to dry out the sweat.

He nodded to Bobby on first, then took his stance. He narrowed his eyes and forced his mind to focus on the pitcher. He'd been watching him. First two pitches he'd snag the corners, hoping for strikes. Sometimes he got 'em. When he did or at least a count of one and one, then he'd put one right down the middle. That's the pitch Jake was looking for.

He took a deep breath and calmed himself so he could wait out the first two. He faked a swing just enough to fool the pitcher on the second pitch. Then he drew back the bat. By his calculations, this would be it. The one he was looking for. And sure enough, there it was.

A big, juicy fastball, right down the middle. Jake let his natural talent take over. Bam! The bat broke as the ball soared over the heads of the infielders, hooked right, and dropped in the corner of right field. Fair ball!

The Buck fielder had been playing it closer to center. He took off, chasing down the ball that had dropped and refused to roll. In the meantime, Bobby Hernandez flew over the bases, heading for home with everything he had. Jake ran to first, hesitated, then got halfway to second before he returned to first base.

But Bobby didn't stop. The third base coach was giving him all the signals to stop, but he kept going. The throw came fast and wide from right field. Bobby dove.

"Not head first!" Jake exclaimed, his gaze riveted on his teammate.

Hernandez flew into home plate along with the ball. The catcher made the mistake of blocking the plate. Bobby didn't let that stop him. He barreled into the Buck, knocking him down. He barely had the ball, when he hit the dirt. The fall knocked it out of his glove. Bobby stopped sliding while he was still on base. SAFE! The umpire called him safe!

The Nighthawks had won the game! Bobby stood up and brushed the dirt off his uniform. Jake blinked several times. He couldn't believe his eyes. Bobby was safe, the game was over and it was only three thirty! Jake ran to the dugout. No time to shower and change. He kept running right into the locker room. He grabbed his jacket, fished out his car keys, stuffed his street clothes under his arm and headed for the parking lot.

"Wait! Wait for me!" It was Skip.

"Me, too!" Nat Owen hollered.

One by one his buddies, except for Dan Alexander, who was still in the medical room, gathered in the hall.

"What the fuck?"

"I've never seen anyone audition for a Broadway show. I'm coming," Skip said.

The others chimed in.

"Besides. You'll need luck. And I'm the luckiest guy here today," Bobby Hernandez said, brushing dirt off his behind.

Jake made a face. "Shit, Bobby, you're going to get that all over my new car."

"Hey, asshole. I probably tore a dozen muscles moving my ass to score so you could go to this thing. The least you can do is take me along."

"What the fuck are we standing here for? It's almost three-forty-five. Let's go!"

Jake broke into a run, as did the others. The five men piled into the car, barely closing the door before the engine roared to life, and the third basemen flew out of the parking lot.

"Take my cell, Skip," Jake said to the man in the front seat. "In case Kate calls. You can tell her we're on the way."

"Got it." He rummaged around the friend's coat pockets until he located the cell.

Jake hit the gas, hoping to make all the lights on Columbus. He knew the lights on Broadway weren't nearly as well synced as Columbus.

"Where the fuck is the theater?" Jake hollered.

"I don't know," Skip said.

"It's the Porter. She gave me the address on a slip of paper. Look in my pockets."

Again, Skip shoved his hand in every pocket until he found it. "Got it Forty-eighth and Broadway."

Jake jumped the gun on a traffic light and hit the gas. He was doing great, making the lights and almost at ninety-sixth street, when he heard the siren.

"Shit! Fuck!" he said, glancing in the rearview mirror. A cop with flashing lights was on his tail.

"Pull over," came the command over a megaphone.

"No time. No time," he muttered, slowing the car.

"If you don't pull over, they'll catch you, arrest you, and you'll never get there," Bobby said.

"I've got an idea. Let me do the talking," Nat said.

Jake pulled over and opened his window. "Yes, Officer?"

"License and registration, please."

Jake handed over the documents, then looked at his watch. Ten minute to four.

"Are you THE Jake Lawrence? The Jake Lawrence who plays third for the Nighthawks?" The officer's eyebrows shot up.

"Yes, sir. I am."

"Officer, there are special circumstances. Can I explain?" Nat leaned over from the back seat.

"And you are?"

"Nat Owen, teammate of Mr. Lawrence."

"You play first base, right?"

"I do. Let me explain."

Speaking fast, Nat boiled the story down to a one-minute explanation. The officer handed Jake's license and registration back.

"Mr. Lawrence. It's three-fifty. I think you'll need an escort if you're going to make that audition on time."

"Bless you, Officer."

"Follow me," he said, then climbed back into his patrol car.

The black-and-white pulled in front of the Hawks and turned on the siren. Jake threw the car in gear and stepped on the gas.

Kate stood in the back of the auditorium.

"It's five of four, Miss McKenzie. Are you ready to go on?"

"My partner is coming. Can we give him ten more minutes?"

The producer looked at his watch. "I can give him five. I have others to see today. Sorry."

She nodded. *He said he'd come. He said he'd come. He said he'd come. He said...maybe.*

If Jake didn't show, she'd have to go on by herself. She inhaled a big breath, then blew it out. It's not like she'd never auditioned alone before. Most of the parts she won, she got by auditioning alone. Those were for regional theater. Small stuff, in her mind, and the mind of every Hollywood and Broadway producer.

She had some credentials, but they weren't anything big, although she got great reviews and showed "promise"—whatever that was—she hadn't cracked the big time. Today was her one chance, and she needed Jake.

The sound of a siren grew louder fast. Then it stopped. Unable to stifle her curiosity, Kate peeked out the theater door. There was Jake, dirty, sweaty, still in his uniform and parked in a no parking zone. He leaped from the car and ran around it.

As if she was seeing an old-time silent movie comedy, four other dirty, sweaty men in Nighthawks' uniforms also piled out of the car and ran toward her. Jake got there first. He grasped her hand.

"Am I too late?"

She shook her head. "Just in time. Come on." She held open the theater door. They moved through quickly. "Who are these guys?" she asked him.

"My teammates, my friends. They wanna watch. Is that okay?"

"Usually auditions are closed to anyone not involved with the show, but Hell, let 'em throw the guys out."

"Ah, Miss McKenzie! I see your partner has arrived. Come up, come up." The man waved them to the stage.

Jake turned to his buddies. "Find a place to sit and shut the fuck up. Not one noise. Not a sound!" he hissed, following Kate.

They ascended the stairs and she made the introductions.

"Are you Jake Lawrence, the baseball player?" Johnny Cleary, the producer asked.

"I am."

"Are those men on your team?"

"They are."

"What are they doing here?"

"They're here for moral support. I hope that's okay."

"As long as they give out autographs after, that's fine. Do you two want to go over it once or twice? I need to return this phone call."

"Thank you, Mr. Cleary," Kate said as he stalked out of the room.

She and Jake did some scales, then the song, and the little dance that went with it. When he heard a snicker from the audience, he turned and raised his voice.

"What the hell did I say about noise? Once more and I swear, I'll throw you outta here myself."

"Sorry," Skip piped up.

"Better be," Jake muttered.

Kate poured a glass of water for each of them from a pitcher and a stack of paper cups on a small table. Jake eyed the vessel.

"I could drink that whole thing in one gulp."

"Jake!"

"We didn't stop after the game."

"Here, have another glass," she said, refilling his.

The producer returned, full of apologies. He was joined by another man and a woman. After ordering a refill for the water, he sat in the front row with the others.

"Are you ready?"

She nodded. Jake gave her a warm stare and a thumbs-up. "You can do this," he whispered.

Confidence transferred from him to her. For the moment, to her, there was no one in the theater but Kate and Jake.

She stuck her thumbs in the loops of her jeans and began the song. Jake chimed in on cue. They sang and did a little dance around each other. Kate relaxed. There was something about him that made her feel like she'd known him all her life. He smiled into her eyes, exuding self-assurance. The words tripped off his tongue.

When they were done, the guys on the team burst into applause. Kate buried her face in her hands while Jake glowered at his buddies.

"Well done. That was great," Johnny said. "Let me talk to my colleagues for a moment." The three left the auditorium.

Kate downed another cup of water while Jake wiped his face on his sleeve.

"Thank you so much. I couldn't have done it without you," she said.

"You were great. You coulda done it in the middle of Times Square."

"When do you sign the contract?" Skip piped up.

"Shut up! Can't you follow orders?" Jake shot his meanest look.

"Sorry, sorry." Skip sat down.

The trio returned.

"Thank you, Kate. That was great. You're an amazing singer, and we loved the way you delivered the song, but we cast the part of Kim this morning. But you're first runner-up. Really. Great job. We wish you much success."

Jake turned to her, but Johnny grabbed his arm.

"Wait a minute. We're missing one male in the chorus. You interested, Jake?"

Kate's mouth fell open. They wanted Jake but not her?

"What?" Jake asked.

"How about giving up baseball for the theater?"

The auditorium was silent.

"You've got to be crazy. Kate's the star here, not me."

"Don't sell yourself short. You've got great potential, my friend," Johnny said.

Stunned, Kate thanked the producers and descended the stage stairs.

"Kate. Wait," Jake called, but she didn't stop. She picked up her backpack and almost ran the rest of the way out the door.

Jake pursued her, followed by the men on the team. When she reached the outside, she let out a sob. Tears blinded her as she headed downtown. Keith's place was in Chelsea. A long walk, but what else did she have to do?

She heard Jake calling her name but didn't stop. Humiliation burned inside her. How could she ever face him, again? Outclassed by a newbie. A guy with no training, nothing. Yet they wanted him and not her. She threaded her way through the crowd, not stopping, except for red lights. A man stopped. "You okay, miss?" She nodded and kept going.

She began to run and didn't stop until she couldn't hear him call her name anymore. She finally reached Keith's place and pushed the buzzer. He released the door from his apartment three flights up. She bolted up the stairs, close to hysteria, as the truth sank in.

She'd gambled everything on this and lost. Her dice came up boxcars. Everything was gone. Keith opened the door and croaked out her name. She fell into his arms sobbing.

Chapter Nine

Jake ran into Times Square, where he got surrounded by fans within minutes. He called and called for Kate, but she had disappeared into the thickening, rush-hour crowd. His heart was breaking. How could this happen? He was a slugger, a crackerjack third basemen, but far from a Broadway star!

As he signed autographs, his heart numb, he kept seeing the expression in her eyes. The hurt, the pain, the betrayal visible in her beautiful blue-greens, made his stomach lurch. Before long, his teammates caught up to him. The number of fans swelled, blocking traffic.

"We gotta get outta here," Skip said, tugging on Jake's sleeve.

"I know, I know. Just one more look," the third baseman replied, scanning the sea of faces, looking for his lover. It didn't take him long to realize she was gone. "Okay. Let's go."

The players eased north slowly, carrying fans with them like burrs on clothing. They tried to shake them off as they signed each autograph.

"If we don't get outta here, my hand'll be too sore to catch tomorrow," Matt said.

When they reached the car, there was a parking ticket on it.

"Figures," Jake mumbled as he unlocked the doors remotely.

One-by-one the men packed the car. Jake was the last one in. He locked the doors and turned the engine over. Slowly they managed to get back on Broadway, heading north.

"That was amazing. I've never seen an audition before," Nat said.

"Where do you think she went?" Skip asked.

"I'm hoping back to my place."

Bobby made a face. "Not likely. She was pretty upset."

"She doesn't have any money. Keith's is the only place she can go."

"Who's Keith?" Matt asked.

Jake explained everything then asked, "Back to the stadium, right?"

"Yep," Bobby said.

"Can you call this chick?" Nat asked.

"Yeah. When we get there."

The men piled out of the car and headed for the locker room, leaving Jake alone. He dialed Kate, but it went to voice mail. He left a message. He called one more time, to be sure. She didn't pick up. He'd like to smash that producer's face. Asshole. How could he break her heart like that? What could Jake do about it? Not a damn thing. He kicked some stones, shoved his hands in his pockets, and hit the locker room.

After showering, he drove home. He had to see if she was there. When he opened the door, the place was empty. He searched every room, every closet, hoping against hope that she'd be there. But found no one.

"Shit." He slammed out of the house and took a cab to Freddie's. He needed a drink and his buddies. No game until tomorrow night, one more the day after, then they'd go on the road for two weeks. If he didn't find Kate before that, he'd lose what they had.

His pals greeted him warmly. Tommy clapped him on the back and gave him dessert on the house for batting in the winning run. The men discussed the game. Jake bought Bobby a beer for going the extra mile. He loved his buddies, they helped soothe his broken heart.

But where was Kate? Why did she run? It wasn't his fault. He ordered a steak and baked potato, but all the food did was remind him of the incredible meal she'd cooked for him. Hunger gnawed at his belly. He ate but nothing tasted good. The beer helped. Then he had a whiskey.

"I shouldn't be giving this to you, Jake," Tommy said, pouring a shot. "But the guys said you need it."

"I'll be all right tomorrow. It's a night game, anyway."

"Okay. But one and that's all."

"Thanks," Jake said, picking up the glass. He needed something to dull the raw pain inside. And he needed Kate. He believed, in his heart, that she needed him, too. Not for his money but for his love. He wanted to be there for her but didn't know what to do.

Skip sidled up next to him. "We'll go on the road and you'll forget all about this chick. Once you meet a few new ones, you'll be fine. The old Jake. No lovesick puppy."

Jake slammed the empty shot glass down on the table. "I'm not a lovesick puppy, asshole. Why don't you shut up? You don't know what you're talking about."

"Hey, buddy, come on. You didn't know her all that long."

"You don't know," his tone softened as sadness filled his heart. "You don't know, Skip. She isn't just a chick."

"Hey, they're all special until the lights are out. Then they're all the same."

"That's a fucking, shitty thing to say. You're such an asshole, sometimes, you know that?" Jake grabbed his jacket and headed for the door.

"You better not let this one ruin your game."

"Don't worry about it. I'll be fine tomorrow, as usual. Nothing disrupts my game."

"Can I count on it?" Skip asked

"Shove it up your ass, Skip," Jake said, shooting his pal a nasty look as pushed through the door. Sure, nothing disturbs the slugger. He'll be knocking 'em out of the park, as usual, tomorrow. Won't he?

After the third strong drink from Keith, Kate calmed down.

"Call him," he said.

"You're right. I should. But what can I say?"

"Tell him you love him, you're going back to him."

"I can't do that. I have no job, no money. I already owe him for two weeks' worth of meals."

"You don't owe him shit. The guy's got millions. Those few meals are chump change to him."

"That's not how I feel."

"How does he feel?"

"I don't know. It's not like he kept track or anything," she said, curling up in the corner of his couch.

"Or asked you for money. Did he?"

She shook her head, chewing on her thumbnail. Keith got up. He grabbed her phone from the coffee table and tossed it to her.

"I'm losing my voice. So this is my last statement. Call him or you're a complete idiot." With that, he turned and headed for the bedroom.

Kate glanced at the clock. It was eleven. He was probably asleep, but she dialed anyway.

He picked up right away.

"Kate?"

"It's me."

"Are you okay? When are you coming home?"

The worry and urgency in his voice broke her heart.

"I'm not."

"What? Why?"

"I have no job, no career, right now. And no money. I need to work. Figure things out."

"Can't you do that living here, with me?"

"No. I can't. You're always taking care of everything. I need to stand on my own two feet."

His voice softened. "You've been standing on your own two feet all your life. Let me help you a little."

There was silence.

"I don't know how to do that."

Even though he couldn't see, she shook her head. "Please try to understand. When I've got a handle on my life, I'll come back to you."

"Will you?"

"Of course. I love you."

"Even after what happened this afternoon?"

"I thought about it. Talked it over with Keith. It's not like you tried to steal anything from me. They simply liked you better. You've got talent, Jake. I can't deny that. It wasn't your fault I wasn't good enough."

"They said you were good enough. If they hadn't already cast the part, you'd a gotten it."

"That's just bullshit. They say that to everyone they turn down. It's just producer-speak for 'You suck, lady. Move on.'"

"I thought they meant it."

"They never mean anything except 'goodbye'."

She heard him sigh.

"Do you still love me?" she asked, a tremor in her voice.

"Of course I do. I don't say that to every girl I date or sleep with. You're different, Kate. So very different."

"Yeah. I'm a bit of a weirdo. I get that."

"That's not what I meant at all. You're better. Different in a good way."

"Thanks."

"We're going on the road for two weeks. Is that enough time? Can I call you after that?"

She laughed. "Hell, I don't know. I have no idea how much time it's gonna take to get things sorted out and plan my next step."

"Can I call you anyway?"

"You can always call me."

"I did today, but you didn't answer."

"I needed time. Still do."

"All right. I don't like it, but I accept it. As long as you'll take my calls."

"I will. I promise."

"I've got to get to bed. Game tomorrow night."

"I understand. Thank you for coming to the audition. It's an experience I'll never forget."

Jake chuckled. "Neither will I. Or the guys from the team."

"Please thank them for me. It was so great that they came."

"I think they just wanted to see if you were as hot as I said."

She laughed. "And what did they think?"

"You'll have to beat them off with a stick."

She laughed.

"Well, can I say goodnight, instead of goodbye?"

"Sure," she responded.

"Goodnight then."

"'Night."

She put down the phone. Tears clouded her eyes. She desperately wanted to hide in the warmth of his arms, to cuddle with him in bed, and blot out the horrible day. But she'd learned, early in life, never to depend on anyone. She'd been let down too many times by those she'd trusted. Now, she refused to go into that place of complete trust. It had been so long, she wasn't sure she could ever trust that way again.

Even so, she missed him. Missed him like hell and wondered how she'd ever get to sleep without him lying beside her. She crawled into bed and let the three stiff drinks she'd had take her to dreamland.

In the morning, Kate woke early. Still groggy with sleep, she reached out for Jake, but he wasn't there. Realizing the bed was empty, she frowned. Without disturbing Keith across the room, snoring, she threw on a robe and padded to the tiny kitchen in the small, two-bedroom apartment.

She put on coffee, yawned, and looked out the window. It was the fourth day of April. Trees outside the window had early spring light green leaves stretching to the sun. The world was awakening after a long winter. But Kate's life had come to a complete standstill. She rummaged around through the papers on the table until she found a copy of *Variety*. Then she opened Keith's laptop and went to Craig's List and a few other sites she knew, looking for a job.

Frustrated at finding nothing, she called her agent.

"Hey, Lacy, Kate MacKenzie here."

"So sorry about that audition, Kate. I had no idea they'd hired someone that morning. She must have been very good, 'cause they said they'd be looking everyone over and deciding next week." Lacy's update only made Kate feel worse.

"Anything on the horizon for me?"

"Nothing at the moment. But you know, stuff pops up all the time. Don't get discouraged. I got you this audition, I'll get you another."

"In the meantime, I need to eat."

"Find a job waiting tables. You have experience, don't you?"

"I do."

"That's where all the best movie stars come from, you know."

"Right!" Kate laughed.

"Seriously, something may come up in Hollywood, you know."

"That would be great!"

"I'm always looking. Honestly, keep it together. You never know."

"Thanks, Lacy. I'll keep my fingers crossed."

Keith didn't get up until eleven. He was much better, and his voice was almost back to normal. He took her to lunch at a small café.

"Keep looking. You'll find something. And keep going to auditions. You can stay with me as long as you like."

"Thank you. Friends like you are hard to find."

"That jock was a good friend, too. And you tossed him out with the garbage."

"It's one thing to be with you. You know I'll pay you back. Chip in for the rent as soon as I'm making some money. But I can't do that with Jake. He won't take anything from me."

"Every woman's dream," he muttered, stirring his Chamomile tea.

"I don't know how to do that, Keith. I never have."

"Maybe you should learn."

She shrugged. He grabbed her forearm.

"I'm going to tell you something you might not want to hear."

She groaned. "A lecture?"

"A new one. And you need to hear it. So listen up, missy."

"Go ahead." She slumped slightly in her chair.

"You need to learn how to let people in. Maybe therapy would help."

"With what money?"

"Shut up, and let me finish!" He gave her hand a playful slap. "You keep everyone out. You think you can't ever depend on anyone else. But that's not true. You shut yourself away, never take anything from anyone—"

"I do from you. Like a place to live."

"Okay. I'm a special case. You've had men falling all over you, all your life. But you shut them out, push them away. You'll be thirty in two years. This is your prime. How do you expect to find a husband, get married, and have a life? You won't until you learn to let go and lean on him a little."

She gazed down at her hands. She knew he was telling her the truth. "Okay. I admit it. You're right. But it's not that easy. Not for me."

"Try. Give this guy a chance. He sounds like a keeper to me. Are you sure he's straight?" Keith chuckled.

"Oh, most definitely. Sorry about that."

They finished their tea and he paid the bill. She hugged him. "Thanks for being such a good friend."

"I'm your only friend. You gotta fix that."

"I know. You're right."

The spring sun had warmed the air and Kate decided to go for a walk. She headed uptown. Jake was playing today, then heading out on a road trip. She sighed. Maybe in the next two weeks, she'd find a job. She said a prayer as she continued north.

Something he had said popped into her head. She hopped the bus with her borrowed Metro Card and hoped against hope. When she got off, she wandered around, lost, until a shopkeeper gave her directions. Sure enough, there was a sign in the window. She went in.

Jake avoided Skip and sat next to Matt on the bus to the airport. They were headed for Atlanta, then Baltimore, then Washington for three three-game series in a row.

He dialed Kate.

"I thought we were taking a break?" she said, her voice as far away as Siberia.

"I know, I know. But I wanted to hear your voice. We're on the way to Atlanta. I'll be back in two weeks."

"Have a safe trip. Good luck."

"We have a good chance to beat the Stallions."

"With you on third, how can they lose?" Her voice warmed a little.

"What about you? How are you?"

"I'm fine. I'm a cat, Jake, I always land on my feet. Don't worry about me. I'll be fine."

"But I want to worry about you," he said, his voice barely above a whisper.

"Knock yourself out."

"Missing you."

There was a long pause.

"I miss you, too."

"Can I see you when I get back?"

"Let's talk then. See where we are."

"I know where I'll be. Waiting outside your door. Curled up like a puppy on the doormat."

She laughed. "That image is hilarious."

"Glad I made you laugh."

"Me, too. I gotta go. Be safe."

"You, too. Love you."

But the phone had gone dead before his last words. Was that a kiss-off? He prayed that it wasn't. Where would he find another woman like Kate MacKenzie? Nowhere.

"How's your girl, Matt?" Jake asked.

"Great. I'm the luckiest man alive," the catcher said, beaming.

"You getting married?"

"Yep. After the first of the year."

"Big wedding planned?"

"Nope. Nothing fancy. I think we're going to do it in Pittsburgh."

"Then your dad can come?"

"That's the idea. How's things with yours?" the catcher raised his eyebrows.

"We're going through a rough patch right now." Jake gazed out the window.

He was still struggling with what happened at the audition. How could she not get the job?

"That was crazy, at the theater, right?" Matt said.

"You read my mind. I couldn't believe it."

"Who'd a thunk they'd want you and not her?"

"I know. Insane. Completely insane."

On the plane, Jake couldn't avoid Skip. The shortstop plopped into the seat next to him.

"Hey, buddy. Look, I'm sorry. Sometimes I say the wrong thing."

"You have a bad attitude about women."

"You didn't think so when we were at bars on the road."

"Yeah? Well that was then and this is now. Kate's not a hooker or a groupie. She's a great woman who needs a break."

"I thought she was amazing at the audition. Honestly. I didn't think you were that hot."

Jake smiled and shook his head. "Friends."

Nat Owen joined them. "I didn't think so either. Must be your looks. Though why they'd want such an ugly guy in the play beats me."

Jake took a swipe at his friend. The stewardess passed out soda, juice, and water then snacks. The guys chowed down and Chet Candelaria pulled out a deck of cards.

"Oh hell? Hearts?"

"Not with you. I gotta keep enough money to pay the mortgage," Dan Alexander piped up.

They landed in Atlanta and took a private bus to their hotel. That night, Jake lay in bed, hands laced behind his head, thinking about Kate. He wondered how she was, worried she'd not be able to eat. He hoped Keith was taking care of her. Taking care of her, he laughed to himself, was like taking care of a wildcat. Thinking about her wild side gave him a hard-on. He needed sleep. They had a big game with the Atlanta Stallions, and he needed to be in top form.

So he took care of business. He didn't like to go solo, but what was a guy going to do? He'd never get to sleep if he left himself like that. Once he'd conjured up an image of Kate in his mind, it didn't take long to bring himself to completion.

After cleaning up, he got back in bed, but sleep still wouldn't come. He pushed out of bed and did fifty push-ups and fifty crunches. Once back in bed, sleep came. And with it, dreams of Kate. The dream turned to a nightmare. He sweated as visions of his girl living homeless on the streets of New York hounded him.

At three, he awoke with a start, bolting into a sitting position as a serial killer raised a knife to Kate. He rubbed the sleep out of his eyes and slowed his breathing. Bad dreams were a bitch. As he lay back down, he knew he'd never rest well again until he knew she was safe.

Chapter Ten

"Now that I've got a job, I should start paying rent," Kate said to Keith.

He put his hand on her shoulder. "Darling, please. You have maybe two bucks in your pocket and you want to give me one. That's sweet as hell, but save it."

"But I..."

"Oh, shut up. Carl and I have the rent covered. We both have reasonably good day jobs. So put your money in the bank, because a job like you have could disappear tomorrow."

Keith made sense, as usual. She relied on him for guidance, and he never let her down. They'd met in college. He'd been a little older as he had to work and save up before he could go. Kate simply took out loans, which she'd been paying off with her work in regional theater.

"What about those college loans?" he asked, putting up a pot of coffee.

"Yeah, yeah. I know. After six years, I'm getting there."

"Sweetheart, you deserve to have a little cash in your pocket, away from your mother."

She nodded.

"What are you going to do with that money?" he asked, handing her a mug of the piping hot liquid.

"I have other debts to settle," she said, adding milk and sugar.

"I hope it's not with that ballplayer. Honey, he makes more in one year than I'll see in a lifetime."

She laughed. "I need some new clothes for the job, too."

Keith's eyes lit up. "I'll say you do. Ragamuffin is not a style that suits you. Let's go shopping together. You know how I love to shop."

"And you have such good taste."

"You need to dress sexy. Better tips," he said.

"I've got two week's pay in my pocket, she patted her jeans. When do you want to go?"

"Carl gets an employee discount at My Girl, the dress shop on twenty-first. Maybe we should start there."

"Good idea. Tonight?"

"Aren't you working?"

"Monday's my night off."

"Perfect. Okay, girl. Time to get you some hot stuff to ramp up that tip jar."

She smiled and sat back. Keith boosted her confidence. The first week on the job hadn't been too bad. In addition to her salary, she'd taken home two-hundred and fifty bucks from tips each week. The singer knew five hundred wouldn't go far in Manhattan, but it seemed like a fortune to her. At least she could buy her own Metro Card and a sandwich.

Keith dressed and went off to his job as an administrative assistant. Kate pulled out one of his books of Cole Porter tunes and sat down at his keyboard. It was time to brush up on her playing and master a couple of new songs.

She threw together a peanut butter and jelly sandwich and hit the streets at one. It was chilly, and she ate her sandwich as she strolled the streets of Chelsea, a neighborhood on the West side of Manhattan in the twenties. Small shops, delis, and mom-and-pop restaurants held her interest. As she passed a beauty salon, she realized she hadn't had a haircut in months.

Desiring only a trim of an inch, she entered. The man serving her gave her a slightly new style which suited her face. Refreshed, she was ready to put some new styles on her luscious body. But first, a mani-pedi. One glance into her wallet told her it would have to be a manicure only as there weren't funds for the pedicure as well as the clothes.

She shrugged and entered the nail salon across the street from Keith's. By the time he got home, she had her 'hamburger surprise' keeping warm on the stove.

"Dinner's ready. Come on. Eat and let's go shopping." She tugged on his sleeve.

Tuesday afternoon, Kate took a long bath and took her time applying makeup. When Keith returned from work, she was dressed in her new turquoise sweater, cut low and long, slinky, black jersey skirt. With four-inch heels, silver jewelry, and makeup, Kate would stop traffic.

"Holy shit! You're hot, baby," Keith said, his eyes widening.

"Oh my God! Who is this? What did you do with Kate McKenzie?" Carl said, opening the front door.

She grinned. "So I look okay?"

"Honey, there won't be a soft dick in the joint," Keith said.

"Good. Horny men leave bigger tips."

"I don't think you should take the subway home, darlin'," Carl said.

"Why not?"

"Looking like that? It isn't safe."

She brushed his worry off. "I'll be okay. I can handle myself."

Keith nodded. "Sure, sure. Like that guy in Long Beach?"

"That was different."

"You're just lucky I work out."

She checked her watch. "Time to go." She kissed each of the men goodbye and headed for the subway.

Once she got to the bar, she put her coat in the back room, got a glass of water, and went to the piano. There weren't many people there at six, but she knew by eight there would be a small crowd. She did an arpeggio, then a few exercises, warming up her fingers.

She recognized a few regulars who strolled in about seven. Some nodded to her, others came over with requests. If she knew the tune, that was fine, if not, she made a note of it and planned to add it to her repertory.

While she waited for the crowd to grow, her thoughts turned to Jake. She hadn't heard from him in a couple of days. She assumed he was busy traveling and playing ball. Maybe he'd met someone new in a bar in Washington? The thought tugged at her heart. She couldn't blame him for moving on.

Her mind replayed the days of their travels together. Before she knew it, she was playing their old song *Friendship* and singing along as if he were there.

The road trip was exhausting. The nightmare about Kate didn't return, leaving Jake to sleep soundly. The games were close. The Nighthawks lost two of the three in Washington. There were errors and no one on the 'Hawks was hitting. A gloomy atmosphere prevailed on the bus back to New York. Jake slept the entire way.

Happy to be home, the slugger unpacked his bag and dumped his clothes in the hamper. His housekeeper, Blanche, would take care of the wash the next day. He'd wondered why he hadn't heard from Kate. Maybe she didn't pay her phone bill and it had been turned off. He dialed. It went straight to voicemail.

The sleep on the bus meant he was now wide awake. He called Skip.

"Dinner at Freddie's?"

"I'm kinda tired," Skip said.

"You're supposed to sleep on the bus, stupid."

"Really? Is that in the player's manual somewhere? Must sleep on bus ride back home? Guess I missed it."

"You know what I mean," Jake said.

"I know exactly what you mean. You got some shut eye, and now you want company. You want to go out tomcatting and don't want to do it alone."

"I was only thinking about dinner." Being alone didn't appeal to Jake.

Skip laughed. "That's a new one. You not cruisin', lookin' to get laid."

"This is the new me."

"I'll believe that when I see it."

"So come to Freddie's with me. You'll see I've changed."

"Maybe."

"Steak. I'm buyin'," Jake said, crossing his fingers.

"You twisted my arm."

"Meet me there in half an hour," Jake said.

"Make it an hour," Skip replied.

"Done."

Jake hit the shower and put on gray slacks, a white button-down and his navy blue sports jacket. A blue and green rep striped tie added color. He was ready. He tried Kate again with the same result as before.

He lucked out, finding a parking spot right in front of the bar. He locked the door and whistled the tune he'd sung on the trip. As he walked up, a voice stopped him. It was female and singing that same song. It was Kate! He pushed through the door and almost dropped his teeth. There she was, Kate McKenzie, sitting at the piano in Freddie's, singing their song. His heart beat doubled as a wide grin stretched his lips. He headed toward the music. When she spotted him, she stopped. She looked different.

"Kate! That is you, isn't it?" His gaze swept over her, taking in her new hairstyle and her prominent cleavage. His fingertips recalled the feel of her supple flesh and sent a zing right to his dick.

"Jake?"

"It is you. You look different."

"I clean up good," she retorted, grinning.

"I'll say. I'm so glad to see you. What're you doing here?"

"I work here, now. Remember when you told me Tommy was looking for someone? I applied and got the job. This is my third week."

"That's fantastic!" He couldn't take his eyes off her. She was more beautiful than ever. Their gazes locked and Jake lost himself in the blue-green beauty of hers. "Can I buy you a drink?" came out of his mouth without him even being aware.

"Ginger ale, maybe. I don't drink while I work."

"Very wise." He signaled Tommy. "Ginger ale here?" The barkeep nodded.

"You were singing our song," Jake blurted out.

"It has become our song, hasn't it?" She played a few notes of the familiar piece.

"I miss you so much. Move back in with me," he spit out before he lost the courage.

Her hands stilled. Her eyes filled. "I miss you, too," she whispered.

"Whatcha having, Jake?" Tommy asked, delivering Kate's soft drink and interrupting them.

"Same, Tommy. The same."

"Game tomorrow?"

"Yeah." Jake whipped out a handkerchief and passed it to the singer. She wiped her eyes and looked up at him.

Tommy's gaze jumped from Jake to Kate and back again before he spoke. "Oh, I see. You two have met before?"

"You might say that," Jake muttered, still staring at her.

"Oh, okay. I'm going." Tommy returned to the bar.

"Maybe we should date first?" she asked.

"Date? That's moving backward," he replied. *Maybe you should move in with me and never leave.* When she stiffened, he held up his palm "Okay, okay. If that's what you want. How about tonight? Burger after you're done here, and I'll drive you home?"

"What about your game?"

"It's a night game."

"Okay. Sounds good. I get off at eleven."

"Wow! You're working hard."

"I'm trying."

"Looking for more auditions?"

Tommy returned with Jake's drink. "Look, Jake, it's not like we haven't been friends forever, but I'm not paying Kate to talk to you."

"You're right. I'm sorry. Just that I haven't seen her in a long time."

"That's your problem. Talk to her after eleven."

"I will," he said, picking up his glass and sitting at a table near the piano.

"How can we talk if we're so close to the music?" Skip asked, sliding onto the seat next to the slugger.

"Oh. Hi. Yeah. It's Kate."

"What?" Skip looked over. "Holy shit, it is! She's lookin' real good." Skip shook his head.

"Yeah. She looks great." Jake sipped his ginger ale.

"You're gone, buddy. Past it. All in, completely insane," Skip remarked looking back and forth between the lovers.

Jake chuckled. "You said it."

Kate could hardly concentrate on the music. Jake looked fine. He cleaned up great. The dark blue of the jacket brought out the blue in his eyes. His shoulders were so broad, she wondered if he had to turn sideways to fit through the doorway.

Looking at him heated her blood. Squeezing her thighs together, she felt dampness. *Crap! He turns me on just by looking at me.* If they'd been alone, she'd have ripped his clothes off and had her way with him.

Her nipples hardened at the memory of his hands on her. Sexy thoughts floated through her brain. Oh yes, things were not finished with this man yet. Not by a long shot. She forced herself to focus on the music and tried to remember the new songs she'd been practicing.

Three new pieces were all she could conjure up by memory. Damn, the slugger messed with her mind and her body. She gave new emotion to the love songs she crooned and attracted some new fans. Two women left their men at the table, talking sports, and wandered over to the pianist. She played a few requests for them, and they sang along.

The women added money to her tip jar, and when they left, their men did, too. Every night the cash grew, as people noticed her and appreciated her sweet, clear voice. Jake hid behind the small crowd gathering and dropped in fifty bucks.

"I saw that, Nighthawk," she said.

"I'm not taking it back. He returned to his table as two steak dinners arrived.

On her break, she checked her cell and noticed a text from Keith:

Take a cab home.

She replied:

I've got a ride. No worries.

He questioned:

With who?

She answered:

Jake. The ballplayer. Don't worry.

Keith:

Good. Much relieved. See you later.

She wondered if she'd see Keith later. Jake wanted to take her home with him and she wanted to go. Why shouldn't she? Wasn't it the same as bunking in with Keith? Except for the fact that she'd be sleeping with Jake and she wasn't with Keith. Big difference.

While her career stalled and she tried to jump start it, why shouldn't she have some fun, enjoy love? Who knew how long it would last? Would she get a call to do a show in California? Would he get tired of her? She smiled. She figured that was more likely to happen than her getting that call to go to Hollywood.

Driven to succeed, Kate had put work above all else. She'd had a few affairs while doing regional theater—short-lived relationships that lasted as long as the run of the show. She'd never had a serious one, nothing with commitment and genuine love. Hell, love had been in short supply all her life.

Her dad had stayed with the family until he couldn't take her mother's gambling anymore. When she turned ten, he had moved out. When she got older, Kate stopped blaming him. Thank God, he'd paid the rent until she left home. Their life had been all about hiding money from her mother so they could pay the rent and buy food. Her mom had been wily and difficult to foil.

She loved her father very much. He'd moved on, remarried, and had another family. She didn't see him or speak with him much, not because he didn't care about her, but because he had a new wife and young children who needed him. Again, it wasn't his fault. She was simply fallout from a bad first marriage. She got that.

Then along came Jake. It wasn't a good time to get involved, her career was just getting off the ground. But it was too late for that. His charm, caring, and sexiness had touched something in her she'd shut off for years. He'd lit a fire, started a hunger for love—physical and emotional—she could no longer deny.

His offer was tempting. Forget about her career. Everyone knows how impossible it is to get to Broadway or the movies. If she ignored that, took her rejection as a sign that she wasn't good enough and settled down with Jake, she'd have a good life.

Of course, Jake wasn't offering that, he was simply opening his door. That welcome could morph into 'get out' in a heartbeat. She needed to have some kind of career or work, and be able to support herself. Life had taught her not to rely on the generosity of others. Outside of singing, dancing, and acting, there wasn't anything else she wanted to do. She laughed to herself. Perhaps nothing else she was any good at, either.

She peeked at him, eating at the table with his friend. They were talking and laughing. Kate yearned to be part of their group. Easy camaraderie, and being accepted by others had always been her dream. But during her high school years, with a mother who gambled, her life had become one of secrets, covering up, and hard work. In high school, she had waitressed to pay their rent.

More people crowded around the piano, blocking her view of Jake and Skip. She played their requests, and they sang along. These women didn't leave tips, but the men did—big ones, too. With a ride home from Jake, she'd have some money to put in the bank tomorrow so she could pay her cell phone bill. A smile lit up her face. It may not be Broadway, but she was performing, sort of, and had an audience. At the end of the number, Jake's applause was the loudest. Life was getting better, wasn't it?

She checked her watch. Only one more hour to go. She glanced at him. He was deep in conversation with his friend. Soon, she'd be the one getting his attention. She smiled as she took another request.

"What happened to you?" Skip asked, adding butter to his baked potato.

"What do you mean?"

"I mean, most of us have off days. Hell, we're lucky if Nat ever gets on base besides drawing a walk, but you struck out like four times this trip. That's not like you?"

"Trying too hard," Jake said, lowering his gaze to his food.

"Trying too hard to hit or to forget some hot chick who sings?"

"Both." Putting a piece of meat in his mouth stopped conversation. Was Skip's question on the minds of all his teammates? What about Cal Crawley, did he wonder the same thing?

"You can't let a chick interfere with your game."

"It's never happened before."

"Get your head screwed on right, Jake. We need you. We're going all the way to the Series this year, and we can't do it without you."

"I know, I know. This isn't news."

"So either get it together or dump this chick."

Jake stopped chewing for a moment and stared at his teammate.

"You're kidding, right?"

"I've never been more serious."

Jake swallowed. "I meet the first girl who's real, and you want me to dump her? Go fuck yourself." He filled his fork with potato.

"I didn't say that. Calm down. I said get your head on straight. Geez. Touchy, aren't you?"

"About Kate, yeah, I am. So watch it."

Skip put his hand on his friend's forearm. "I'm happy for you, Jake. I am. I'm just worried about the team. Fuck it. Maybe you should marry her." Skip sliced another piece of steak.

"That's the first intelligent thing you've said." Jake glanced at his watch. Eleven.

He heard Kate's announcement. She thanked the patrons of the bar, picked up her tip jar, and closed up the piano before joining Jake.

He rose and pulled out a chair for her.

"Looks like a fine haul. Your fans appreciate you," he said. "This is Skip Quincy, our shortstop."

She took Skip's hand and eased down onto the chair next to Jake.

"What do you want to eat?"

She sucked her bottom lip between her teeth and picked up the menu. Tommy wandered over.

"Nice job tonight, Kate. We had a big crowd."

"Thanks, Tommy."

"What'll you have? It's on the house," the barkeep asked.

"Thanks. How about a cheddar burger with sweet potato fries and a Coke?"

"Coming right up. Jake? Skip?"

"Nothing for me, I'm done," Skip said, pushing to his feet.

"Coffee for me, Tommy. Thanks."

"I'm on it. 'Night, Skip. Good luck tomorrow." With that, the bar owner headed back to the kitchen.

"I'm going to leave you two lovebirds. I'm sure you won't miss me," he snickered.

"Nice! You embarrassed her."

"Hey, if she's gonna be your babe, she'll have to get used to us crude guys, right?"

Jake simply shook his head.

"Thanks for the steak, Jake. Hey, that rhymes! Goodnight, Kate. Great music!" Skip said, then left.

"Ah, to be alone with my beautiful girlfriend," Jake sighed, taking her hand.

"Am I your girlfriend?"

"Of course you are. Right?" A note of uncertainty crept into his voice.

"Maybe. We'll see."

"You're not still mad about the audition?"

She shrugged. "Win some, lose some. There's a ton of rejection in this business."

"I didn't mean to do well. I mean, I did, but I didn't think they were listening to me. Not when you were there, looking so gorgeous and sounding so perfect."

"Who knew? I'm not mad. If you can't handle the rejection, this isn't the business for you."

"I could never take it," Jake said.

"Did you ever get any rejection in baseball? Wasn't there ever a team you wanted to be on that didn't take you?"

He blushed as red as a tomato. "Actually, no."

"Oh, wow! Geez. I have no idea what that must be like."

"I worked really hard. Baseball was everything. I did school and baseball and nothing else."

"Geez. I worked hard, too."

"You've been in stuff, though, right?" he asked.

"I have. Regional theater. Different shows."

"So you didn't always get 'no', did you?"

She smiled. "You're right."

Tommy placed a plate in front of her. "Here you go."

"Thanks." She dug into her food.

"Never had a girlfriend?"

"I've had a lot of them, but nothing serious. Mostly for a couple of weeks, a month or two. That's all. You ever been engaged or anything?"

She laughed. "Uh, no to both engaged or anything. I've had a few flings. When you're in a show, it creates a closeness, ya know?"

"No, I don't. Maybe like the team, though. Kinda like a family."

"Yeah, yeah, that's it. You get close to people, even though you know it's only for a short time. And stuff happens. You have a thing, an affair. Then the show's over and you move on."

"I can't imagine any guy wanting to move on from you."

"Thanks." She offered him some fries. He took one but kept eye contact.

"When you're finished, come home with me?"
She stared at him as she chewed.
"Please? I need you."
"Does anyone ever turn you down?" She narrowed her eyes.
"Not often."
"Like ever?"
He blushed. "A guy doesn't kiss and tell."
"That's what I thought." She lowered her gaze to her plate.
"You're different."
"Oh? I don't think so."
"But I do. And it's my opinion that counts."

She stopped eating to look at him. He picked up her hand and kissed her palm.

"Please? I don't usually have to beg."

"Begging looks good on you." She hesitated long enough to take another bite of her burger, chew, and swallow. She enjoyed keeping him in suspense. "Okay."

He beamed at her. "Yes!"

His stare heated her. She touched his fingertips with hers. Who knew how long it would last? Would he get tired of her? Forget about her when he was out of town? She shrugged. For whatever it was, she was in. There was no way she could turn away the man who lit her fire and warmed her heart.

Chapter Eleven

Once back at his building, Jake gave the doorman a friendly greeting. When the elevator doors closed, he grabbed her. His mouth was on hers, urgent, hungry, devouring her. Desire flooded Kate's veins as she clung to him, clutching his shoulders, pressing her hips to his.

He backed her against the wall. Then the ding sounded. They jumped apart as the elevator doors opened.

"Going down?" a man asked.

"No. Up," Jake replied.

The man stepped back and the elevator continued to the slugger's floor. Jake fumbled around, trying to get his key in the lock while kissing Kate. Finally, she pushed away and he opened the door.

Slamming it behind her, he was on her again, walking her backward to the bedroom. He kept going until her knees hit the mattress. She fell backward, and he landed on top of her.

"Oof."

"You okay?" He supported himself on his hands.

"Not as long as you're dressed. Shed those clothes," she said, licking her lips.

Jake pulled off his clothes and dropped his boxers. He sported a healthy erection. Then he approached her.

"I've been wanting to do this all night," he said, yanking down her sweater. Her breasts rested in a purple bra that made him gasp. He eased her back down, assaulting her chest with his lips and tongue while his hand crept up her leg. Though she wore a long skirt, he had it up to her thighs in no time. He glided his fingers up the smooth skin to her damp panties, then shoved them aside, leaving her open to his exploration.

"God, you're wet!" He raised his head for a moment.

She caressed his shoulders, easing her fingers through his short, dirty blond hair. Everywhere he touched her lit a fire. She arched up and he grabbed her panties, ripping them down and off. She unbuttoned the skirt and he removed that, too. Then the sweater went flying.

"Leave that on," he said, nodding toward her bra.

She laughed. "Now I know. Purple lingerie."

"Yeah. On you. Then off you," he said, unhooking the bra. He parted her legs and leaned against her, the hair on his chest tickling her nipples, making them harder. She loved the feel of his hard muscle against her soft flesh. She bent her knees, while he raised up on his. His shaft poked at her entrance.

"Do it. Take me. Now. Oh, God, I need you, Jake!" she cried out, wrapping her legs around his middle, putting him in position. One thrust of his hips and he was inside her. She arched and cooed.

"Oh, God. It's so good," she breathed while he pounded into her.

"Baby, baby, oh, I've missed you," he muttered, burying his face in her neck. She hugged him to her and undulated her hips to match his movements. They rocked together faster and harder until the electricity inside her coiled up and exploded into an orgasm that made every muscle shudder.

She cried out his name. He lowered his mouth to hers in a savage kiss, taking her, possessing her mouth. She slid her hands along his back, through a fine sheen of sweat, feeling the muscles work as he pumped in and out of her.

When he could hold out no more, he released her lips, raised his head and gave a loud groan. He sank down on top of her like a deflated balloon, resting lightly on her chest.

"There aren't words," he mumbled.

She laughed. "Uh, yeah. Right."

She kissed his shoulder while he nuzzled her neck. "I love you, Kate," floated to her ear. Her heartbeat increased, sweat between their bodies made their skin slippery. She clung to him, holding him tight. She swallowed the words dancing on the edge of her lips, held them back to hide her heart. But they had rolled off his tongue easily, embracing her, bringing her to him. A tear of gratitude slipped out of the corner of her eye and down to her ear.

He pushed up to make eye contact.

"Is it too soon for you?"

She shook her head. Although she tried to hold back, the words forced their way out. "I feel the same about you."

"You do?" His face, at once boyish and eager, lit up.

"Didn't you know?"

"You said it once, but that was a while ago. I hoped you still felt the same, but hey, who knows, right?"

Her fingers combed his hair back from his damp forehead, her gaze perused his face, taking in every handsome detail. His nose was straight and not too long, his jaw firm, scruff even. There was a small scar on his jawbone. She touched it.

"What's that?"

"Fell off a swing when I was four."

She leaned forward and brushed her lips against it. His blue eyes followed her every move. His lips, sensuous and inviting pecked the tip of her nose. She ran a fingertip against his scruff. He fitted his hand over hers, trapping it against his cheek.

"I want to stay like this forever," she muttered.

"Me, too." He stroked her hair before pushing up and rolling off her. He trotted off to the bathroom to dump the condom. When he returned, he wiggled his finger.

"Come here," he said, climbing back in the sack.

She slid across the mattress and he snaked his arm around her, pulling her up close. He dragged the bedcovers over them, kissed her temple, and sighed.

"It's late, baby."

"I know. You've got a game tomorrow. Goodnight, Jake."

"Goodnight, Kate."

And that was the last she heard until morning.

Jake was up at nine and let Kate sleep. When she awoke, there was a note saying he'd catch breakfast at the stadium and would be there practicing for the day. The night game was scheduled to start at seven.

She went food shopping and fixed a stew for dinner. Happy to be paying for the food with her own money, Kate bought the best quality she could find. As she cut up carrots and peeled onions, she sang, practicing her new songs.

By four, the meal was ready. She took a bowl into the living room and ate in front of the television. She left a dish covered with plastic wrap and a note for Jake. At five, she'd fished her performance outfit out of a small duffel she brought, changed, and headed for Freddie's. Her work began at six.

On the subway, she wondered how they would work out their different schedules. Kate hoped he didn't have too many night games. Day games might work better. If the game was over by three, he'd have to shower and race home to make dinner at four. She couldn't eat any later and make it to Freddie's on time.

She chewed her lip. One stage manager had cautioned her. "Don't get involved with anyone outside the theater. You'll never make it work." His words worried her. Now that she was living with Jake, could they manage around two such different schedules? What about his trips out of town? When he was on the road, would he stay faithful to her?

She didn't doubt her ability to remain loyal to Jake when he'd be away. She'd been so careful about men, avoiding entanglements as much as possible. After her childhood, she'd been left with trust issues. And her lifestyle, moving around from show to show, didn't lend itself to a commitment. She smiled, but she had that now, or at least on her part.

Kate had always wanted a solid relationship, a happy family of her own. Was she headed that way now? What about her career? As the train pulled into the station, she rose to leave. Perhaps it was best not to think about those things right now. She deserved to enjoy life a bit, especially after what she'd been through. Kate resolved to push disturbing thoughts away and simply be happy with Jake and her little singing job. At least the gig at Freddie's would keep her voice in shape, in case something bigger and better came along.

She grabbed a ginger ale and warmed up her fingers on the keyboard. Her cell rang. It was her agent.

"Hey, Lacy, what's up?"

"Two auditions. One this week and one next. I'm texting you the info now."

"That's great! Thank you."

"Good luck. Let me know what happens."

Perhaps good fortune was smiling on her, for a change. She grinned, happy to know she might be trading up her job for some real performing soon. A man in a blue suit sidled up to the piano.

"Do you take requests?"

"Sure do. What do you want to hear?"

After a lively night at Freddie's, Kate decided to splurge on a taxi. She called Uber and waited outside the bar. While she waited on the sidewalk, an uneasy feeling crept over her. Two men approached her.

"Hey, honey. Looking for a good time?" the taller one said.

They were drunk. Fear spiked in Kate.

"No. Thanks. Waiting for a cab."

"Don't worry about getting home. You can spend the night with us," he said, smirking.

Fortunately, the Uber car pulled up. The driver rolled down the window.

"Kate?"

"Yep. My ride's here," she said to the men as she hurried to the car. The shorter one stepped in front of her.

"Get out of her way or I'll call the police!" the driver yelled.

The man jumped back in surprise, and Kate darted into the car, slamming and locking the door. The driver sped away.

"That's not a great place to be waiting, miss," he said.

"I guess not. Thank you so much for speaking up."

"Sure. No problem."

Arriving at Jake's building, she was glad to see the doorman. A quick ride in the elevator and she entered the apartment. It was dark and quiet. Jake had gone to bed. She undressed and slipped, naked, between the sheets. He was on his side, with his back to her. She crept close to him, putting her hand on his bare shoulder.

"Huh? Wha...?" he mumbled, rolling onto his back.

"Hey, babe. Wanna make love?" she whispered.

"Now? It's the middle of the night. Early day," he mumbled, his voice heavy with sleep. He returned to his side and was snoring softly before she could answer.

She sighed. Being turned down for sex was new to her, and she didn't care for it one bit. She hunkered down under the covers. She guessed they'd have to adjust their sex life along with their dinner plans. Would the complications destroy their tenuous love?

Refusal to ponder heavy questions at midnight, she closed her eyes. She'd had a busy day and sleep came quickly. During the night, Jake rolled over and slung an arm over her. She stirred, smiling at his touch. She cuddled up to him, and he drew her against his chest. Yanking the blankets over her shoulders, she sank back into a restful slumber.

At seven, Jake cast a guilty glance at the bowl of stew he'd discovered when he returned home at eleven. He'd grabbed a quick burger at the Stadium after the game. He'd never expected Kate would have left dinner for him before she went to work. He'd undressed and eased into bed, tired from a day of practice and a tense game with the Carolina Tigers. The 'Hawks had won, but only by one run in the bottom of the ninth.

Sipping on fresh coffee he'd made, he sat in the living room, staring out the window. A foggy memory poked at his brain. He needed to remember something, but what was it? It hit him like a wrecking ball. Kate had approached him for sex last night, and he'd turned her down.

Shit! Turning down a hot woman in his bed was not his usual practice. He scrunched up his face and shook his head. What was he thinking? Of course, it had been after midnight and he had an early day, but still. *She must feel terrible.* Every man knows what that kind of rejection feels like—and it ain't pretty. He'd inflicted pain on his lady love. *What an asshole!*

Before rushing to apologize, he had to give himself a Get Out of Jail Free card on this one. Baseball had to come first. He needed to be awake and ready to roll today. They had another game with the Tigers, one they needed to win. Well, hell, they wanted to win them all, but that'd never happen. Jake had always taken training and baseball seriously. He'd followed the rules for food, liquor, and lights out. His attention to those things helped him succeed.

He needed to explain things to Kate. They'd have to work out a schedule. Ugh. Planned sex. He loved spontaneity, especially when it came to his love life. He figured he had a choice, give in to scheduled sex or lose Kate. Losing the love of his life was not an option. He took a deep breath, another slug of coffee, and headed for the bedroom. No time better than right now to clear this up, before she got mad, or hurt and took off.

He stopped in the doorway. Kate appeared innocent and lovely, like Sleeping Beauty. He wanted to wake her with a kiss. Well, actually, more than a kiss, but she'd been up late and probably wanted to sleep. He lowered himself on the side of the bed and placed his hand on her shoulder. The skin was cold under his warm palm.

She stirred, her eyes cracked open.

"Morning, beautiful," he said, caressing her neck.

"What time is it? Too early," she muttered and rolled over, shutting her eyes.

"Kate, honey. Sweetheart. About last night," he began.

"Hmm?"

"When you came to bed?"

"Arrgh. I need sleep."

"I'm sorry I wasn't up for lovin'. It wasn't you. Just when I have an early day..." he continued.

"I get it. Now go away."

She slid away from him to his side of the bed, then slammed the pillow over her head to shut him out."

If he'd wondered if she'd been mad, now he knew. He bent to kiss her, pushing the pillow up to get to her face. She kicked her legs, and he chuckled.

"Sleep, sweetheart. I'm off to the stadium."

He threw his gear in his backpack and closed the door softly behind him. The drive was short. He soothed himself with the notion that he'd show up at Freddie's tonight and speak to Kate then. Unless the game finished early. Maybe he'd find her home and in the mood. He cracked a grin. The very idea of making love to her got his blood pumping and his dick's attention.

Whatever he had to go through to keep this relationship on the front burner, he'd do. She was worth everything. This wouldn't be the first test he'd faced in his life and probably wouldn't be the last. But it would be the first in his love life. Could he give Kate McKenzie the same devotion he'd given baseball? He guessed he'd be finding out real soon.

He ambled into the locker room. He was early and took his time putting his stuff away.

"Hey, Jake! How's it goin'?" Skip Quincy asked, from the doorway.

"Good. You?" Jake shut his locker.

"Great. How's that new girl? Getting enough?"

Actually, he hadn't been getting any for a day or two, but he wasn't about to admit that to his friend.

"She's hot as ever."

Skip slapped his friend on the back.

"How about you, Skip? Time you settled down, isn't it?"

"Nah. I'm good. Haven't met anyone anyway."

"Maybe if you got your ass out of the bar, you might," Jake volunteered.

"Ah, go fuck yourself, Lawrence. Not everyone has your luck."

Jake laughed. "Got that right."

"Someday I'll meet the right girl."

"You wouldn't know the right girl if she fell in your lap," Matt Jackson piped up.

"Fuck you, Jackson."

"Thanks, but I've got a much better deal goin' than makin' it with you, Quincy," Matt chuckled.

"Dusty's way too hot for you, Matt," Jake said, shaking his head.

"Be jealous, all of you." Matt snapped a towel at Skip's butt.

"I keep hopin', every time I come in here, there'll be a naked girl waiting for me, too," Skip shot back.

Jake and Matt laughed.

Nat Owen joined them. He opened his locker. "Did you hear? Emerald Albright is singing the national anthem today."

"That hotshot singer?" Jake asked.

"Yeah. God, she's hotter than hell," Nat replied. "Think she's married, though."

"If you like that sort of thing. I'm happy with what I've got. Best lookin' girl in the U.S."

"I disagree, Jake," Matt shot back.

"Damn good thing we don't all like the same girl. Or I'd have to kill all'a you," Skip said.

Chuckling, the men headed for the workout room.

Kate awoke at eleven. She padded into the kitchen and reheated the leftover coffee. When she opened the fridge to get milk, she spied the bowl of stew she'd wrapped and left for Jake the night before.

"Didn't eat my stew?" She raised her eyebrows as she drew out the carton. "Didn't want to have sex? Bloom is off the rose already?"

The excitement of preparing for an audition turned to gloom as she figured she hadn't made a dent in the life of star slugger, Jake Lawrence.

"I love you, yeah, right," she sniffed aloud to herself. "Don't think so."

She finished the brew and didn't bother with food as her appetite had evaporated like mist on a sunny day. Time to get ready for an audition at one. She showered, dressed in a slightly sexy new dress she'd bought for try-outs and attempted to shake her downer mood.

She hit the street, showered with a warm, May sun. She stared at her phone, repeating the lines of the short speech she'd be expected to recite for the producers and director. A new off-

Broadway play was being cast. Although there was no music, her experience qualified her for a look-see.

She approached the entrance to the subway and descended the steep staircase to the platform. Nerves kicked up, as they always did when she was trying out. After boarding the train, she was lucky to find a seat.

Things with Jake had hit a rough patch, maybe heading for the end. As the car rolled along at breakneck speed, she shoved thoughts about her man out of her head so she could master the words for this new show.

Opening the theater door, she made her way to the front. A woman with glasses, wearing jeans shoved a clipboard at Kate.

"Here. Sign in, then take a seat. You're number twelve. Only four more to go before you get your turn."

Kate filled out the information and slipped into an aisle seat, her gaze trained on the stage. She'd not often been privy to the auditions of others. She watched each one, critiquing the performance in her head. At two, she checked her watch. By two thirty, the woman wearing the specs gestured toward her.

"Kate McKenzie? You're next."

Kate stood, brushed her hands down her dress to smooth out any wrinkles and strode up to the stage with what she hoped was a confident gait. After the reading, she walked to the subway.

"I won't get it. That's okay. It's straight acting and I'm a singer and dancer," she said aloud to herself as she descended the stairs to the train. Kate always told herself she wouldn't get a part because it made it easier when she didn't and a wonderful surprise when she did. Except for that new musical. She'd never wanted a part as badly as she had wanted that one.

It still hurt to think about it, so as she sat on the train she opened her phone and pulled up a book she was reading. Anything to distract her from negative thoughts. When she got back to Jake's place, it was time to grab some stew, change, and head for Freddie's.

Eating alone in the kitchen, she missed the slugger. They had shared every meal on the road. She'd gotten to know that he always salts his food, he drinks water with his meal, he takes a little sugar and a lot of milk in his coffee and prefers fried eggs to scrambled. She wondered when they would break bread again. Was it over, already? She sighed. This time she wouldn't be the one leaving. She didn't want to lose Jake and would stick it out until he called it quits, no matter how much she wanted to run. This time, wanting to stay beat chickening out by a mile.

She warmed up her voice on the way to the bar and grill, humming, and doing scales. A few people on the train stared at her, but most ignored her singing. This was New York City, people were used to all kinds of crazy people. Most New Yorkers kept to themselves, wrapped in their own cocoon—removed from others.

Not Kate. She smiled and said "good morning" or "hello" to people all the time. Some returned her greeting, others stared at her as if she were an escapee from a mental hospital. It didn't matter to her. Kate had set her mind to the fact that she'd not bury her human side, just to ride the subway or walk the streets of New York.

"Hiya, Kate! Right on time. Harry's special tonight is fried chicken."

"My favorite! Give him a kiss for me," she said, hanging up her light jacket.

"Kiss him yourself. Make his day. Ginger ale?"

She smiled. "Yep." At the piano, she did her warm-up exercise as Tommy trotted over with her drink. Maybe she'd be rehearsing a new show soon, instead of singing at a bar and grill. With a slight toss of her sexy locks, she discarded the idea. Hope was a luxury she couldn't afford. For the time being, Freddie's had to be good enough.

In the bottom of the ninth, the Nighthawks tied up the game with the Carolina Tigers. It went to extra innings. Not playing his best game, Jake had Kate on his mind. He tried to focus and was successful most of the time. But he'd committed an error on a routine grounder to third, bobbling the ball for a split second and throwing high to Nat Owen at first, allowing the runner to beat it out.

He was one for three at the plate. Nat had squeaked out a single and was languishing on first base as Skip and Bobby made out. It was the bottom of the twelfth inning. Jake was dog tired, but he was up at bat.

One look at the third base coach and he knew the hit-and-run play was on. He glanced at Nat, who gave him a nod. Usually, the hit-and-run was designed to move the runner one base, two at the most. Today, Jake prayed it would land in the farthest corner of the outfield, allowing the speedy 'Hawks first baseman to make it all the way home.

Jake set his jaw and narrowed his eyes at the pitcher. The first two pitches were balls. This was a new reliever, fresh from the bullpen. His control should be on target. The third pitch came straight down the middle above his waist, just the one Jake had been looking for. He swung and connected and followed through on his swing, pulling the ball to the left field corner.

Nat had made it almost to second when Jake let loose. As the ball sailed and the outfielders took off, full speed to get to it, Nat ran like the wind. Jake pushed his tired legs to run faster but was surprised by the speed Nat showed. Like a ghost in pinstripes, he flew from second to third. By the time he was nearing home, the ball had been fielded and was rocketing it's way to home plate. Luck was on their side. The possibility of such a long throw being right on target was slim. And this one was no exception. The ball came in a little high, allowing Nat to slide into home just under the tag.

The fans went wild as the team hit the field, mobbing Nat and Jake. And the game was over. The two heroes had first crack at the showers. Jake put on his watch. It was six-fifteen. *Kate will be at Freddie's by now.*

"A beer at Freddie's?" Skip asked, towel in hand.

"Yeah. I'm going now. Gotta talk to Kate," Jake said.

"I'll catch up with you."

The third baseman drove past the bar. It looked crowded. He had to drive four blocks away to find a parking space. The night air was pleasant. Memorial Day weekend was coming up. His thoughts turned to the next road trip. He'd be heading to Ohio, by plane, then a bus back through Pennsylvania. Ten days out of town.

He sighed. He'd have to tell Kate. How would she take it? Would she stay faithful while he was gone? A beautiful woman, like her, singing in a bar full of drunken, horny men. He swallowed. How would he know? He stopped to wait for a green light. He'd know. He'd always known. There was something different about a cheating woman. A man could always tell if he opened his eyes.

Sure, women keep secrets. But there are secrets and there's infidelity—totally different. Guilt did strange things to women and trying to hide something that big might be too much of a challenge for most women.

Kate appeared honest, to a fault. He grinned as he recalled the time she told him they needed to stop in the next town and get him a haircut. The road trip had been telling. Hard to hide anything when you're with someone twenty-four/seven. And in close proximity, like a car. She'd spoken her mind all the way across the country. And sometimes he got pissed at her comments –but they were honest. No, if Kate cheated, he'd know right away.

He pushed through the door and there she was, singing *Piece of My Heart*. Warmth filled him. *Yes, take my heart. You've got it anyway.* He didn't want to interrupt and tiptoed over to the table with the *reserved* sign on it. That table was always reserved—for Nighthawks. He sat down and caught Freddie's eye. The barkeep waved.

A couple of people hung on the piano, singing along with Kate. Her tip jar looked full. He smiled. She deserved success, even if it was only in a bar near the stadium. When she finished, there was applause and a few bills flying.

He strolled over.

"Can you take a break?" he asked.

She looked up at him with uncertainty in her eyes.

"I suppose. Sure." She pushed to her feet.

"Do you want a drink?"

"Coffee, maybe?"

Jake got a coffee from the bar. "Let's go outside," he suggested, handing her the mug. He held the door and followed her out into the early evening. He took her hand and directed them to a small park around the corner from Freddie's.

There were people on two of the four benches. He led her to an empty one and sat down.

"What's up, Jake?"

Chapter Twelve

"First, I want to apologize for last night. I wasn't prepared, I mean, I didn't expect you—"

"To proposition you in the middle of the night?"

"Right."

"I'm the one who should apologize. I forgot you had an early day."

"I didn't mean to shoot you down. I'm kinda strict about some things about baseball, food, alcohol, sleep, and stuff like that."

She stroked his forearm. "I know. You're right."

"In the morning, you were too sleepy to take up where we left off."

"Right. I'd gone to sleep real late."

"It's okay. I guess we're going to have some timing problems."

"Maybe you want to call it quits?"

"What? No. No! Where'd you get that idea?" He took her hand in his.

"I mean, I left you a bowl of stew. You didn't touch it. You didn't want to fool around..."

"I told you about the sex thing. The stew? I didn't know you'd been cooking all day. It looked great, but I'd eaten at the stadium. I put it away to have later."

"Really?"

"I was surprised. You cooked for me? That's awesome."

"I did. But I thought you didn't like it or want it. And then in bed," her voice grew shaky.

"What?"

"I thought you didn't want me. I tried to say it was because of your early day. But I've never gotten 'no' before. It hurt. So if you'd rather stop now, I understand." She took a deep breath.

"Stop what? Us?"

She nodded.

"No, no! What are you talking about?"

"I just thought—"

"You thought wrong. You don't want to break up, do you?"

She shook her head.

"Well then, what are we talking about here?"

"I guess, I don't know."

He stroked the back of her hand with his thumb. "We're just getting started. Don't pull away from me, Kate. Please."

Her chin quivered.

"Please, baby," he said, folding her in his embrace.

"I don't want to," she whispered, her voice shaking.

"I love you, honey. Don't you feel the same?"

"I do, I do, Jake. I just thought, maybe you'd changed your mind." She rested her head on his strong shoulder.

"Never, baby. Never." He brushed her hair out of the way and kissed her neck. He felt her muscles relax against him.

"Good. Because I don't want to move on. I'm happy with you."

"We might need to make schedules or something."

"Schedules?" She leaned back, her gaze searching his face. "Like for sex?"

He could sense the heat in his face. "Well, maybe. I mean with you working nights and me sometimes days, and sometimes nights, and some days out of town."

"When's your next road trip?"

"Funny you should ask. We leave on Friday. We're playing Saturday in Cleveland, then a doubleheader there on Sunday. Monday we leave for Pittsburgh, play three games there, then Philly, then home."

"Wow!" Her eyes widened.

"Yeah. We play a lotta games."

"When you play a night game, you can pick me up at Freddie's and we can go home together, right?"

"Yep. That'd work."

"Could you put a calendar on the fridge? For, like a month? Then I'll know where you are, and when you'll be home and stuff?"

"I could do that." He nodded.

"When you're on the road, no fooling around. Okay?" She straightened up.

"Right! And you, too," he said, wagging a finger at her.

"Of course not. Who am I going to cheat with, anyway?"

"A bar full of horny guys, that's who."

She laughed.

"I mean it. Don't you get propositioned there?"

She shook her head. "Nope. I don't flirt with anyone."

"That doesn't stop some guys."

"Freddie's got a bouncer. If anyone gets out of line, I simply motion for Sam. He gets rid of them. Problem solved."

Now it was Jake's turn to laugh. "See? You have had men coming on to you."

"A couple of times. No biggie."

"No woman who looks like you do doesn't have men hanging around."

"Okay, okay, I admit it. There've been a few guys. But I set them straight. I'm not available and they take it well. I'm not shy about telling people about you." A small smile graced her lips.

His heart swelled. "You tell guys about me?"

"Of course."

"And when I'm gone?"

"I'll do the same. I'm no cheater, Jake. What about you?"

"Me, neither. With a girl like you, what could I possibly find on the road?"

"You found me on the road," she replied, narrowing her eyes.

"That was a different kind of road. I was kinda looking then. Not anymore."

"That's good. Because if I find out you're cheating..." she said, making a fist.

He covered it with his big hand. "Never happen, baby. Never."

"Can I take that to the bank?"

"You can. Now let's finish up your night and get home."

"Hmm, one of those horny guys at the bar?" She cocked an eyebrow then stood.

"How'd you guess?" He took her hand.

"Just lucky." She grinned.

He leaned over and whispered in her ear. Her face flushed.

"Uh, let's go. We need to get home. In a hurry."

"You might say that," he replied, chuckling.

He took her in his arms and kissed her, then they scurried along back to the bar to finish her last hour. Jake ordered a steak and a salad with blue cheese dressing. He ate quietly, watching her, listening to her silvery voice and pretending to pay attention to Skip's chatter. All the third baseman wanted to do was kiss his girl, climb in bed with her, and make passionate love. Although he'd have to wait, he knew it would be worth it.

In the car, he took it easy, dodging people on bikes and aggressive cars. They pulled up to a red light. Kate leaned into him, rubbing her breast against his arm. She closed her fingers around his upper thigh.

"Can't you go any faster?"

Her lips so close called to him. He kissed her, losing track of the light, which turned green. A teen in a car next to his yelled out the window. "Get a room!"

Jake jumped back. Honking horns behind him urged him to step on the gas. Kate laughed as they zoomed ahead, beating out the next light, which had turned orange.

"Shit," he muttered.

She tightened her grip on his leg and licked her lips. Jake's dick responded, leaping to life.

"If you continue, I won't be able to get out of the car," he said.

"Let the doorman be jealous," she purred in his ear.

Jake focused on the traffic, zigging and zagging in and out of cars, speeding up when he could. He needed to get home fast before it was all over in the car. Damn she was sexy, and she knew exactly what to do to drive him crazy.

When he pulled into the driveway at his building, he maneuvered Kate in front of him as he tossed the keys to the valet and nodded to the doorman. When the elevator doors closed, he pounced on her like a hungry cat on a mouse.

He pushed her into the corner, his mouth crushing hers, his body trapping her. His erect shaft poked her belly. Kate softened against him. Luckily, there were no other riders and they rode up express, and alone. He walked her backward down the hall, never taking his mouth from hers until they reached the door. He fished his keys out of his pocket but fumbled with the lock.

Kate could barely stand the heat coursing through her veins. Jake's arm trembled, shaking the key. Frustration took over, and she pushed his shoulders, then grabbed the key and jammed it into the lock. She turned it and opened the door.

He pursued her, reaching out, but she eluded him. Wagging her finger at him.

"Uh, uh, uh," she said.

"Oh, yeah?" A salacious grin on his face, he lunged for her. She dodged him and ran for the bedroom, with Jake close behind. She took a flying leap for the bed. Laughing, she rolled over in time to dodge his airborne body aimed at the bed. He landed next to her, making her bounce up. When she came down, he was there, trapping her legs between his, her torso between his arms.

She lifted her hands to either side of his head and gazed at him. Lust sparkled in his eyes. The longer she stared the warmer his look. Something she swore was love mixed with the desire in his baby blues as his hungry look stripped her bare.

A thrill shot up her spine at the realization that she loved this man, and he just might love her back.

"I want you," he croaked, his voice husky.

"Come and get me," she uttered, her hands pulling at his shirt. Sitting up for a split second, he yanked his shirt over his head and rifled it to a chair. "Now you," he said, nodding at her chest.

She pushed up on her hands. "You do it."

"My pleasure." He slipped his fingers under her sweater and eased it up over her rib cage. She giggled as his soft touch tickled. She lifted each arm and he slid it off, then jerked it over her head and tossed it. With one hand, he unhooked her bra and watched it shimmy down her arms. When she was exposed, he stared, moving his hands to touch her.

Kate arched her back, pushing her flesh into this palms. "God, Jake! Touch me, take me. I want you bad."

He focused on her breasts, kissing her neck, then inching his lips down. When he reached a nipple, she pushed him back and sprang up off the bed.

"Last one naked is a rotten egg," she said, attacking the zipper on her long skirt. He wasn't far behind, unzipping his pants but staring at her. She bumped her hips at him while she eased her skirt down. He shoved his pants and boxers to the floor in one move.

"You lose," he said.

She quickly slid her panties down and stepped out of her skirt. She had worn sandals and had no stockings on.

"Nope. You lose," she replied, pointing to his socks.

"Damn!" He sat on the bed and ripped them off his feet, tossing them wherever.

"Rotten eggs make the best lovers," he said, sliding on his butt back against the headboard and pillows. "Come to this egg, lady." He motioned.

She licked her lips. He was an amazing specimen of a man. Broad shouldered, firm chest, with just the right amount of blond hair on his pecs. Strong biceps and forearms. His thighs were lean but muscular as were his calves. And his shaft pointed up, calling to her. She curled her fingers around it.

Jake pushed her away. "No, no. No way this time. Next time. Not happening this time." He grabbed her securely at the hips and lifted her up. Settling her on his thighs, he spread them, reaching under her.

"You're wet and ready, honey."

"Duh. I've been like that since the red light."

Talking was over. He covered himself, rubbed himself against her to lubricate his dick, and then eased inside her. She pushed up on her knees to give him room, then lowered herself onto him. Her knees straddled his thighs and hips. She sat up as if she were riding in an English saddle. He clutched her middle and guided her. Her nipples tightened as he pushed in and out. Emitting a groan, she arched, steadying herself with her hands on his shoulders. Face to face, they gazed at each other.

The intensity almost overwhelmed her. Lust and love joined in her. He slid his palms up her sides until his thumbs came in contact with her nipples. She widened her eyes at the additional stimulation.

"Good?" he asked.

"Fantastic," she breathed. "Don't stop."

He chuckled, then leaned in to claim her lips. She kissed him with a hunger that had been pent up for years. She wanted this man in every part of her, especially her heart. She took his mouth, meeting his tongue with her own. With his free hand, he squeezed her breast, then slid it down her flat stomach to press against her nub. She gasped, her eyes fluttered shut as his touch ratcheted the heat up to an inferno. She sensed her orgasm forming, growing tighter, gathering in intensity.

As the climax gripped her, she pushed off him to tilt her head back and give out a roar that ended in his name. He sucked a peak into his mouth hard, extending the contracting and flutter of her muscles around his dick.

Panting to catch her breath, she opened to stare at him. The look on his face started another fire. Color crawled up his chest into his neck and cheeks. As she bounced on him, controlled by his hand their rhythm started her up. She watched him reach his peak, as he slammed into her three times, then held her down as he sweated through his release.

He muttered her name, his eyes closed, and his hands clutching her butt. A mini orgasm whipped through her as he came. She'd never had such a totally mind-blowing sexual experience before. The anticipation had sent her into overdrive. Wanting him had piqued her sensitivity to the touch of his fingertips and lips. Each caress created a small fire, which burst into a huge blaze when he touched her in the right places.

He was out of breath, too. She lowered her forehead to rest on his shoulder. He stroked her back and kissed her hair.

"I didn't know it could be like this," she whispered.

"Only with you, baby. Only with you."

He closed his arms around her. His warmth, mixed with a bit of sweat, surrounded her. This was her safe place. Lying in Jake's arms, nothing bad could happen to her. He was her protector, the man who could ward off evil spirits and disasters. He made everything whole again for her.

She pushed up and off him. He trotted off to the bathroom. Kate stretched out, pointed her toes and pushed her arms up over her head. Everything felt good, every part of her hummed. When he returned, he pulled down the covers and slid her in like a letter in an envelope.

"Will you hold me all night?" she asked, hope growing in her chest.

"Of course. Come here." He motioned to her, opening his arms.

Lying there, nothing bad existed in her life. Protected against the world, Kate snuggled into her cocoon with Jake, savoring every second.

"Comfortable?" he asked.

"Very."

"Good. Me, too." He eased down, holding her to his chest, stroking her bare shoulder. "Your skin is like silk."

She smiled. She said a prayer of thanks before her eyes drifted shut, and she enjoyed the best night's sleep she'd had in years.

Jake awoke with new energy after a night of making love with Kate. They had both stirred around three and had had a shorter but also intense encounter. The clock said seven, so he bounded out of bed and headed for the shower.

When he padded back into the room with a towel fastened at his waist, he stopped for a moment to watch his sleeping beauty. She rolled over, exposing her breasts to his view for a moment, before turning on her side and covering up. If he lived to be a hundred, he'd never get tired of looking at them.

Time was a wasting, so he trotted into the kitchen and started coffee and cracked a couple of eggs into a frying pan. Then he turned on his laptop and printed out a calendar. After retrieving it from the printer in the den, he laid it on the table.

As he ate the eggs, he pulled out his pocket schedule. One-by-one, he wrote each game on the calendar. When he finished the month of June, he stuck it on the fridge using two magnets. He downed his eggs, another cup of coffee then threw on sweats.

Kate rubbed her eyes and sat up when he hit the bedroom.

"You're leaving?"

"Game today," he said.

"Oh. Okay." Even hazy with sleep, Kate was pretty. Jake couldn't take his eyes off her.

"It's a good thing you're asleep when I have to leave," he said.

"Why?" She cocked an eyebrow.

"Because if you were awake, I'd never be able to go." He leaned down to kiss her.

"Pick me up tonight?"

He nodded. "I'll be there."

"I love you, Jake."

"Love you, too, honey."

The valet had his car ready. Jake sang the song *Friendship* as he drove to the stadium. He wished all his teammates could be as happy as he was, but, that wasn't to be. Dan Alexander was on his cell in the locker room.

"I know, Mom. Yes. No, I don't want a fancy wedding either, but no one asked me. What? Yes, yes. I know that. Really, Mom? No. I don't care. That's right. Please, can't you let it go?" Dan paced. "Okay. I'll see what I can do." He shoved his phone in his pocket and let out a breath.

"What's up?" Jake asked.

"Stupid, fucking wedding," Dan muttered.

"Really?" Jake's eyebrows rose.

"It's not Holly. It's her pain-in-the-ass mother. She wants to have some gigantic wedding costing a mint. My mom is appalled. They can't afford anything fancy and she's afraid they won't even be able to pay for the rehearsal dinner. I told her I'd pay for it, but she's adamant. Women." Dan shook his head.

"Are you pitching today?"

Dan nodded.

"How's the leg?"

"Healed."

"You'd better get your head in the game and away from the wedding, buddy."

"I know. But when everyone's bitching at you, it's not so easy."

"Just visualize your future mother-in-law in the face of every batter," Jake teased.

"I'll get thrown out for intentionally hitting the guy," Dan retorted.

Jake laughed and patted his teammate on the shoulder. Matt Jackson was scowling, banging his locker shut.

"What the fuck?" Jake asked as he got to his locker.

"Dusty's playing in Pittsburgh, then Columbus, Cleveland, and Philly."

"Miss her?"

"Yeah. She's spoiled me. Not used to going so long, sleepin' alone."

"I know what you mean."

"You and that road trip chick still together?"

"Yup. She's playing at Freddie's."

"Not bad," Matt said, nodding.

"At least it keeps her here."

"Not like Dusty," Matt said, frowning again. "It had better not rain."

"Didn't you promise her you weren't going to be a pain-in-the-ass about her being on the road?"

"Yeah, yeah. But promising was easy. Not worrying about the safety of her fuckin' bus is something else." Matt shoved his cap on his head, pulled the visor down, and headed for the field. Jake watched him walk away, thanking his lucky stars his girl was in New York, didn't have much family, and loved him. He was sorry for his friends but wouldn't change places with either of them.

He hung his backpack in his locker and ambled toward the workout room. Skip and Nat joined him. Bobby Hernandez was the last of the infielders to warm up at the treadmill. Within forty-five minutes, Jake was in the batting cage.

At one o'clock, they started a three-game series with the Boston Blue Jays. Jake expected to beat them easily. Their star pitcher was on the disabled list, along with their starting centerfielder and their shortstop. But the lack of their strong players simply motivated the others to work that much harder.

Dan didn't have his usual edge. Matt appeared grouchier than ever, but the slugger had no problem concentrating. No worries about Kate entered his mind. Peace in his personal life gave him the freedom to put all his energy into baseball. His focus was sharper than ever.

They got good wood on a few pitches, racking up a score of four to three by the bottom of the eighth inning. Cal Crawley was grumbling on the sidelines. Jake stepped up to the plate. Skip and Nat were on first and second base.

Jake shouldered the bat. He turned steely eyes on the man on the mound and waited for his pitch. He didn't have long to wait. Two balls and a strike later, there it was, sailing low down the middle. Jake swung and lofted the ball high in the air. It soared toward the stands. He ran half-way to first and stopped. Nat and Skip hugged their bases, waiting. The right fielder raced full speed to the warning track. The ball came down as fast as it went up, dropping in the far corner.

That was all the men needed. Skip took off, with Nat right behind. Jake followed, careful not to pass Nat Owen. Skip flew across third and slid into home. Nat stopped at third and Jake at second. The game was tied. And Matt Jackson came to bat.

Jake gave a nod to Matt. Although he didn't have the highest batting average on the team, he was their clutch hitter. The 'Hawks could count on Jackson for a hit when they needed it most. Jake took a healthy lead off second, crouching a bit with his knees bent. He had to be ready to go at any moment.

Keeping his eye on Matt and each pitch, Jake took a breath. Swing and a miss by Matt Jackson. The third baseman glanced at Skip, then back at Matt. The signals from the third base coach were for a long fly ball, to bring in Skip.

The pitcher went into his windup. Jake noticed Skip switch his weight to the balls of his feet. That meant this would be Matt's pitch. The ball sizzled across the plate and the catcher swung. He connected and the ball took a shot to right field—

exactly where he was supposed to hit it. The right fielder backed up to the warning track and reached up. Skip and Jake tagged their bases. As soon as it was caught, Skip took off.

Jake did as well, hoping to confuse the Blue Jays and distract from Skip racing toward home. But the other team didn't get confused. The right fielder rifled the ball toward home. But it took a bounce, slowing and slicing to the left. Skip slid into the catcher who was blocking the plate—which is illegal.

The shortstop knocked the catcher down, and the ball whizzed over Skip, missing him. The catcher fell backward, unable to field the ball. Jake loped into third standing up. Timeout was called while they checked that the catcher was okay. Skip got up and dusted his uniform off. He was grinning from ear to ear. Jake raised his hand and shouted to Skip, who returned the sign.

The Blue Jays were not able to come back in the top of the ninth, so the Nighthawks won. Skip and Matt were mobbed and teased in the locker room. Jake couldn't wait to get to his girl.

"Out of the way, move aside. Man with a woman waiting, here," Jake said.

"Go fuck yourself, Lawrence," Chet Candelaria, center fielder, said.

"Okay, okay. Go ahead. You need a very long shower," Jake said, a smile teasing his lips.

"Fuck off."

"Who's waiting for you, Chet?"

"About a million women who haven't met me yet, asshole," he said, stepping in front of Jake.

The third baseman laughed and moved aside, giving his teammate the last available shower.

"The longer she waits, the hotter she'll be," Matt said.

A few minutes later, Jake stepped under the warm spray, his mind crowded with thoughts of Kate. Looked like living with her was good for his game. He'd never been more confident, more invincible, than he had been against the 'Jays.

He dressed in his best blue button-down shirt, khaki pants, and stuffed a green tie in the pocket of his navy blue blazer. He slid his feet into soft, Italian, black leather loafers, twirled his car keyring on his forefinger, and waved farewell to his teammates.

There was a parking space right in front of the bar, which he took as a good omen. He headed for the Nighthawks' table after a brief wave at Kate. She wore a silvery, shimmering long strapless dress. His mind immediately imagined what he could do to a dress like that. His dick twitched at the thought of yanking it down and off.

She was singing a song from the new Broadway show whose producers had turned her down. She told him that even though she didn't get hired, she still loved the music. He had to admit it was catchy, and he found himself tapping his foot to the melody.

Tommy brought him a beer and took his order. While he sipped, he took a long look at his girl. She'd used money she was making at Freddie's to expand her wardrobe for this job. She had good taste. The silver dress made her look like a movie star—maybe from a glamorous movie from the '40's or something. Jake didn't know what, exactly, but he knew she looked stunning and every male eye in the room was glued to her.

Nagging doubts as to how she'd fare being faithful to him while he was on the road returned. He had to believe her. When he entered the bar, he'd lingered by the door and watched her for a minute before making eye contact. She'd been smiling at the clutch of folks around the piano, but not in a flirtatious way.

He'd breathed a sigh of relief. Then she spotted him and her face lit up like a Christmas tree. It warmed his heart to see her response. Yep, he'd made the right decision about her. She was one in a million.

Waiting for his food, he sauntered over to the piano and leaned down to kiss Kate when she finished her song. She ran her palm over his cheek and shot him a questioning glance.

"Yeah. We won."

"Yay!" She raised both arms with fisted hands and cheered.

The people at the bar asked for his autograph. He obliged, as always. Tommy dropped his burger at the table and an extra, too. Jake sat down in front of his plate. He checked his watch.

"Yes, she's off in five minutes. So I thought she might like to join you. Hers is comped."

"Thanks, Tommy."

Kate wound up her song, thanked the patrons and joined him. While they ate, he regaled her with details of the game. She listened, making eye contact, showing her interest. He asked her about the evening.

"There was one guy Sam had to escort out, but otherwise, it was a nice group."

"If I'm here and someone tries to move in on you, I'll take them out. With my fist," he said, popping a fry in his mouth.

She smiled. "I love how protective you are, but it wouldn't be worth hurting your hand on some idiot, sweetheart."

She called me 'sweetheart'. He swooned, quietly to himself.

When they finished eating, Jake paid the bill and took her hand, lacing her fingers with his. He drove carefully because he had precious cargo. Once they were inside the door, he had his way with her dress. They made love in the light of the summer moon.

Chapter Thirteen

Jake sat back next to Skip Quincy on the bus to the airport. Confidence in his relationship made taking a road trip no big deal. He'd miss Kate, but he'd call her. He figured he'd call her every night. Simply saying "goodnight" would ensure he'd sleep soundly.

He played cards with his teammates, joked with the trainers, but didn't flirt with the stewardesses. Flirting with other women was over. He had the best woman in the world. He'd be damned if he'd screw it up by flirting with some groupie in a bar. He wondered if that would be hard to give up, but on his first night with Skip and Nat, he found he had little interest in the women who buzzed around his teammates.

He'd even stopped participating in the hot chick search during slow games. He threw in his five bucks, but he didn't bother perusing the stands. He knew, without looking, there wouldn't be any women there who could compete with Kate McKenzie. But he didn't want to turn his nose up at his friends' game. So he tossed in a fiver and congratulated the winners.

Every night, whether he'd had a night or a day game, Jake drove to Freddie's to pick up Kate. It wasn't safe for her to take the subway or even wait outside to get a taxi. Some nights they'd come right home because he had to be up early. He'd already eaten the dinner she'd prepared earlier in the day and left for him. On his early days, he'd look forward to seeing what she'd made for him. She'd bring home a burger from Freddie's. When they arrived, she'd eat, then they'd hop into bed for a quick cuddle before sleep.

Curling himself around Kate brought on the deepest sleep he'd ever had. Since they slept naked, he had access to her soft skin all night long. In her sleep, she'd fasten a hand around his bicep or flatten her palm on his chest, bringing a smile to his face. Her touch brought happiness.

Days breezed by. Their unusual schedule evened out. The calendar helped them keep track of each other, and missed meals stopped. Middle of the night propositions occurred only on nights before evening games. Jake's batting average climbed, his fielding percentage remained steady, and errors charged to him dropped to almost zero. His coach noticed.

"Keep up the good work, Jake," Cal said, slapping Lawrence on the back.

He smiled at his manager.

"You been practicing regular and it shows," Crawley commented.

"Yeah. Bein' happy doesn't hurt, either," he mumbled.

Cal laughed, shook his head, and headed for his office.

Jake hadn't expected living with Kate would be so perfect. Thoughts about making it permanent floated through his mind. Sure, he knew it was early. But when something was as right as this, why wait?

It didn't take his buddies long to figure out something was up. In the shower next to him, Skip piped up.

"So, when you gettin' married?"

"What?" Jake's head snapped up.

"You heard me. Gonna walk up the aisle with this chick?"

The third baseman laughed. He wasn't ready to reveal his thoughts, even to his best friend.

"We all know you been thinkin' about it. See it in your eyes. You have that 'married' look."

"Oh? And what the fuck is that?"

"I dunno. Just something a guy gets. Around the eyes. You know?"

"No, I don't."

"Yeah, kind of a melancholy thing. Sort of like a puppy dog."

Jake threw a bar of soap at Skip. "Fuck you! I'm no puppy."

"Maybe you're a tomcat with his balls cut off. Cuz you sure look pussy-whipped to me."

Jake rinsed his hair once more, then stomped out of the spray, and grabbed a towel. Damn him! He's spoiling it. Jake dressed quickly without uttering a word. He didn't want to see Skip and talk about his plans. *So what if the guys think I'm crazy? None of their fucking business.*

He drove to Freddie's, waved at Kate, and took a seat at the Nighthawks' table. He ordered the special, chicken parmigiana with spaghetti and a beer. While he waited for his food, he studied his lover. She wore a short dress in a sparkly teal color, silver necklace, and earrings. The dress almost matched the elusive shade of her eyes.

The oldest of three children, he wondered what his parents would say when he told them what he had planned. His younger brother and sister were already married. His brother had a kid, too. Jake chuckled to himself. They'd probably say, "It's about time!"

He hadn't seen his family since the holidays last year. Once the season started, he played every day or almost every day. There was no time for vacations or family visits. They understood and were proud of his achievements. Besides, his siblings lived nearby and spent plenty of time with his folks. How would Kate fit into his family?

His mom taught school and his dad was in his last years of coaching at a local college. They lived a couple of towns away from Willow Falls. Although he'd loved growing up in the country, now he was a city guy and enjoyed living in the Big Apple and being on a high-profile professional ball team.

Although he'd been in New York for a couple of years, he had yet to take advantage of all it had to offer. He hoped Kate would help him discover the treasures of New York. He sighed, looking at her and imagining picnics in Central Park, nights at the theater, Christmas on Fifth Avenue. His dreamy thoughts were interrupted by the sound of a familiar voice.

"Well, hello there."

Raising his gaze, his heart sank and his pulse kicked up.

"Angela! What are you doing here?"

"We used to be dating, remember?" She pulled out a chair and sat down. "Or am I no longer welcome at the Nighthawks table?"

"Of course, of course. Sit down." *Oh shit!* She was the last thing he needed to tip the delicate balance of his perfect life.

"Can I have a glass of wine?"

"Certainly." He motioned for Tommy.

Angela asked for a wine list and took her time going over it, looking for the rarest and most expensive wine, he guessed. She always did that. She was such a snob, spouting off about this vineyard or that, why it was good or why she'd never let their product touch her lips. He hated her pretense. And when she did it in front of the other guys, she embarrassed him. He could see them glaze over and shuddered to think how much grief he'd take about her in the locker room the next day. None of his teammates liked Angela. Skip actually cheered when he heard she was going to Europe for four months.

"Maybe you can find a normal chick while she's gone," he'd said, not knowing he was echoing Jake's sentiments exactly.

Now she was back and he needed to get rid of her as fast and as quietly as possible. He cringed at the idea of the fuss she'd make when he made it clear they were through. She had had it coming for months. She wasn't nice to his friends, insisted on spending his money like water, although she came from a wealthy family, and was lousy in bed. Angela looked down on the world. Very few were her equals in her eyes. She said sex was messy. He'd laughed. His response, "Especially if you do it right." She hadn't returned the chuckle.

He'd often wondered why she was with him but never had the nerve to ask. Now he wanted her gone and fast, before Kate came around asking questions.

"How was your trip?"

"So-so. Europe isn't what it used to be. So many low-class people there now. It's disgusting."

"That's too bad. What are your plans now?"

"I thought we'd take up where we left off." She reached for his hand, but he pulled it away.

"Angela, things have changed," he began, glancing over at Kate, who was facing him, her eyebrows raised. *Oh shit! Fuck! Damn you, Angela.*

And it was break time. He heard the arpeggio Kate always played before she took a bathroom break. She'd be heading over to his table. Sweat started on his forehead. Jake wiped his face with his hand.

Angela looked at Kate, then back at him. "Her?"

Jake nodded. Dread filled him. Kate sashayed over and bent to kiss him. He closed his eyes, avoiding Angela's glare.

"Who's this, Jake? Aren't you going to introduce us?" Kate stood next to him, resting her hand on his shoulder.

"I'm his girlfriend, Angela. And who the hell are you?"

Kate stepped back as if she'd been punched. "If you're his girlfriend, where have you been?"

"In Europe for four months. Jake knows that." Angela looked Kate up and down. "You've made a nice little stand-in, I see. But I'm back. So you can crawl back under your rock now."

Jake pushed to his feet. "Angela! Don't talk to her like that. She and I are together. You and I are through. You knew that months ago. We had this discussion on the phone before I left California."

"I didn't take that seriously. You were pouting because I was leaving. I figured you needed to sow a few wild oats and so I let you. But now I'm back and she can mosey along."

"For two cents, I'd punch your lights out," Kate muttered, her face growing red.

"Angela, we're done. We've been done for four months. We were done before you left."

"Oh? I didn't think so as you fucked me the night before I left."

Jake raked his hand through his hair. "This is getting ugly. I'm not going to have a fight with you here. I'm telling you we're done and that's it. Kate is living with me and that's the way I want it. We didn't have anything when you left and you know it."

"I thought we did."

"Well, you were wrong."

"Don't you have any dignity? The man flat out told you it's over. Wish him well and walk away gracefully," Kate put in.

"Who the hell are you to tell me about dignity, you little whore?"

That was it. Kate took a step forward and slapped Angela across the face. Sam, the bouncer, appeared out of nowhere.

"This woman giving you a hard time, Kate?"

"Yes, she is, Sam."

"Lady, it's time to leave." Sam stood between them, his massive arms folded across his chest.

"Jake, are you going to let this man throw me out?"

"Yep. I am. You've behaved badly. You deserve to go."

"Lady, you can do this the hard way or the easy way. The choice is yours," Sam said, reaching for her arm.

Angela pulled away from him. "I'm going. Who needs to hang out with trash like this? She looked at Jake and Kate. I've got better things to do." She huffed her way to the door with Sam following.

Kate narrowed her eyes and looked at Jake.

"Is what she said true? Is she, was she, your girlfriend?" Her eyes filled.

"No, no. I told her we were done when she left. She was never anything to me. We dated for a couple of months, that's all. Angela could never be competition for you. Please, Kate, believe me. It's you I love. Don't let her come between us."

He whipped a handkerchief out of his pocket and handed it to her. Her hand shook as she dabbed at her eyes.

"I'd like to believe you."

"Then do. She's nothing to me. Nothing."

"We'll see." She glanced at her watch. "I've got to get back."

Kate returned to the piano. She motioned for Tommy. Jake overheard her order a vodka tonic. He frowned. Kate never drank when she was singing. He checked the time. One more hour before he could take her home and explain, in private, how she'd captured his heart.

He finished his beer and settled up his bill. Dan Alexander joined him. Jake was happy to spend the rest of the hour listening to Dan moan about his family and Holly's

"The hardest part is finding the right girl. You'd think the wedding would be a slam dunk, right? Wrong. Women." Dan shook his head, then took a slug of beer.

Jake sighed. If he and Kate got married, he wouldn't have any of Dan's woes. Nope. Kate's mom didn't have money, probably didn't care if her daughter married or not. They could have a nice, quiet little wedding upstate at his folks' place, then take a great honeymoon to Paris or the Caribbean. He grinned, but not for long. After a questioning, unhappy glance from Kate as she played, *I Love Paris,* he wondered if she'd be around long enough to propose to. *Damn you, Angela.* He shot a tentative smile back, wondering what was going through her mind.

Kate's hands trembled as she held them above the piano keys. She elected to play an instrumental as her voice shook too much to sing. She wanted to run from the place and never return. But years in show business taught her that the show must go on, and she had to suck up her feelings and continue until the gig was over.

Pain sliced through her heart. Was that witch really Jake's girlfriend? How long had they dated? Was he still committed to her when Kate met him? And did that mean his commitment to Kate was only good until the next woman came along? Though she tried to force herself to concentrate, questions circled in her brain.

Finally, she clamped down, turned her mind to the revival of *Guys and Dolls* in Seattle where she had played the lead. She sang tunes from that show, the words flowing easily because she'd done the music so many times. A few people wandered over and joined in. Sam hovered on the periphery of the little circle and shot her a thumb's up. He'd protect her from anything. She smiled. But who would protect her heart from Jake Lawrence?

She saw him glance her way, his brows knitted, and his smile tentative. Did that mean he was worried about what she thought or he was rethinking being with her? Once again, she focused on the song, *If I Were a Bell*.

At eleven on the dot, she closed the piano and bid farewell to the disappointed patrons. She needed to get out of there and talk to Jake. When she stood, he was waiting for her by the door, his car keys jingling.

"Come on, honey. I've got to get you home," he said, taking her elbow and ushering her out before Tommy could deliver food. Sam raised his hand and she nodded back at him. They were quiet on the ride home. Kate wanted to gather her thoughts before speaking. Her heartbeat quickened as they rode up in the elevator. Now she knew how a condemned prisoner felt on his last walk to the electric chair.

"Smile, baby. You're not being executed," Jake said.

Might as well be. She managed a thin smile.

He opened the door for her. She headed for the liquor cabinet and nabbed a bottle of vodka.

"There's chili left over. It was really great. Can I heat up a bowl for you?"

"I'm not hungry," she said, reaching past him to grab a bottle of tonic.

"That's not a good idea, babe," he said, removing the alcohol from her hand.

"Now I can't have a drink?" She straightened.

"Can you wait until after we talk? You might feel differently."

Frowning, she slumped down into a chair. "You want to talk? Talk."

He took out a bottle of apple juice and filled two glasses, then handed her one.

"In case you're thirsty. I mean after all that singing."

She sipped the liquid, her eyes large, staring at him. Fear coursed through her and she gripped the arm of her chair to keep her hand from trembling.

He glanced down at his palms, then up at her.

"I love you, Kate. With all my heart. I hope you're not letting what Angela said get between us."

"When did you break it off with her?"

"I'm not sure, exactly. But it was before the road trip, 'cause I remember feeling really free when I hit the highway."

"Before you met me?"

"Way before." He palmed his phone. "Do you want to check my cell? It'll have the date of my last conversation with her on there. Go ahead. It's okay. I've nothing to hide."

She held up her hand. "No. That's okay."

"Angela and I never had anything serious. She's a wealthy chick looking for kicks. She was slumming with me, dating me because she knew her parents wouldn't approve."

"How did you meet her?" Kate's pulse slowed to normal.

"At a charity event. She was coming on to me. Frankly, I was in the mood to get laid, so I played along."

"And?"

"And she wanted more. I didn't have anyone else and hey, free sex when I wanted was hard to turn down."

"Was she good?"

"In bed?" He chuckled. "Selfish people are selfish everywhere, honey. It was okay, but nothing to brag about. I had some fun at a few snooty affairs she dragged me to. Loved the look on the faces of some of the people there when I told them what I did for a living," he said. "Baseball? You play a children's game for a living?" God, those snobs cracked me up.

"They really said that?"

"Hell, yes. Baseball is big business, but those assholes had no clue. Too many heads up their own asses, for my taste." He finished his juice.

His story was plausible. From what she knew of Jake, he was, number one, a very bad liar, and number two, an unpretentious guy. He made a shitload of money and after spending time with him, you'd never know. Tension drained out of her body, slowly.

"Can I have that drink now?" she asked.

"You're not gonna hit me, are you?"

She shook her head. He handed her the bottle, and she filled a glass with ice.

As she put the tonic back in the fridge, Jake came up behind her. He folded his fingers over her shoulders, his lips to her ear.

"I don't want anyone but you, Kate. And I doubt I ever will. Please don't leave me. Don't let Angela drive us apart."

He kissed her neck and stepped back. His face was pathetic, worry clouded his eyes, and formed little lines at the corners of his mouth. His sweet gaze touched her heart. How could she turn away from this incredible man and the love he promised?

She cupped his cheek. "It's okay. I get it. I understand."

"You do? That's fantastic!" he said, relief flooding his voice. He kissed her. His kiss told her everything she needed to know. Men can't fake kisses. She could distinguish lust from love in a man's kiss. Jake had both. She eased up against him.

"Why don't you bring that drink into the bedroom," he suggested, tugging gently on her sleeve.

"Great idea." She followed him.

Putting her drink down, she slipped her dress up over her head and closed the door.

Kate awoke at nine, stretched her arms over her head and smiled. The memory of passionate lovemaking from the night before filled her head, crowding out any negative thoughts about the fact that her life was going nowhere. Jake lay beside her, sleeping.

She tiptoed out of bed, slipped on a robe, then opened the window. Cool morning air drifted into the room. Jake had a night game, so they'd have some time together. He didn't have to be at the stadium until one.

Kate padded into the kitchen and put up a pot of coffee. She'd learned a lot about cooking during her waitressing days. The singer hummed the song *Friendship* as she prepared pancake batter. After setting the table, she pulled out a container of pure maple syrup and plucked two paper napkins from the holder on the counter. She enjoyed cooking, especially for Jake. He scarfed down every morsel she put in front of him, raving about how much he loved it. Almost everything about Jake Lawrence made her happy. Everything except his schedule. She figured that, over time, they'd adjust. In the meantime, she focused on how wonderful he made her feel.

Her cell dinged. A text from her agent, Lacy.

Call immediately!

Probably another audition, Kate guessed. It could wait until after breakfast. She poured a glass of juice and went to sit by the big windows in the living room, while Jake slept. Another text arrived.

Call now! Urgent!

Kate had never gotten a message like that from her agent, even when she'd won a role. She shrugged, then dialed.

"Hi, Lacy. What's the big emergency?"

"Are you sitting down?"

"Yes."

Lacy proceeded to share the biggest news in Kate's life. She sat there, frozen between pure joy and overwhelming sadness.

"So think it over tonight—like you'd ever turn this down, right? Give me your final answer tomorrow."

"Thank you."

"Thank you? I deserve more than that. How about some flowers or a trip around the world?" Lacy laughed and hung up.

Kate's appetite went south. She pushed to her feet, pinched herself hard enough to believe she wasn't dreaming. She wanted to jump for joy, then she wanted to cry her eyes out. Tears overflowed, the happy ones mingling with the sad.

Thank God Jake was sleeping. She'd need to get herself together before he got up. What did she want to do? Torn, she sat back down and stared at the city below. This was her big chance. She'd worked for it and waited for so long. How could she turn it down and be true to herself? How could she turn away from the one thing she'd been working for all her life?

What about Jake? He offered love, devotion, support, protection—all the things she'd yearned for as a child. She had it all with him, didn't she? How could she leave him now?

She dialed Keith. He was the only one she trusted. She told him.

"You know what you have to do. Why are you calling me?"

"I don't know. Honest."

"This may never come along again, Kate. And if you're serious about the theater, then you have to do it. Don't pester me with all that lovey-dovey crap. This is business."

"But Jake."

"I repeat. You know what you have to do. I'm hanging up now," Keith said, and the line went dead.

Kate put the cell down and faced the window again. She wiped her wet cheeks with her hand. Keith was right. He was always right. She took a deep shuddering breath. For the second time in twenty-four hours her heart hurt.

"Hey, baby. Last night was amazing," a deep voice behind her said.

She jumped. Jake snaked his arms around her waist. He kissed her neck. Kate twitched and trembled at his touch.

"What's wrong?"

She glanced over her shoulder, then avoided eye contact. Her throat closed up and the waterworks returned.

"Talk to me, Kate," he said, his brows knitting, his lips compressed into a frown.

"I got a call today from Lacy." She still had her back to him.

"Okay." He took her shoulders and turned her to face him.

"The show we auditioned for?"

He raised his eyebrows.

"You remember. *Call Me Sunshine*?"

"Oh, yeah. The assholes who offered me a part in the chorus. Yeah. So?"

"The show is a big success. They're forming a road company." She hesitated, the words stuck in her throat.

"And?"

"And they're offering me the lead," she spat out fast, then held her breath.

"That's terrific! Congratulations! Aw, honey, that's wonderful!"

He kissed her, then headed for the kitchen.

"Is it? It means going on the road for a year, maybe two."

"What?" He stopped dead, turning to face her. "What?" His voice almost a whisper.

"I haven't seen the contract yet. Lacy'll go over it. Maybe it's less. Maybe six months?"

"Six months, a year, without you?"

"Or I could turn it down," she said.

He smiled. "Turn it down?"

She nodded.

"Something you've been waiting for all your life?" He shook his head. "I don't want the responsibility."

"What responsibility?"

"Of being the one you gave up your big chance for. That'll kill what we have. I can't do it. You have to take it."

"But what about us?"

"I don't know." He poured a cup of coffee, then sank down on a chair at the kitchen table. "Do you have any ideas?"

She shook her head. "I don't want to leave you."

"That makes two of us. But I don't see that we have a choice."

She covered her face with her hands and sobbed. Jake eased her onto his lap.

"It's not that bad. We'll figure it out. Somehow. We'll figure it out." His voice quavered as he held her tight against his chest.

Chapter Fourteen

It was disorienting to wake up and find yourself in a nightmare. But that's exactly where Jake was. This couldn't be happening. He finally found the girl of his dreams and now she's leaving. And it's not because they don't love each other, it's life. Career. Achievement.

A little voice in his head begged him to ask her to stay, turn down the role of a lifetime. He ignored it. It didn't go away, it screamed louder and louder. *Don't go! Don't take the part! Stay here with me.* All he heard was the echo in his head, not a syllable came out of his mouth.

Emotion gathered in his chest, choking off words. Tears stung at the backs of his eyes, but he blinked them back. Stuffing down the pain in his heart, he reverted to his teens when he was convinced that boys don't cry. He'd learned to shove emotion somewhere and lock it away. He grappled with that as he considered what lay ahead.

Life without Kate. How cruel to let him have this time, live with her, be together day after day and then yank her away, far away for such a long time. Begging occurred to him. And/or proposing marriage. The things he could do to keep her there, like threatening to throw himself in front of the subway, flitted through his mind. His rational self discarded each one.

Words from his father echoed in his head. It happened in high school when Jake broke up with a girl because she wouldn't sleep with him. He'd complained to his dad, who had taken him aside for a heart-to-heart.

"Son, love means being unselfish."

"But Dad, she wouldn't—"

His father raised his palm. "Hear me out."

Jake had nodded, full of answers and little patience.

"If you're going to love a girl, it means not getting what you want all the time. It means being giving, unselfish. You have to take her feelings into account. If she's not ready to be intimate with you and you truly love her, then you'll wait until she is. If you don't, then you should move on. Never force a girl who isn't willing."

"But she says she loves me."

His father had chuckled. "Oh, my. Yes. Love at seventeen. It's not about how much she loves you but about how much you love her. And if you do, you'll be patient. You'll wait. She's very young for that kind of thing, son. I know how boys are, but girls come to the same point a little slower."

"Not Mary Lou Schafer," Jake had snickered.

"We're not talking about her, are we?"

"No, sir."

Jake had been too young to wait for the young lady's "no" to turn to a "yes". So he'd moved on and broken her heart—something he later regretted. He'd run into her at a reunion and she'd snubbed him. Yes, he'd been an asshole, but he wasn't anymore.

Jake's feelings for Kate were not puppy love. They were the real thing. He recalled his father's words. The third baseman had to "man-up". If he wanted Kate, he'd have to let her go, no matter how painful that was.

The twosome sat in the kitchen, clinging to each other, not talking. He closed his fingers over her shoulder and kissed her hair. Kate sighed, her tears wetting his chest.

"What do you want to do today?" he asked, rubbing his palm along her back.

"I don't know. I thought of a movie. But it's hot out. Let's stay here. Watch a movie on TV."

"And order in food. You've cooked enough."

"Okay, from the gourmet place down the block?"

"Wherever you want," he said, sadness ripping at his heart. "When do you have to leave?"

"I don't know yet. Lacy hasn't discussed the contract with me. She'll probably know in a day or two. She said something about being ready to go by the end of next week."

He gave a slight nod. "What movie?"

"A romantic one. How about, *While You Were Sleeping?*"

"Don't know that one."

"It's a chick flick. An old one. Is that okay?"

"Anything you want today is okay, honey."

Kate pushed to her feet. Jake took the menu out of a drawer and handed it to her.

"I'll go find the movie on demand. It's gotta be somewhere. You order food."

"What do you want?"

"Surprise me. Order lots of food. Charge it to my account there."

"Thank you." She kissed him and pulled out her cell.

Jake headed for the living room and his monster television. A chick flick would give him a legitimate reason to cry. He blew out a breath and grabbed the remote. He had a week to figure out how he was going to live without Kate. The enormity of the task overwhelmed him.

Jake hated to leave Kate for the ballpark. He resented every minute they had to be apart. He showed up in the locker room grumbling, itching for a fight. He changed in silence, refusing to talk to his teammates. He didn't trust himself not to end up brawling with one. When he hit the gym, Vic Steele greeted him.

"What's eating you, Jake?"

The third baseman glared at the trainer.

"Okay. Let's take it out on the machines?"

Jake nodded and followed Vic. After twenty minutes on the treadmill, he hit the machines. Pushing the weight up, he hit his limit and kept going.

"Hey, hey, you're gonna tear a muscle doing that. Slow down," Vic said, raising his palm. Jake stopped and the trainer adjusted the weight down. "You must'a had a bad night." Once the weights were where they should be, Vic backed off.

"I feel like I could bench five hundred today."

"Take it easy or you'll end up on the DL," the trainer said.

When he was finished, Jake wiped his face and neck with a towel. He'd worked off the anger. Now all that remained was sadness, squeezing his heart, threatening tears. Oh, God, no. He couldn't cry in front of his teammates.

"I need a shower," he announced as he sought refuge under the spray where tears flowed undetected. He dried off fast and suited up, hitting the field just a heartbeat behind his teammates. He scanned the stands for Kate and picked her out easily. Standing with his cap in hand, resting over his heart, he sang the national anthem but stared at Kate. She stood up and raised her voice as well.

We're smart. We'll figure this out. We have to. I can't lose her.

"Get your head in the game," Skip said, glancing at the stands then back at the slugger. "We need you to win, buddy." Skip clapped the third baseman on the shoulder.

He was right. Jake knew it. He took a deep breath and narrowed his eyes. He needed to focus. Slinging his cap on, he grabbed his glove and headed for third. They were playing the Philly Bucks. It would be a three-game series, and the 'Hawks had to win. They were on track, right where they should be, to make the playoffs. There was no room for screwing up.

The Bucks' first baseman stepped up to the plate. Jake remembered Matt Jackson's words, "This asshole was known for grounders to third, many ended up foul, but a few would cross the baseline into fair territory, a dribbler into right field good for extra bases." Jake bent his knees, shifted his weight to the balls of his feet and rested his hand and glove on his knees.

As Manuel Gonzalez, the Nighthawks' pitcher, went into his windup, Jake's body jerked to life. He narrowed his eyes and opened his hand, ready for anything. At the crack of bat on ball, the third baseman straightened up. Matt Jackson had been right. This time a line drive flew right at Jake. He raised his glove and thwack, made the catch, then fired the ball around the horn, starting with Nat Owen on first.

The game was close. The Nighthawks squeezed out a win in the tenth on a single by Bobby Hernandez and a double by Matt Jackson. Jake hadn't played his best. Disgust at his lack of concentration caused him to rifle his mitt at his locker. Then he kicked it.

"Hey, we won, didn't we?" Skip asked.

"Yeah, but I played like an asshole."

"Everyone has an off day. Forget it," Nat said, clapping his teammate on the back.

Jake showered and dressed, knowing that it was Kate's leaving that had screwed up his game. He had to get a handle on his personal life. Losing focus on the field was a recipe for disaster. Jake had worked hard for too many years to become the best and to maintain that reputation. To lose it now would mean he'd wasted his time.

Kate waited for him by the entrance. He turned hostile eyes on her. She straightened up.

"What's wrong?"

"I played like an idiot."

"Everyone makes an error sometimes."

"It's your fault."

Blood drained from her face, then returned in a fury. Her cheeks reddened. "What do you mean it's my fault? I was sitting in the stands not doing anything."

"Your leaving is fucking up my game."

"Really? Jake, you've got to be kidding me."

"I'm not. I'm totally serious."

She stopped and stared at him.

"Falling for you was a mistake. I should've known you'd get your break and leave me in the dust. And now you are and I'm fucked. Personally and professionally." He kicked a rock.

"Well, pardon me!" She positioned her hands on her hips and shifted her weight. "What do you think it's doing to me? Do you think I'm overjoyed about leaving you?"

He took her by the elbows. "This is the answer to your dreams. And it's going to be the end of mine."

Her eyes got wide. "No! Don't say that!"

"My concentration was off by a mile today. Because of you."

"That's not fair, Jake."

"Maybe not. But it's true."

Her eyes clouded, brimmed with tears. "I'd never hurt you."

"Not on purpose. But you have. I need to walk away." He stepped toward his car.

Water spilled onto her cheeks. "Go ahead. I wouldn't blame you."

As if she'd thrown a spear straight through his heart, he almost doubled over. His feet froze.

"I can't." His throat closed.

She chased after him and fell against his chest. He wrapped his arms around her.

"Don't, Jake, don't," she choked out. "We'll work it out. Somehow. We'll figure it out."

He stroked her hair. How could he give her up? The scent of her teased his nose. His fingers caressed the soft skin of her neck. When she touched him, he came to life. He needed her. He didn't want to, it would be easier not to, but he did.

There was no calling it off, he knew that. He'd only said it to hurt her like he was hurting. He'd be a fool to think that breaking up with her would be any less painful than being thousands of miles apart. What a rotten asshole he was! How could he be so mean to the woman he loved?

"I'm sorry, Katie." He buried his face in her hair. "I didn't mean it."

"Sometimes love hurts like hell."

"Yeah, like now," he replied.

He kissed her hair. They broke apart, but Jake slung his arm around her shoulders, and she snaked hers behind his waist as they headed for the car.

He put it in gear. "Freddie's?"

"Can we get take-out? I'd rather be at home with you than in a crowd."

"Sure, honey. Whatever you want."

As soon as she had accepted the role, Kate had called Tommy to quit her job. When they pulled up to the curb, she noticed a sign in the pub's window, advertising for her replacement. When they entered, Tommy greeted them loudly. He called everyone's attention to the couple and led a cheer for her. They placed their order. Tommy wished her good luck when he handed them the food and they left.

Once in the car and on the way home, Kate blew a few strands of hair out of her eyes.

"Whew, wow. That was intense."

"Get used to it. You're gonna be a celebrity."

"Nah. Just the star of a regional show and have steady employment for a while."

"Don't put it down. Not everyone gets a chance like this. You worked hard for it."

"I just hope I don't blow it."

"You won't."

They ate in the kitchen. Kate flipped through the guide on the television, looking for a movie."

"Wanna watch a movie?" she asked, wiping her lips with a napkin.

"I wanna watch you get undressed," he said, a smirk on his face as he chewed.

"You know, you chew cute. Have I ever told you that? You look cute when you're chewing."

"Really?" He raised his eyebrows.

"Yes, you do. It's a guy thing, I guess."

"So, movie or getting undressed?" he asked before popping two more fries in his mouth.

"Getting undressed first, then a movie."

"Early day tomorrow."

"Okay. I got it."

"We should make a schedule for phone calls and texting and shit like that."

"You mean sexting?" She wiggled her eyebrows.

He sensed a flush in his cheeks. "Hadn't thought about it. I could be up for that."

"How about Skype sex?"

"Holy Hell! Yeah!" He grinned. "When can I call you?"

"Hmm. Performances every evening at, like, eight. Wednesday and Sunday, matinees. No show on Monday night. How about you?"

"I can give you the game schedule. When we're out of town, you can call me when we're traveling. Except when I'm on the plane. We have to shut off phones for a while."

"So I can call you in the morning?"

"Uh, most mornings I've got practice and workout. Games are twelve, one, two. Like that. Or night games at like seven or eight."

"Hmm. Do you ever have days with no games?"

"Travel days. Sometimes we have double headers. Two games in one day. It would be hard to reach me on those days."

"Does your team have a schedule for the rest of the season?" she asked.

"Yeah. Somewhere. I'll ask Cal for one tomorrow," he replied.

Kate ate her last two fries. Jake let out a breath.

"This isn't going to be easy," he said, staring into her eyes.

"Nothing worth it ever is, is it?" she countered, holding his gaze.

He leaned forward and kissed her. "You're right. It never is."

"I love you, Jake. And I always will."

He took her face in his hands and kissed her. A small prayer that he'd still hear that six months from now winged its way from his heart.

Jake and Kate took their time making love. No reason to hurry. Afterward, they took an early night and shut off the lights at ten. She loved the way he curled himself around her, protecting her, making her feel safe. The warmth of his skin on hers kept the cool night air at bay. The pillows, the quilt, the fine quality cotton sheets created a comfort she had never known. She rested well in Jake's bed, especially after making love. His energy and passion brought her to new heights, guaranteeing a satisfaction that seeped down all the way to her soul.

She had hoped their road trip would continue as a journey through life together. Now, the future was uncertain. The thrill of her new role in the theater blended with the fear of losing Jake, making her bounce from high to low and back again.

At three o'clock, Kate threw off the covers and padded to the bathroom. When she returned, sleep eluded her. She sat up in bed, watching Jake snooze, tattooing his sweet image on her brain so she'd never forget. After a few minutes, he stirred, rolling over, then back again. He opened his eyes.

"What the hell?"

"You up?"

"I am now. Geez, you're staring at me. Why?" He rubbed his eyes and sat up.

"Sorry. I can't sleep." She went over to the window and opened it wider.

"How come?"

She shook her head. "Too much going on in my head."

Jake patted the mattress. "Come here. Tell me."

She returned to his side. "What if I'm no good? What if I can't cut it? What if I get fired? Like on the first day?"

He chuckled. "No one gets fired on the first day."

"You know what I mean."

"You won't get fired. You're good. Really, really good."

"But what if I'm not good enough?"

He pulled her head against his shoulder. "Honey, don't worry. You *are* good enough. And if by some horrible, tragic mistake they do fire you, you can come home and marry me."

"What? Marry you? Is that a proposal?"

"Sort of. I guess. Yeah. It is."

"But I'd be a failure. My career would be over."

"You'll never be a failure to me."

Her heart swelled and words caught in her throat. She stroked his face. "How did I get so lucky to find you, Jake Lawrence?"

"You got that backwards."

In the dim light, she made out his face, located his mouth, and then kissed him. "I love you, Jake, with all my heart and soul."

"That proposal is good if you're a success, too. Which I'm sure you will be."

"I like that. An all-purpose proposal," she chuckled.

"If you believe in us, it'll happen. Just tell all those horny directors, producers, and actors to fuck off and leave you alone," he said rolling the ends of her hair between his fingers.

"Fine. As long as you peel off all those bar bunnies who cling to you after games."

He laughed. "None of them are in your league, baby."

"But they'll be there and I won't."

"You'll be in here," he said, tapping the left side of his chest.

"You'll still love me if I fail?"

"How I feel about you has nothing to do with your theater success."

"And the short answer?"

He chuckled. "The short answer is 'yes'."

She snuggled down, under the covers, plastered up against him.

"Remember, when you leave you're my fiancée now."

"Did I say 'yes'?"

"I thought you did. Didn't you?" The note of controlled panic in his voice amused her.

"If I didn't, then 'yes, I will marry you, Jake Lawrence'."

"Good. You had me going there for a minute. I don't have a ring. I hadn't planned to do this now. But then, I hadn't planned to be up at three having a heart-to-heart, either."

"Best not to have a ring now anyway."

"Why?"

"Because I'd have to take it off when onstage. Easy to lose it that way."

"But then, all those horny guys would know you were taken."

"Hey, an engagement ring doesn't keep someone from cheating," she replied.

"No, but it's a deterrent."

She laughed. "Not really. If they want to have sex with you, some guys don't care if you're engaged or married. As long as you're breathing."

He laughed. "Men are whores, aren't they?"

"Damn right. I'm on to them. So you'd better be careful. I'll know if you cheat," she said.

"I won't. Don't worry," he said, his tone firm.

"Good. Same goes for me."

"Better not. I'll tear apart any guy who lays a hand on you," he said, balling his fingers into a fist.

"Oops. I forgot to tell you that my co-star has to kiss me in the show."

"As long as it's onstage, fine. But not off."

"Definitely not off. I think he might be gay, anyway."

"That suits me," Jake said.

"You're so possessive," she said.

"Damn right. And don't you forget it."

"I won't, sweetheart, I won't."

Jakes words soothed her. He repositioned himself and was breathing steady within minutes. Kate's eyes closed, but questions about her own ability didn't fade away in the cool of the night.

The week passed quickly. Jake had a game Sunday at noon. That night, he'd be leaving for a road trip and Kate would be leaving for Seattle. That was their first stop on the tour. Cal had given Jake permission to meet up with the team in D.C. that night, so he could return home after the game and see Kate off. He'd planned to take them to the airport together.

There was no time for breakfast on Sunday morning, as Jake had to leave early for the stadium. Kate didn't have much stuff and finished packing in an hour. She ordered in a corned beef sandwich and munched in front of Jake's game, cheering and booing as if she were sitting in the stands.

When he came to bat, pride swelled in her heart. She sat up, her gaze riveted to the screen. He looked good, eyes narrowed, tough, focused, and in control. She called that his "slugger" face. It meant he was on his game and that pitcher didn't stand a chance.

Damn, that man in the batter's box was sexy! Watching him turned her on. They'd never done it in the stadium, and she regretted that slip-up. A vision of him in the shower danced through her mind. *We'll fix that when I get back.* She crossed her fingers that she would return.

She expected Jake at four. Her plane left at eight, not leaving them much time. She took the chili she had made two days earlier out of the freezer. They'd have time for a quick bowl. Food wouldn't be on Jake's mind when he got home after the game. The Nighthawks lost to the Boston Blue Jays by one run. It wasn't Jake's fault, the Jays were on their best game and the 'Hawks pitching left something to be desired.

Kate made a trip around the apartment one more time, to check that she hadn't left anything behind. When she finished, Jake thundered through the door.

"We lost! But I don't give a shit because I want my woman!" He ran to her, embraced her in a vise-like grip. His passion ignited a hunger in her and she reacted. She jumped up, wrapping her legs around his waist. He supported her butt and carried her into the bedroom.

He tried to disengage to lower her to the bed, but she wouldn't let go. Jake lost his balance and the couple fell on the bed together, laughing.

"Take off your clothes," he ordered his lips on her neck.

"You, too."

"Last one to strip is a rotten egg," he said, pushing up from the bed.

The two lovers ripped at their clothing. Watching each other with hot eyes, they added a few bumps and grinds to the action as they shed layer after layer. Kate finished first. She raised her fists above her head and did a little nude dance before she placed her hands on Jake's waist and shoved his boxers to the floor.

"You win," he said, closing his arms around her naked midriff and lifting her off the ground.

Heat raced through her body as her behind hit the mattress. Jake's mouth was all over her. She squirmed, trying to get her arms free, but he had them trapped.

"Oh, no. Our last time and it's gonna be my way, first."

She laughed. "Yes, master!"

He raised his head, his eyes twinkling, and said, "It's about time you recognized that I own you."

"I suppose now that we're engaged, you sorta do," she admitted.

"Damn right I do. And I'm claiming my due now."

"And that means I sorta own you, too," she retorted.

"That's only fair. You can take me the second time," he said, between nibbles of her breasts.

Kate's eyes drifted shut as she gave in to her senses. He was everywhere at once, or so it seemed. She heard the drawer in the nightstand open a few seconds before his tongue hit her hot flesh. It sent her to the moon as tension pooled in her core. God, she wanted him, wanted him bad.

"Hurry," she hissed, opening her eyes.

He raised his head, tore at the condom packet and covered himself in a flash. Then he threw himself down, back against the headboard, and grabbed her hips. He positioned her above him and lowered her onto his shaft.

"I want to see you. This last time. I want to see you."

She swore she saw tears mixed with lust in his eyes. "Do it. Do it, Jake. Take me. Hard, fast. I want to remember."

"Oh, baby, this is one you'll never forget."

He rammed her down hard. She held onto his shoulders, steadying herself as he moved her up and down. His eyes bored into hers, his look intense, loving, possessive, demanding. A thrill shot up her spine. She moved her hips in concert with his hands, pushing down on his shoulders, rising and falling faster and faster.

With her climax building, she grabbed his head and fastened her mouth on his. He consumed her with his lips and tongue. Steadying her with a hand on the back of her head, he devoured her, with a moan here and a grunt there. The fingers of his other hand closed around her breast. He squeezed a little hard, drawing a gasp from her.

"Sorry, sorry, honey," he whispered.

"Don't stop," she breathed in his ear.

The intensity pushed her to the limit, then exploded inside her. She groaned his name, loudly, as pleasure streamed through her.

"Oh, God. Jake, I love you so much," she whispered.

"Now it's my turn," he said, plastering her against him with one hand, and rolling them over with the other. Once she was on her back, he loomed over her, pushed up on his hands, his hips moving. She peered up at him from under her lashes. Sweat coated his forehead, his eyes glowed the brightest blue she'd ever seen. He wore a smirking, sexy, dirty smile as his gaze darted from her face to her breasts.

"Oh baby, baby, baby," he muttered, thrusting into her, harder and harder.

Kate arched into him. He lowered his chest until her nipples rubbed lightly against his skin. The sensation shot tingles through her as her peaks hardened. She snaked her arms around his chest, raking her nails down his back. He shivered and broke out in goosebumps.

"Shit, man. When you do that..."

She snickered, tilting her chin up to make eye contact. His blues turned smoky. She could tell he was getting close. Tightening her muscles inside made him groan louder. Finally, he gave one hard push, then dropped his forehead to her chest, groaned her name and stopped. Sweat dripped off his brow. His lips sucked at her neck.

"That was the most amazing sex ever," he said, blowing out a breath.

"God, yes," she responded.

"Time to get ready," Jake said, throwing down the covers.

"Yep," Kate mumbled, swinging her legs over the side.

The pair dressed in silence. Jake grabbed his travel suitcase.

"You pack ahead?" Kate asked.

"I have extra clothes, shaving stuff, and crap. I keep it in a separate bag. I'm on the road so much, this means I don't have to pack up and find shit at the last minute. I grab this and go."

"That's so amazing. I mean, I thought guys didn't plan?" She rested her hand on her hip.

"They don't. This way I don't have to," he said, his gaze sweeping her nakedness. "And if you don't put some clothes on, we're both gonna miss our planes."

"Oh, sorry." She bustled over to the chair where her jeans were.

Within twenty minutes, they were dressed and out front, waiting for the car service. They sat close together, their hands laced. Neither spoke. Kate divided her attention between Jake and the scenery. His eyes looked clear and shy.

"I'm getting a ring."

She shook her head. "That's okay. I don't need a ring. We're together."

"I want you to wear a ring. I want people to know you're mine," he said, tightening his grip on her a tiny bit.

"Okay, then. A ring would be great."

He leaned toward her and planted a sweet, gentle kiss on her lips.

"I love you," he whispered. "Don't forget me."

"I couldn't, wouldn't." She fought to keep the quaver out of her voice but was unsuccessful.

"Things are crazy. I know you're scared. So am I. I believe in you. I know you can do it. And no matter what happens, you'll always have me to come home to."

She touched his face, running her thumb over his cheekbone.

"I don't deserve you."

"You deserve so much more."

Her cell rang, shattering the warm feeling. She checked the screen. Her mother.

"Hi, Mom. What? I'm on my way to Seattle. Yeah. I got a starring role with the road company."

Silence.

"I don't know, Mom. I'm going to have a lot of expenses. Just stay away from the track and you'll do fine. We're pulling up to the airport. Gotta go." Kate clicked off the phone.

She looked at her lap and took a deep breath.

"She's kinda in your face, isn't she?"

Kate nodded. He cupped her cheek and kissed her. "Take care of yourself first, honey. You'll be working hard. You don't need to be worrying about her. She can take care of herself."

"I know. I need to cut her loose."

The car pulled up to the curb and stopped. The couple got their luggage and headed for the security line. They held hands as they followed along. Jake was recognized by a handful of people and signed autographs. He leaned down to whisper in her ear.

"Soon you'll be the famous one and everyone'll push me aside to get your signature."

She laughed. "Don't hold your breath."

Once they passed safely through the metal detectors, they checked their boarding passes. They were heading in opposite directions. While Kate had twenty minutes to boarding, Jake only had fifteen. The moment she had been dreading had arrived.

"Time to say goodbye," she said, her eyes filling.

"Not goodbye. See you later?" Jake pulled her into a hug.

Kate clung to him as if it were the last time she'd ever see him.

"Hey, baby, don't break my ribs," he chuckled.

"Sorry, sorry," she said, loosening her grip. "It's just that..." she stopped.

"I know. I know. It'll be okay. We can do it."

"Can we?" She raised wet eyes to him.

"I'll come to you after the series."

"That seems so far away," she said.

"It's not. You'll see. You'll see," he said, stroking her hair.

Kate buried her face in his chest and sobbed. Jake clasped her shoulders.

"I love you. We'll be together."

She rummaged through her purse for a tissue. Jake yanked a handkerchief out of his back pocket and thrust it into her hand. "Here."

She wiped her face. "I'll wash it and get it back to you."

"See? That means we'll be seeing each other again."

"You've got to go," she said, glancing at her watch.

He kissed her as if it was the last time. People stopped and watched. Some actually applauded when they separated. Jake ran to his gate while Kate raised a palm, tears streaming down her cheeks.

Then it was her turn to run. She made it, wending her way to her seat. She plopped down next to the aisle and fastened her seatbelt. Numb, she stared straight ahead but saw nothing. She clutched Jake's hanky in her right hand and shoved her purse under the seat with her left. The doors closed and the plane taxied to the runway.

Her journey to a new life had begun, and she'd take it alone.

Chapter Fifteen

Kate settled quickly in Seattle. Rehearsals started right away. They'd play in Seattle for a week, then on to Portland. A week in each city until they reached Denver, where they planned to stay for two weeks, if reviews were good. Then straight to Chicago. The schedule after that was grueling, one week in each, smaller city, two weeks in the larger ones like Dallas and Houston.

After Chicago, they'd depart for Milwaukee, Indianapolis, Columbus, Cincinnati, Pittsburgh, then south, to Texas, and moving east to New Orleans, and smaller cities on their way to Atlanta. They'd head north through a few stops in the Carolinas, and Tennessee, then D.C. The final swing would be to Philadelphia then home.

The company was friendly, making the fourteen-hour work days easier. To avoid unpleasant scenes with randy producers, and crew, Kate made her engagement public. She hoped that would discourage any man who had sexual ideas on his mind.

To her relief, Bart McQuinn, her co-star was gay. They became friends immediately. He was as new to the road trip experience as she, so they clung to each other for support. He had a wicked sense of humor, which put Kate at ease right away.

There were three weeks of rehearsal before opening night. Kate studied her lines during her few hours of free time. At night, she'd text Jake. With the three-hour time difference, she rarely found him awake. In the morning, the first thing she did was open her phone. There it was—his answer to her text from the night before.

Tough day. Struck out twice. Miss you.

Touching base with Jake through texts made getting up easier. His responses, sometimes funny, sometimes sexy, made her smile as she met the day.

Sore muscles after rehearsal. Miss you.
Cold, then hot bath. 2 for 4 today. Miss you, too.

When she wasn't on stage dancing, singing or going through her lines, she was sitting in the auditorium, thinking up clever texts for Jake. Sometimes they were available at the same time. Those were the best.

Waiting three hours for my dance.
Waiting for rain to stop. Rain delay means I can text. So not so bad.
When I kiss Bart on stage, I pretend he's you.
Don't overdo it. He might get ideas.
He's gay.
Thank God!
Hate sleeping alone.
Hate having sex alone!
Me, too!
They're rolling up the tarp. Miss you. Love you.
Choreographer arrived. Miss you and love you, too.

What seemed like endless rehearsals ended when opening night loomed. Kate had been focused on getting things right and doing her part perfectly, she had not paid attention to the calendar. Days had blended together into one big run-through with a few moments taken out to eat, sleep, and text Jake.

She woke up that morning with a slightly sick feeling in her stomach. It wasn't flu or food poisoning, rather first night flurries. Kate recognized the combination of euphoria and total dread mixing in her belly. Opening night! This would be the night that determined everything—success or flop? Great review or total pan? She hit the shower then joined Bart for breakfast.

"I can never eat anything on opening night," he said, ordering the jumbo breakfast.

Kate ordered bacon and eggs and wondered if any of it would pass by the lump in her throat. When the food arrived, Bart chowed down as if he had been starved for weeks. He consumed bacon, eggs, sausage, a pancake, hash browns and a small serving of fruit salad. Kate's eyes grew wide as she toyed with her food and watched him.

"See? I mean normally, I eat twice as much," he said.

She burst out laughing.

"There you go. Feel better?" he asked.

"Yeah. You did that for my benefit?"

"Hell, yes. You looked like you were on your way to the guillotine."

"That's how I felt," she said, taking a forkful of eggs.

"Honey, you can't perform on an empty stomach. You need fuel. This is no walk in the park. A lot is riding on tonight."

"Tell me about it. How do you deal with the nerves?" She picked up a piece of bacon.

"I usually go out and get laid."

`Kate almost spit out her food.

"But since I'm in a relationship, that's out of the question." Bart kept a straight face as he polished off the fruit salad.

"It would be great if Jake was here."

"Got a picture?"

She nodded and swiped on her phone. She had several, including a couple that weren't for sharing. She pulled up one of him in uniform, holding the bat in his stance, looking determined.

"God, he's gorgeous!"

"Yes. And I don't share," she said, with a smile, picking up her coffee mug.

Kate took a short nap, then met the rest of the cast for dinner before the show. When she headed for her dressing room, a member of the crew stopped her.

"A delivery came for you. I hope you don't mind, but I put it in your dressing room."

"That's fine. Thank you."

Who's sending me something? She couldn't imagine what it was until she opened the door. There on her dressing table stood a big vase holding two dozen red roses. She plucked the card off the top and read,

Break a leg tonight. Love you. Jake

She got giddy. Never had she experienced this when she opened in small, regional theaters. A queen, a princess, a diva, a Broadway star got roses on opening night, not Kate MacKenzie, little miss nobody!

There was a knock on the door.

"Come in!" she yelled.

A young man with a toolbox under his arm joined her at the table and began the magic of greasepaint and eyeliner to make her look real, onstage. Of course, they didn't actually use greasepaint anymore, but it sounded authentic.

Confidence, buoyed by her lover's sentiment, and his flowers, flowed through her veins. As if he had been there to hug her and tell her she was great, his love washed over her. She picked up her phone and checked her watch, then the schedule she'd taped to her mirror. Nope. He was playing right now, no phone call, she sent him a text, instead.

Thank you for the flowers! You're my All Star. Love you to pieces.

Before she had time to think, another knock on her door and the call, "Five minutes," spurred her to touch up her hair, smooth down her skirt and head for the door. She stopped to sniff the red blooms once, sucking in the sweet scent of love before she exited to take her place on stage. As the curtain went up, a burst of energy flew through her. In that moment, she knew she could do it.

All her lines, the lyrics, the dance steps, even the kiss with Bart went off without a hitch. If she was going to blow it, it'd be because her performance wasn't good enough, but not because she forgot anything. Like automatic pilot, everything she had learned flooded back, the way it always did. Fear blended with excitement, creating a new energy. She flew across the stage executing each step perfectly.

Kate connected with Bart, creating chemistry that sizzled and humor that bubbled. Audience laughter and applause spurred them on to the best performances possible. They got five curtain calls and a standing ovation! She floated on air, hugging Bart and every member of the cast. The cast party was down the street.

Combing her hair, Kate grinned in the mirror like a monkey. Although the producers and the show's backers would care about the reviews, Kate wasn't worried. She knew she'd done her best and that it was good. The audience has a way of telling you if you've succeeded or failed. And this appeared to be a big win.

Her door opened and Bart McQuinn blew in, like a gust of fresh, spring air.

"Darling! You were great. I think we're a hit! Now let's go and get drunk." He settled his attractive butt into a chair.

"Be ready in an instant," Kate said, removing her makeup with a damp sponge, baby wipes, and soft paper towels.

Her cell rang. Happiness welled up inside her as she grabbed the phone.

"So, how did it go?" Jake asked.

"Great! We got five curtain calls! You would've been proud of me," she said, suddenly breathless.

"I'm always proud of you. That's terrific! Congratulations."

"Wish you were here to celebrate."

"Me, too. We won tonight."

"Congratulations to you!"

"Yep. But it was nothing compared to your opening night."

"Your roses helped so much. It was like you were here with me."

"I'm glad. I love you, Kate. I know the show will be a hit."

"I'm coming back to you. Don't forget that."

"You'd better."

"Bart's waiting for me. We have the opening night cast party. I've gotta go. Love you with all my heart, darling," she said, closing her eyes.

"Have a good time, but not too good a time," he chuckled.

"I won't."

"Love you forever, honey," he said and hung up.

Because he had had a night game the day before, Jake slept in until nine the next morning. He sprang out of bed, washed, dressed, and had breakfast in front of his laptop. He searched the net for reviews of *Call Me Sunshine*. Bam! Pay dirt! He found two listed, one in the Seattle Times and one in the Seattle Post Intelligencer, now an online newspaper. First the Times:

A new star is born! Kate MacKenzie in Call Me Sunshine shone like a glittering nova in the galaxy. Opening night for

this revival, Miss MacKenzie lit up the stage with her energy, her beauty and her talent.

He skipped down to the closing paragraph.

We will be looking for more from Miss MacKenzie in the future. Expect her star to shine over Broadway.

If you're looking for a bright, fresh play bursting

with music and dancing, Call Me Sunshine, is for you.

The review in the Post-Intelligencer was equally glowing. Happiness and pride filled Jake. He had known she'd be a hit.

Worry clouded his thoughts. This meant she wasn't coming home anytime soon. He sighed. Torn between wanting her to succeed and the desire to have her home warred in his heart.

Was it wrong to love her and want to keep her for himself? Was he being monstrously self-centered? The answer was "yes", but did he care? Wasn't love a selfish emotion? Did you want to possess the object of your adoration and not share her with the world? Of course, you did, but what about her? Would that kind of devotion smother her, robbing her of her day in the sun? Wasn't she entitled to the freedom to seek her own success at something in life that didn't revolve around him?

He poured himself another cup of coffee. Would he want to be hooked up with a woman who wasn't her own person? He'd been raised to seek a partner with no ambition beyond being a wife and mother. But being in New York and meeting the women his teammates were dating and marrying had changed his mind.

He could love a woman who only wanted to be his wife and the mother of his children. But a woman who wanted more? Damn, she was exciting! Watching her perform, turned him on. He couldn't wait until her show overlapped in at least one city so he could see her on stage.

Listening to her clear, stunning voice in the car, then at the audition had humbled him. Sure, he had talent, amazing talent, but here was a woman with the same amount of talent, but in another career. That had knocked him out.

Where could he find another woman like her? Nowhere, and that was the rub. He sighed, realizing he was stuck loving Kate. Because she was the gold standard and nothing less would do. He had a top-of-the-line, talented woman as his partner, his equal, his lover. Soon to be his wife, maybe.

He dressed and headed to the ballfield to work out and practice. They had a three o'clock game. It was already eleven. He needed to get it together. This was number three in the playoffs.

The slugger had to be in shape, had to save the game, had to perform at his best. His team, his buddies and Cal Crawley were all counting on him.

Jake parked his car and loped to the gate. He was ready to prove that he was as good as Kate. Well, almost as good. The words of the reviewers rang in his ears. He grinned and shook his head. Who would have thought little Jake Lawrence would have a shot at the World Series and the love of a talented musical theater star? Wouldn't they be surprised at home?

"Where you been, Jake? Shag a few at me," Skip said.

In Jake's opinion, his friend was the best shortstop in the league. And that was saying something, considering how hard short was to play. Jake hit balls for half an hour, then warmed up on the treadmill and the track for half an hour.

They broke for lunch in the clubhouse.

"Kate got great reviews."

"Reviews?" Skip asked before taking a bite of his sandwich.

"Last night was opening night. In Seattle." Jake sipped his juice.

"Oh, yeah. Great news."

"Can we get free tickets to the show?" Nat asked.

"I doubt it. Besides, she's in Seattle right now. It'll be a while before she's back in our area."

"What's a while?" Bobby asked.

"Months."

"Okay, guys. Listen up. We gotta knock off the Sharks. We're close. Ahead two games to zip. If we win today, then just two more and it's the Series."

The men cheered. Jake was pumped. The team was primed and ready. He knew they could take the Miami team. They had to. Jake wanted the Series so bad he could taste it. And this time they'd win. He knew it. Something about Kate's success stoked his fires. Bring on the Sharks, he'd harpoon 'em with his bat.

Homerun fever infected Jake Lawrence, and the other team had damn well better look out.

The Nighthawks had won the first two games in Miami. Today they had home field advantage. The broadcasters and odds-makers were predicting a 'Hawks' sweep. The Miami Sharks came to bat first. Dan Alexander had pitched the first game. It was crucial to win in Florida, but they couldn't use him because he was still on rest. Cal needed him for the first game of the World Series.

Manny Payton was the starting pitcher for New York. Rodrigo Jimenez started for Miami. Manny struck out the first batter. Jake remembered Matt Jackson's words after the last game. Seems as if this batter often struck out his first time at bat in a big game.

"He was going for it. Trying too hard'll kill you every time," Matt Jackson had said.

Jake nodded, slipping a piece of gum in his mouth. That's exactly what the idiot had done. The third baseman smiled—he had no objection. He kept his eye on Matt. The catcher signaled him to move a little closer to the bag, which Jake did. Good thing, too, because the second batter shot a line drive right at Jake, who caught it with ease. Two away.

Third batter struck out, too, and the Nighthawks came to bat. Nat Owen started the top of the lineup. He wasn't a long ball hitter but was pretty reliable in the one-bag hit department. And he was fast. A bit shorter than some of the others, Nat was quick. He and Bobby Hernandez tied for the most stolen bases.

Sure enough, Nat punched one to right field and beat out the throw. The 'Hawks had a man on. Jake licked his lips.

"Getting' ready?" Matt asked him.

Jake nodded.

"Relax. You've got a few minutes before you bring him home," Skip said.

Jake watched Bobby draw a walk. Skip struck out and returned to the dugout, cursing. As he passed his buddy, he whispered, "It's up to you, Jake."

The slugger nodded. Energy flowed freely as Jake Lawrence took his stance. He stared at the pitcher, who was wiping his face on his sleeve.

The bastard's nervous. Serves 'im right. He should be. Confidence held Jake upright as he shouldered the bat and narrowed his eyes at Jimenez. Not knowing what to expect because the guy was new, Jake decided to jump on the first pitch.

And what a great decision! He connected with a fastball right down the middle, chest high, exactly in Jake's zone. The crack of the bat was felt all the way to his toes. The ball soared at top speed, heading straight for the third tier. Jake took off. He loved the home run around the bases routine. Nat and Bobby waited for him. The three players tipped their caps to the fans before descending the stairs into the dugout.

That was all the action. The Sharks got one home run, but Jake's three-run baby won the game. He got mobbed in the locker room.

"Celibacy keeps you sharp, Jake," Skip said.

"Shut the fuck up, Skip. Oh, no. Wait a minute. You'd know all about that, right?" Jake tossed a towel at his friend.

"Damn right he does," Nat put in.

"What would you know about getting laid regularly?" Bobby asked.

"Now, Dan and I are a different story," Matt snickered.

Four wet towels were rifled at Matt Jackson's head.

Jake shook his head. He couldn't wait to get home. Managing to get out before his teammates pranked each other, Jake hit the gas pedal in his fancy car and took off for home. He preferred to text his lady when he was alone. He tossed his keys in the bowl in the foyer and headed for the fridge. He filled a large glass with orange juice and sat down to text Kate.

We won game 3! I had a 3 run homer.

He had to wait until eleven to get a reply.

Fantastic! Congratulations! Blowing a kiss.

Wish you were blowing something else. Ha ha.

Very funny. Wish I was, too.

We killed in Portland and Denver. Next stop Kansas City.

Awesome! But I'm not surprised.

How many games until the Series?

Two more. Wish you were here to be my good luck charm.

Me, too. Sending you positive thoughts, babe.

Love you.

Love you, too, Jake.

They had game four the next day. The Nighthawks were pumped. Jake couldn't sit still. He was salivating to get the Miami Sharks on the field and beat the shit out of them. This playoff was going to be theirs, and they were going to go on to the series, no matter what.

The men got to the field early. They warmed up, they trash talked the Sharks, they fed each other positive vibes. But sometimes, things don't go as planned.

Chapter Sixteen

From somewhere, the Sharks put it all together. Maybe coming from behind was their thing? They beat the Nighthawks, three to two. Jake couldn't hit shit and there were two costly errors in the field, one infield and one outfield. Matt Jackson, coolest head on the team, dropped a ball rifled at him to tag a runner out at home. He bobbled, then dropped it. Charged with an error, the catcher lost it, swearing at himself and almost got ejected from the game.

The Nighthawks were still ahead, three games to one. Jake vowed that they'd get them in this next game. He texted Kate.

We fucked up. Lost. Now we have to win tomorrow or go to Miami.
I'm so sorry!
We can't lose tomorrow.
That's a shame. Call me on the plane.
Yeah. I hope you're still doing great. Miss you.
I'm fine. Denver was okay. Not as good as Seattle.
Good reviews?
Yeah, but not five star. KC will be good. Sleep well, darling.
I will. Love you.
Love you, too.
Kick butt in Kansas City, honey.
Night, Jake.

They had to win the last game in New York, but they didn't. The score was three games for the Nighthawks and two for the Sharks. Jake went home to pack. He was furious, enraged. How could his wonderful team collapse like that? How could he have screwed up and struck out, not once, not twice, but three times?

He wanted to hit himself, throw himself against the wall. But that wouldn't help. All the while Kate was knocking audiences out, bringing them to their feet. What would a star like her want with a loser like him? They had to win. Had to defeat fucking Miami. He paced, popped open a beer and sat back, watching the game, which he had recorded.

He looked for the problems. Studied the pitcher to see where he missed the signals. He couldn't concentrate. *It's all her fault. If Kate were here, I wouldn't have messed up like I did.*

Shame filled him. His loss had nothing to do with her. Of course, if she'd been there, he would have been more confident, but he'd been blazing baseballs into the stands long before she came on the scene. Sure he missed her, but his bad game was simply his own damn fault.

As he watched, he saw where his teammates messed up, too. Skip had an error at short. Their pitcher kept walking the Sharks. Seemed like he couldn't hit the box no matter what type of pitch he threw. It all added up to a lousy performance and win for the Sharks.

He needed to talk to Kate. Not a text conversation, but a real one. Once they got in the air, he was free to use his cell, but would she be performing? It was Sunday, matinee day! Perfect! No evening performance, so he could call her. The thought of her voice put a smile on his face. He'd have to find a quiet corner, away from his nosy teammates. He shook his head, a private conversation in the air would be impossible. But he'd try.

The Nighthawks needed to win in Miami. If they did, then they'd go on to the World Series. If only he could touch Kate. Hold her hand, kiss her once before the game. He'd gain strength and get his confidence back. But she was winging her way to Kansas City, so that would never happen. He sighed. Love was hard. He had never known how hard.

Life would be easier if Kate had been traveling with him. No matter how much he missed her and wanted her with him, he had to admire her talent and gumption.

Kate had picked herself up and kept going, trying, believing in herself. Now she was on the road to stardom, the big payoff for years of deprivation, striving, and heartbreaking disappointment. He smiled. If she could do that, who the hell was he to give up, to throw in the towel because he had had a bad game or two? What a pissy little crybaby he was!

The comparison strengthened his resolve. He needed to make himself and Kate proud. He needed to get back in the saddle and start blazing 'em out of the park again. There was no time for self-pity or wound-licking. He had to man-up now.

If the Sharks won twice in Miami, then they'd go on to the World Series and the Nighthawks would be a bunch of losers left sucking their own dicks. He pulled out his travel bag and threw in some clean underwear.

Kate had breakfast at a diner on the way to the theater. She wanted to be alone to think about Jake and reread his texts. After their conversation the night before, as he was flying to Florida, her heart ached. Although he'd appeared happy-go-lucky, confident, and calm when she left—last night he expressed self-doubt, apprehension, and nerves about today's game.

This Jake was a stranger to her. His insecurity rocked her as much as it surprised her. She'd leaned on him, he'd been the strong one. But on the phone, Jake had needed her reassurance. She recalled part of their conversation.

"I know you'll do okay today," she'd said.

"Okay's not enough. I have to get it back. I need to hit at least one out of the park today. And no more errors. Shit, I don't know what's happened to us."

"Every team has bad days. Days when everything goes wrong."

"That doesn't happen when you do a show, does it?"

She had laughed. "Are you kidding? Wardrobe malfunctions of all kinds. Losing your voice in the middle of a song. Geez, you'd be amazed."

"Yeah? Tell me about it."

"One time one of the spotlights blew up about two minutes before curtain time. Just last week, someone spilled something on the stage and my leading man slipped and fell flat on his ass in the middle of a dance routine!"

Jake had laughed, relief in his voice.

"You laugh. Crap like that gets written up in reviews. Critics then call the show an 'amateur' production. You get branded. Ticket sales fall off to nothing by the end of your run."

"People are so unforgiving?"

"Of course. Haven't you seen guys get booed when they strike out? Or pitchers, when they walk someone? Audiences can be demanding bitches."

"Of course, they expect the best from athletes."

"Same is true of performers."

"I'd never thought of that. A lot of stress for you," he'd replied.

"I try not to think about it. I assume every performance is going to go off without a hitch. And ninety-nine percent of them do. It's those few that don't, that scare the crap out of me."

"So you're saying the same is true of the Nighthawks?"

"I am. Look at how well you guys have done all season."

"That's why we're in the playoffs."

"Of course. But you can't go on forever, performing at that level, and never having an off day, can you?"

"I suppose not." His voice got lower.

Kate wracked her brain to find the right thing to lift his spirits but came up empty. She'd never thought he'd need encouragement. Embarrassed with herself for being so self-involved and thinking him super-human, she faltered in her efforts to buck him up.

"If I was there, I'd give you a big hug." She frowned at her lame reply.

"If you were here, you'd give me a helluva lot more than that!"

She laughed. "Yeah. That, too. I love you, Jake."

"Me, too. Break a leg, honey."

When she'd hung up the phone, she wasn't convinced she'd cheered him up. Perhaps there wasn't anything anyone could do in this situation. At least telling herself that relieved a bit of her worry. She'd chewed on her lip. Being far apart had turned out to be harder than they'd thought. But she wasn't going to give up. He was the best thing to happen in her life. Kate McKenzie didn't walk away from a challenge. She simply hunkered down and figured it out. This time would be no exception.

She finished her coffee and picked up her cell. There was something she had to do before the matinée at two. When she finished, warmth spread through her. She headed for the theater wearing an impish grin.

Shark Stadium, Miami

Kate chewed a nail as the taxi jerked to a halt. She shoved the cash in her hand through the opening and threw open the door. Grabbing a small bag, she dashed up to the entrance.

"You can't go in there, lady," the man in the box office said. "Game's about to start. We're sold out, too."

"I have to see Jake Lawrence before the game starts." She struggled to keep desperation out of her voice.

The man shook his head slowly. "Don't see how you're gonna do that. They're singing the national anthem right now."

"You've gotta let me in there."

The security guard sauntered over, eyeing Kate.

"What seems to be the problem, lady?"

"Jake Lawrence is my boyfriend. This is a long story."

"I'm not going anywhere," the guard replied.

"There isn't time. Look, he needs to see me, if only for a few minutes."

"How do I know you're his girl? Anyone could say that."

She rummaged around in her purse, yanking things out, searching for her cell. She scrolled through her pictures until she found ones of her with Jake—on the road trip, in Freddie's, one with her wearing his jersey and nothing else. A furious heat filled her face as she flashed that one in front of both men.

They cleared their throats. The security guard looked down.

"Guess you are his girl," said the ticket seller.

"How can I get in there? I only need to see him for a minute."

"Only way now is through the locker room and the tunnel to the dugout," replied the guard. "All the gates are locked."

"Which way?" She asked.

"You can't go in there."

"I'll take her," the guard said.

"We've got to hurry." She grabbed the man's arm. "Let's go."

He led the way to the locker room. Pushing open the door, the guard stuck his head in and called out. "Anyone here?" Silence greeted them. He nodded to her and held the door. Together they made their way to another door.

When he opened that, she heard the faint noise of a crowd cheering. *The anthem must be over. They'll be here in a moment.*

"Team's coming," he said, rushing forward down a wide tunnel toward the field. Kate followed. "Hurry up!"

Kate got there as the men dribbled in. They showed surprise when they saw her. Jake was the last one in. He stopped before descending the few steps and rubbed his eyes.

"Kate?"

"Yep." She grinned.

Cal Crawley. "No women in the dugout, miss."

Jake took the stairs two at a time. He grabbed her elbow and escorted her to the connecting alleyway.

"What are you doing here?" He stared as if she were a mirage.

She launched herself at him, throwing her arms around his neck. Tears burst forth.

"I had to come. You needed me."

"Kate," he said, quietly, nuzzling her hair. He drew her up hard against him.

"I love you so much," she murmured, squeezing her eyes shut to stop the water flow.

"Me, too. But what about the show?" He stepped back.

"The theater is dark on Monday night. I'm flying back tomorrow morning."

"You'll stay the night here? With me?"

She nodded.

He grinned from ear-to-ear. "This is my lucky day, baby."

"It is. Now go out there and kill those Sharks," she said.

"You know I will."

Cal Crawley stuck his head in. "Let's go, Jake. Nat's on second, Skip's on first, and Bobby's at the plate."

He kissed her deep, with passion, before breaking away. "Gotta go." Jake blew her another one as he loped down the hall and disappeared into the dugout.

She stepped back and nodded. The polite clearing of a throat reminded her that the security guard was waiting for her.

He reached in the pocket of his pants. "Here. They gave me this in New York. I've been carrying it with me to give away. But I forgot. Front row, honey."

Kate took the ticket. "Thank you so much!" Together, they hurried out to the stands.

Kate handed the man fifty dollars, but he refused the cash.

"Consider it my contribution to true love," he said.

"Thank you. You're an angel."

He took her to her seat. She got there just in time to see Bobby Hernandez walk and Jake come to bat. He walked to the box with his old swagger. Her heart leaped into her throat as she watched him take his stance. He swung a couple of times, rotated his wrists, shifted his weight back and forth between his feet, and then stopped. He turned his head toward the pitcher.

She swore to herself that the old Jake was back. He took two pitches, both called balls. Then it came. A fastball, sailing high and outside. He swung hard and connected. She heard the crack and watched the baseball soar up, up and into the second tier seats. A grand slam home run! The fans rose to their feet. The cheering was deafening. She danced a jig with the man in the seat next to hers.

Then she stopped to watch. As he rounded the bases, approaching his teammates who waited by home plate, the crowd simmered down. Kate was the only one left standing. Jake was mobbed by his buddies, but he stopped to doff his cap to the fans. Then he turned and blew a kiss straight at Kate, who blew one back. A new cheer reverberated around the stadium, causing her to blush.

The Nighthawks went on to grind the Sharks into the ground, winning eight to three. Kate let the others exit ahead of her as she lingered to meet Jake by the locker room door. Men dribbled out with wet hair and huge grins. The Nighthawks were going to the World Series. Joy beamed from the faces of the players as they headed back to the hotel for a celebration.

Finally Jake came. He picked her up and twirled her around.

As his fingers gripped her waist, belief seeped into his brain. Kate was really here. She'd flown all the way from Kansas City to be there for this game, and to spend the night with him. Doubts, fears, and worries melted away. Coupled with their amazing win over the Sharks, his unexpected grand slam, and now, Kate—could life get any better?

When he set her down, he whispered, "I'm the luckiest guy on Earth."

She beamed up at him.

"You really flew all the way from Kansas City just for one day?"

"And one night," she snickered.

"Oh, hell, yeah."

A group of his teammates waved. "Coming, Jake?" Skip called. "We've got a celebration at the hotel. I had no idea you'd be here."

She waved her hand. "No problem. Can I come?"

"Of course! You don't mind?"

"We'll have all night."

Her sentence sent heat through him. He was beyond horny. "Maybe just one glass?"

"Of course. We have to celebrate!"

He took her hand and joined the others on the bus.

"No fair! Lawrence gets to have his girl here," Bobby Hernandez called out.

"You hit a grand slam, Bobby, and I'll get you a Playboy Bunny," Cal Crawley said.

The team cracked up. Everyone chattered away about the game. Jake held Kate's hand, listening to the guys while keeping his eyes on his girl. Something about her was different. Her hair style was new, shorter, kickier. He guessed it had something to do with her role in the show. Her face glowed, happiness radiated from the smile that never left to the shining of her eyes.

In an instant, he knew what it was. Success—she oozed success and confidence. Pride in her filled his heart and gratitude that such a talented, hot babe wanted to be with him. His gaze fastened on her breasts. His fingers twitched. God, he wanted to touch her, but he'd have to wait.

"Lawrence is too horny to rub his slammer in your face," Skip said.

Bobby glanced at the third baseman. "Damn right. I would be, too."

"Jealous?" Jake cocked an eyebrow, then leaned over to kiss Kate.

"Damn right!" Nat piped up.

It wasn't long before the bus pulled up in front of the hotel. They'd be flying out in the morning, so tonight, all hell would break loose. The men headed for the private room where champagne bottle after champagne bottle rested in tubs of ice. Platters of cheese and crackers dotted tables around the ballroom. A huge bowl of cold, fresh shrimp and a giant silver server of delectable pastries graced a round table in the middle of the room.

As fast as the servers poured glasses of the bubbly, the men polished them off. Jake kept his arm around Kate as if he let go, he was afraid she'd vanish. Her scent teased his nose. Remnants of the lilac perfume she wore tantalized him, sending signals to his groin. If he didn't get her upstairs soon, he'd develop a huge boner right in front of his teammates.

He joined in on the toasts, shook Cal's hand, hugged his buddies then steered his girl toward the door.

"We need to leave," he whispered in her ear.

"But the food is so good."

"If we don't leave now, I'm going to take you on the floor in front of everyone."

He chuckled as she blushed. "Oh, I see. Good reason to go." She plucked four mini eclairs from the tray and wrapped them in a napkin.

When they got to the lobby, he pushed the button for the elevator. His fingers pressed into her waist, rubbing against the silky material of her dress, while his other hand held her small overnight bag.

Impatience mixed with a growing desire, making time stand still. Or so Jake thought. Finally, it reached the fifth floor. They exited, and he moved them down the hall at a rapid clip. He jammed the keycard in the lock. When the little light turned green and buzzed, he rammed down the handle and flung the door open.

The room was comfortable but not sumptuous. Fortunately, the bed was a queen. He dumped her bag on a chair and faced her. Kate barely took off her jacket and put down her purse before she was in his arms.

His body burned. Ravenous for her, he closed his lips over hers. His kiss was demanding, hungry, and her response met his. They fairly ripped off their clothing, trying their damnedest to keep their lips locked.

Jake ripped down the covers.

"Condom," she panted, her chest heaving as she reached around to undo her bra.

"Thought you were on the pill?" He unzipped his pants.

"Stopped it. No reason to take it when I'm away from you for so long," she said, tossing her bra on the chair.

Jake's gaze clamped on her chest. He stopped, his mouth watered. He reached for her. "I've been missing those."

"And they've been missing you," she said, shooting him a smoldering stare.

While she was down to panties only, Jake still had his pants on, unzipped, but on. He shoved them down with his boxers and climbed on the bed. Kate joined him.

"Take those off," he demanded.

She peeled them down, slowly, watching his eyes.

"Temptress," he said, grinning.

"I like to torture you."

"I'll show you torture," he said, grabbing the delicate lingerie and ripping it from her body. Kate gave a squeak.

"I'll buy you new ones."

"I'll come commando, next time," she laughed.

"Oh, shit," he said, shaking his head. His slightly erect penis jumped to attention and hardened before his eyes as the image of her on the plane, commando, danced through his head.

She leaped onto the bed, bouncing toward him. He grabbed her waist and tucked her beside him. His fingers closed over her breasts and he groaned as he massaged her.

"That's sooo good," she cooed, closing her eyes.

He nudged her thighs apart with his knee and inched his way up until his leg pressed against her center, making her gasp.

He lowered his mouth to her breast, taking the peak into his mouth. His other hand, opened flat, glided up and down her side and stomach. The soft, silky feel of her skin aroused him almost as much as her nipple in his mouth. God, he'd dreamt about this and now it was happening. His dick was like a concrete pole.

When he raised his head, she captured his mouth.

"Do it. Do it. Oh, Jake, you're torturing me."

He pushed his leg against her harder. Kate raised one leg and hissed in his ear.

Jake broke from her and leaned over to the floor. Fiddling with his pants, he finally located his wallet and the condom he always carried inside.

"That your only one?" she asked.

"I wasn't planning on needing one. I always have one in my wallet. Old habit."

"Thank God!"

He applied it and faced her, wearing a shit-eating grin. "Now, where were we?"

She closed her fingers around his hardness as he plunged two into her.

"Crap. Jake. Let's do it."

He lay back on the bed and grasped her hips. Raising her up, he lowered her on his dick. She bent her legs, settling one on each side of him. As he entered her, desire flamed in his body.

Her eyes drifted shut as she moaned his name. Her palms flattened on his chest to steady her. He slid his up to her smooth shoulders, down her arms all the way to her wrists, then back up her thighs to her hips. God, her skin felt good! The texture and her scent ratcheted up his heat level until he feared he'd come before she did.

Kate balanced against his chest and pumped her hips up and down on him. He ground his teeth as his balls tightened, desperate to hold off.

"Oh, God, Jake! I'm gonna come," she said, a tremble jerking her torso.

"Do it. Do it, babe."

He felt her inner muscles clench around him briefly, then flutter against him. He watched her nipples harden and stand proud as her hips ground out their own rhythm.

Love and lust blended in his heart as his body took over. A powerful release gripped him, arching his back a bit as he held her firmly in place. He groaned, uttering her name and shutting his eyes. The power of the orgasm stole his breath. It had been a long time.

Panting, she dismounted and fell, limp beside him. He lay, breathless, by her side, staring at the ceiling, his hand feeling for hers. They laced fingers.

"Holy hell," he whispered when he could.

"Yeah."

"That was the most amazing..." they began together, then stopped to laugh.

She cozied up to him. He took the hint and scooped her into his embrace. The warmth of their skin-to-skin contact soothed his heart. He'd thought he'd known how much he had missed her, but he'd been wrong. He closed his eyes, committing every feeling, every touch to memory. Who knew how long those images would have to live with him until he had her in his arms, and his bed, again?

"I'm sorry, Jake," she muttered softly.

He drew her to his side and faced her. "Sorry? About what? You don't have a thing to be sorry about."

"I did this. I broke us apart. I miss you so much." Tears clouded her eyes.

"Baby, baby, baby," he said, hugging her to his chest. "Please. Don't apologize for your success. I think it's great. I'm so proud of you. We'll get through this. We have so far."

She kissed his pecs. "I know. But it's hard."

"Damn hard. But worth it."

"Is it?"

"It is for me. I don't want anyone but you. Don't you feel the same?"

She smiled, wiping at her eyes. "I do. Just didn't know how you felt."

"You're the one," he said, making eye contact.

He threw on sweats and made a quick trip to the lobby to buy more condoms. When he returned, they cuddled under the covers until sleep claimed them.

The couple awoke during the night and made love again. They slept until seven, then shared a sweet shower before room service arrived with breakfast. At nine, there was a knock on the door.

"Hey, buddy. Bus leaves in an hour."

"Thanks, Skip. I'll be there."

They dressed in silence. Ready early, Jake sat on a wing chair and beckoned Kate to his lap. She curled up under his chin, her fingers clasping his bicep. Sadness squeezed his heart.

"I know you can't be there for the series. Can I come see you, maybe travel with you on my own dime after it's over?"

"Of course! I'd love that. As for the series, I don't know. Let's wait and see."

"Okay."

One more knock and the lovers picked up their luggage and headed for the lobby. Kate rode on the bus with the team. Jake held her hand tight as if his grip could keep her from leaving. The men were quiet, subdued. Many were hung over after their celebration. The World Series wasn't scheduled to start for several days, so they had time to recuperate.

When they unloaded the men and luggage, Kate and Jake separated from the crowd for a more private farewell.

"I don't know when I'll see you again," she said, her gaze searching his.

"I love you, honey. It'll probably be sooner than you think."

"If the series goes for seven games..."

"And if we lose in four straight, then it'll be before you know it," he said.

"Don't say that!" She put her finger over his lips. "You'll win. You've got to."

"I hope so. Thank you so much for coming. Will you make it back in time?"

She checked her watch. "My flight leaves in half an hour. I should be fine."

They kissed as if it was the last time, then parted. One thing for certain, no other woman could take her place. He watched her walk away. She stopped at the door, turned and waved to him, then was gone. The hand of Cupid crushed his heart.

"Come on, Jake. Time to board," Cal said, shepherding one of his flock.

"Yeah, yeah. I'm coming." He turned to follow his manager. Back to business as usual. Baseball needed to occupy his mind and heart. He sighed as he sank into his seat. No magazine or book could divert his thoughts from Kate McKenzie.

"Come on, Jake. I haven't taken your money lately," Skip said, holding a pack of cards.

Jake waved him away.

"Don't be like that. Feeling sorry for yourself won't help."

"What do you know about it?" Jake cocked an eyebrow at his friend.

"Think you're the only one ever got his heart busted? Grow the fuck up. Come on. You owe me a couple a games."

Jake pushed up from his seat. "Don't think this means you're gonna win."

Skip chuckled. "Yeah. That's exactly what it means."

"Yeah? How much cash do you have on you?"

"Enough to take you on."

"Get your checkbook ready," Jake said, settling into a seat between Nat and Bobby.

Skip laughed. "You're kidding, right?"

"Deal, asshole. And shut the fuck up," Jake replied, ordering coffee from the stewardess.

Chapter Seventeen

Cal Crawley gave his men two days to get over their celebration before they had to report for practice for the World Series. Everyone was pumped. They were slated to play the San Francisco Pirates for the championship, serious business.

Matt Jackson ran base-stealing practice. The men took turns attempting to steal and then throwing out their teammates. Vic Steele, their trainer, ran the men through some rigorous exercises. Every morning they ran to warm up. Then they had sprints, to increase their speed. He even had them doing agility courses, so they wouldn't trip over their own feet while running bases or chasing after the ball.

At the end of each day, Jake fell into bed, exhausted, and asleep by nine. He didn't have much time to miss Kate. He'd talk to her during his morning break. Sneaking off to the parking lot, he indulged in a few sexually charged conversations with his honey.

"I know you're blushing," he teased.

"You can't be sure. You can't see me."

She laughed before signing off.

He focused his energy on his skills. When it was over, he had plans for Kate McKenzie, but he kept mum about it. No way could he confide in his teammates. There wasn't a good secret-keeper in the bunch. They shared everything and didn't see any reason not to. Fine, then. He'd keep his plans to himself.

Because San Francisco had a better record and clinched the playoffs in fewer games, the first two games of the series would be played there. Home team advantage was not to be sneered at. Jake wished they were starting off in New York. He loved the New York fans. A rowdy, profane, loyal bunch who stood behind the Nighthawks, win or lose.

After playing cards on the plane, some of his teammates went to sleep. Jake found a quiet corner and dialed Kate.

"How did Kansas City go?"

"Great! We got a terrific review in the Kansas City Star. They have booked the theater for an extra week and the show is sold out already."

"Wow, that's something. Did they mention you?"

"Yes," she paused. "Not to brag or anything, but they said my performance was the best they'd seen all year."

"Oh, honey, that's great. You're a star. A superstar!"

"I'll send you the link so you can read the whole review. The show is doing really well."

"What can I say? I'm not surprised."

"Thank you. There's some buzz about a movie, but it's probably just talk."

"A movie? Really?" His heart sank. A movie would take her farther away.

"Yeah, but I'm sure it's just gossip."

"Oh, okay. Bad enough you're traveling around the country. But a movie, well, hell. That would take you to the West Coast and keep you there." He wiped sweat from his forehead.

"Don't worry. It's just a rumor. When are you coming out?"

They discussed the schedule for the Series, and he promised to fly out after it was over. First two games in San Francisco, then back to New York for three games. If more were needed, they'd go back to San Francisco for the final one or two. The league had scheduled two days for travel since there were major time changes involved. Seven games stretched over ten days.

"Are you off in a corner? Can you talk?" she asked, her voice seductive.

"I guess. What did you have in mind?" A lusty grin spread across his face. He leaned back, resting his right hand behind his head, his phone in his left.

"A little striptease?"

"What are you wearing?"

"T-shirt and shorts."

"Underwear?"

"Yes."

"Where are you?"

"In my dressing room."

"How fast can you take it off and put it back on?" he asked.

"Wanna find out?"

"Yep. Can you send me a picture?"

"Better. I can do it live on video."

"Holy shit!"

Chet Candelaria snored softly in the seat facing him. Cupping his hands around the device, Jake held the phone so that no one else could see it. His cock twitched as he watched Kate hum a tune and slowly peel off her clothing. She wasn't wearing much and it didn't take long for her to be completely naked.

"Ta-da!" she said, throwing her arms wide, then closing her fingers on her hips and striking a sexy pose.

"Wow," Jake said, his mouth watering, blood pumping between his legs.

"Just don't want you to forget what's waiting for you when the series is over."

"Are you kidding?"

A tap on the door drew her attention. Jake laughed as she called out for the person on the other side of the door to wait and scooted into her clothes a hundred times faster than she took them off.

He watched as she let a man in.

"Parker Havens wants to see you," said a young man.

He left and Kate turned to the phone.

"Who was that?" Jake asked.

"Go-fer. The producer wants to see me. Hope it's not bad news." She chewed her lip.

"How could it be? You're a star!"

"Thanks, babe. Gotta go, sweetie. Love you."

"Thanks for the show. Love you, too," Jake replied. The screen went blank.

He did deep breathing to calm down his dick and return his body temperature to ninety-eight point six. Then he looked out the window. Although most of his teammates snoozed away, sleep eluded Jake. He missed Kate. The brief mention of the possibility of a movie made him squirm. He shifted in his seat.

Kate in a movie? Definitely possible. She sure had the looks and the talent to do it. He pressed his lips together. If she became a movie star, what would she want with him? Sure, he was a big man now. Slugger, home run hitter, vital to the Nighthawks, but what about five years from now. Okay, maybe ten? He'd be a washed-up ball player with no career, no status, nothing. Maybe he'd have some cash put away, but that's it. And Kate? Hell, she'd be breaking box office records year after year.

Guilt crept into his heart. How could he worry about himself when this might be the biggest break of her lifetime? How could he begrudge her going for the brass ring? If it was him? Hell, he'd do it in a heartbeat. Being on top mattered to Jake Lawrence. He worked his ass off to get there and was still working night and day to stay.

He had to be honest with himself. He could be magnanimous about her going on the road with the show, but becoming a movie star was a different deal. Nope, he couldn't be generous about that. Didn't he get a say about this stuff? He wanted her with him, even if what he had to offer couldn't compete with the entertainment world.

He looked up to see Cal Crawley slip into the empty seat beside him.

"How you doin', Jake?" The older man asked.

"I'm okay."

"You sure?"

"Yeah."

"We need you. These two games are crucial."

"I know. I'll be there, Cal."

"Focused? Thinking about baseball and only baseball?"

Jake shrugged. Hard to lie to his manager.

"Don't worry about her, son." Cal patted Jake's knee. "She'll be there when the season's over. She'll be waitin' for you."

"How do you know?" Jake couldn't help himself. He had to challenge Cal's easy words.

"'Cause I saw the look in her eye when she looked at you. That's a girl who's got her man. She'll be there. Trust me. I'm old. I know these things."

Jake had to smile. Cal's wisdom was famous in baseball. But what did he know about love?

"I hope you're right."

Cal stood up. "Focus, Jake. We gotta win here."

"I will. You can count on me."

Intimidated by the Pirates' record, the Nighthawks lost the first game by one run. Inspiring words from Cal and determination brought them a win in the second game. Then it was back to New York.

They split there, two games for New York and one for San Fran. The team bitched about having to fly back to the West Coast, but Cal simply shrugged.

"Hey, if you'd a won all three at home, we'd be out celebrating right now instead of sittin' on this damn plane."

The Pirates picked up the next game and now it was tied, three games apiece. The last game would clinch the series. Nerves were taut, tension crackled in the air, and the Nighthawks vowed to reach into their guts for every last ounce of energy and skill they could muster. Jake led them in a cheer as the bus ferried them from the posh hotel to Pirates' Stadium, one last time.

Kate was winging her way to Dallas. She and Jake had connected for one last conversation before he boarded the vehicle. Every seat at the ballpark was filled. As the final splash, Lucy Albright, the brand-new, number one country music singer, was there to do justice to the national anthem.

Single guys on the team drooled over her revealing dress, slit up the side and cut down to her navel, showing off a fine pair of "D's". Nat Owen nudged Skip Quincy when the singer came out on the field. She walked right by them, winked at Nat, and kept going to her mark.

Nat's face got red.

Jake leaned over. "Don't come on the field, Owen. Geez. Keep it in your pants, will ya?"

"That is one fine woman," the first baseman replied.

"Focus on the game, numb nuts," Bobby Hernandez hissed.

"I am, I am. But I got eyes, Bobby."

"Asshole," the second baseman mumbled.

"We're counting on you, Nat," Matt Jackson said.

Nat had been especially strong during the series. His batting average was up and his fielding near-perfect. His stretches at first had enabled him to get five men out who would have been safe had someone else been tending the base.

The roar of the crowd was deafening as Nat walked to home to start the game. Fans cheered so loud, Jake wondered if anyone could hear the calls at the plate. But after the Pirate released the first pitch, called a ball, they settled down.

The game was tense, no score on either side. What started as a pitchers' duel, was busted wide open in the top of the ninth when Jake hit a ground rule double, bringing home Bobby Hernandez who had walked his turn at bat, then stole second. The slugger glanced at his manager, who nodded. The third baseman was disappointed he hadn't hit a homer. The break-through started things. Matt Jackson brought him home on a long ball to the right field corner that dropped before the fielder could get to it.

Chet Candelaria beat out a dribbler to the shortstop. Matt was held to second base. The Pirates' pitcher struck out the next two batters. With two men on and two out, Jake wondered how they were going to bring them home. It was the pitcher's turn at bat. Jake cringed. Dan Alexander, the Nighthawks' pitcher, couldn't get a hit if his life depended on it.

Matt was on second. Dan begged the manager for a chance to bat. A pitcher who wants to take a swing? That wasn't the norm. Jake sidled over to listen in on their conversation.

"Please, Cal. I know I can do it. Matt and I have been working on my bunt. I know I can move him to third. Give me a chance."

With two men out on the disabled list, Jake wondered what choice Cal had. In most games, he'd have pulled Dan at the end of the seventh. But this was the last game of the year, any way you sliced it. Nothing to save Dan's arm for until Spring Training in March.

"Please. I'm begging you," Dan pleaded.

Jake expected the ace pitcher to go down on his knees at any moment. With two outs, Dan couldn't settle for a sacrifice, he had to make the bunt work and get safely to first base.

"Okay, okay. Just don't fuck it up." Cal shook his head but motioned Dan to the plate.

Jake shot a look at Matt, who was smiling and making the thumbs up sign. Dan raised his hand. The fans went berserk to see the pitcher coming to the plate with the 'Hawks two runs ahead and two men on base. Jake shuddered. The double-play possibilities were huge. He crossed his fingers and held his breath.

Nat, Bobby, and Skip came up beside him.

"If he pulls this fuckin' miracle off, you're next, Nat," Skip said.

"He'll never make it," Nat replied.

"Don't be so sure," Jake put in.

The Nighthawks were on their feet in the dug-out. Jake and his buddies stood at the edge, riveted. The slugger watched Dan's mouth tighten, his lips compressed into a fine line in response to the smug look on the pitcher's face. Matt was reading the signals the Pirate catcher was sending. The Nighthawks' men had practiced just this scenario. Jake had seen it and marveled at how well it had worked.

Matt simply nodded for *swing* and shook his head once for *take*. Sure enough, the first pitch was a pitchout. Dan took all the way and Chet and Matt hugged their bases. Ball one.

After another ball, then a strike, Matt nodded. Jake tensed. There it was, right down the middle. Dan squared off and laid down the perfect bunt. He took off like his butt was on fire, heading for first base. The ball dribbled along the third base line. The catcher followed it, waiting for it to roll foul, but it never did. By the time it stopped, Dan was safe on first.

Matt had slid into third and Chet hit second. The Nighthawks went nuts in the dugout dancing around and screaming. The crowd was on its feet. And Dan Alexander grinned from ear-to-ear. Cal Crawley shook his head and laughed.

Nat Owen came up to bat.

"You can do it!" Jake shouted. He, Bobby, and Skip stood waiting. Sweat dribbled down Jake's face. He knew exactly how Nat felt. Two out, bases loaded, top of the ninth, last game in the World Series. Hell, was there ever a situation with more pressure than this? He doubted it.

Nat wasn't known as a long ball hitter. Even a single would bring home Matt, increasing their lead to three zip. But that wasn't enough to guarantee a win. Nothing was. Jake knew that in situations like this, men often became superhuman, pulling out skills they didn't even know they had. He shut his eyes and muttered a prayer.

"Nat can do it," Skip said, nodding.

"He has to do it," Jake agreed.

Their teammates stood at the entrance, some paced. Most held their breath. The first pitch. A strike! Skip let out a breath.

"Shit," Bobby said.

Jake raised his palm. "Give him a chance."

Second pitch, a ball. Jake let out the air he'd been holding. Tension thickened the air, Cal paced. Skip and Jake moved up to the stairs. Sweat poured off Jake's neck and down his chest.

The 'Hawks expected Nat to be taking the next pitch. Suddenly, his bat cut through the air and connected. With a loud crack, it soared far and fast. It wasn't too high. The players gasped as the center fielder raced to the warning track and made an amazing leap, almost connecting with the fly. Jake held his breath. The ball barely grazed the top of the man's glove. The tip had the opposite effect than the Pirate wanted. The ball went straight up in the air, two feet, but still traveled fast, and landed in the stands. Holy Hell, Nat Owen had hit a grand slam homerun!

Matt, Bobby, and Dan waited at home plate, high-fiving and chest-bumping each other while a stunned Nat Owen ran the bases. When he reached home plate, the entire team poured out of the dugout to mob their first baseman.

The umpire signaled for the men to clear the area. Bobby Hernandez was up next. He popped up to the third baseman, and the Pirates came to bat.

Dan Alexander was still pitching. Pumped up by his amazing bunt single, he appeared energized, not tired. He struck out the first batter. The crowd tensed. Two outs away from winning the World Series.

Jake's mouth got dry. He pulled his cap up to improve his vision, crouched, and put his weight on the balls of his feet. He needed to be ready for anything. The wind-up. The pitch and blam! A line drive right shot right at the first baseman. But there was Nat, his glove almost smoking from catching that powerful hit. Two down. The fans grew restless.

The windup. The pitch. Dan walked the next batter. Bobby, Skip, and Jake were on high alert now. They needed to get this guy out. The next pitch was hit. The ball aimed toward third. It took a funny hop, heading right for Jake. He jumped a foot in the air and caught the ball on the bounce. In mid-air, he twisted and rifled the ball to Skip, who was covering second.

Boom! Out number three! The Nighthawks' had won the World Series! The team mobbed Dan Alexander, the circle of men leaping and yelling, expanded like a balloon filling with air. News media hovered around Nat Owen. He was the obvious choice for most valuable player in the series.

Lucy Albright, who had stayed for the game, sauntered over to Nat. She gave him a huge hug and kiss, to the clicking of the cameras. She mugged for the news media, draped all over Nat. He grinned but didn't speak.

Jake chuckled and shook his head as he watched his friend stare at Lucy's cleavage, then at her face. *Poor Nat. Doesn't know what to do.* After all, she was a big star and Nat was simply a little guy from a small town, who happened to be an excellent baseball player.

Twenty minutes later, Nat returned to the locker room. He opened his hand to reveal a crumpled business card.

"Lucy Albright gave me her card. She told me to call her," he said, a note of wonder in his voice.

The men laughed. "You scored in more ways than one today," Bobby said.

"Let me see that," Chet said.

"Over my dead body," Nat said, chesting the card.

Jake was first out of the shower. He couldn't wait to call Kate. When he nabbed his cell from the shelf in his locker, he found there were three calls from her already. He grinned. Not a selfish bone in her body. Hmm, her body. The grin widened. Soon he'd be joining her, traveling with her on the road for month.

Jake needed the rest and figured what better way than to tag along with Kate? Although the idea of a new hotel every week turned him off, being with her would make up for it. And it was time to put forth his agenda.

He joined the team for a big celebration at Freddie's, on the Nighthawks. Champagne flowed, steaks, chops, and grilled chicken filled the buffet table. The bar and grill was closed to the public for this once-in-a-lifetime party.

Jake sat with his buddies as they recounted the game. Dan and Matt talked about their coup getting Dan on base. Cal congratulated each team member. The men demanded a speech from shy Nat Owen.

Lucy Albright showed up at the party. Nat, with two glasses too many in him, asked her out in front of everyone, and she accepted. The men cheered, then settled down and let her sing a song to Nat.

Seeing her at the piano made Jake nostalgic for the days when Kate used to play and sing. Loneliness separated him from the crowd. He hugged his teammates then hailed a cab back to his apartment. Hell, he needed a good night's sleep.

After the ticker-tape parade the mayor of New York City had arranged to take place in a week, Jake would wing his way to his girl and a few nights in Dallas.

Before he turned out the light, he checked his phone. There was a text message on it from Kate. She was performing at that time, so he couldn't call her back.

Can't wait to see you next week. I have a big surprise!

Jake frowned. Was she going to do the movie? What could her big surprise be? It surely couldn't be anything as big as the surprise he had cooked up for her. He tucked the covers around his chest and closed his eyes. Today had been the biggest day of his life. But he had a hunch that here might be an even bigger day in store for him real soon.

Epilogue

He didn't expect her to be at the airport, but there she was. Wearing glamorous sunglasses and a sexy little pink sundress, there she stood, waving at him. He had been stopped for autographs by several people at the baggage claim. People wanted to chat with him about the game as they awaited their luggage.

He only wanted to be with Kate. He scooped her up into a bear hug and twirled her around. She laughed into his neck, tickling him, her arms fastened around him. God, it felt good to have her up against him.

"Let's go someplace," he said.

"My hotel room?" she suggested.

He shot her a salacious grin. "I thought you'd never ask."

A taxi took them into town. They kissed and whispered in the back seat the entire way. Once she closed the door behind them, Jake grabbed her. His hunger for her took over and he stripped her bare in seconds. Then he shed his own clothing.

Finesse went out the window as need ruled his body. He took her quickly and passionately. When they had exhausted their desire, they lay, propped up in bed, each sucking down a bottle of water. Dreading her answer, he knew he had to ask the question.

"Okay, so what's your surprise?" He took a breath to calm down.

"The surprise? Oh my God. You're gonna love this. At least I think you are," she said, casting a skeptical glance his way.

"Shoot." He wiped the sweat from his forehead with a tissue.

"So I told you about the movie thing, right?" She faced him.

He nodded, an ache forming in the pit of his stomach.

"You'll never guess what happened."

"The suspense is killing me."

"Okay, okay. So, yes, they've decided to do a movie version of the show."

His stomach dropped.

"They asked Ella, the woman starring in the show on Broadway. The one who originated the role. Right? They thought it would make the movie stronger to have the original star in it. Everyone wants to see the original star, right? So they offered it to her."

"And she turned it down?" His mouth got dry.

"She accepted!"

He shot her a quizzical look.

"This is the great part. When she accepted, they offered me her role on Broadway!"

"What?"

"Yeah! They're gonna put her understudy in my place in the road show. They said I have more experience in front of an audience."

"Oh my God. Really?" His heartbeat doubled. "This means you're coming back to New York?" He was afraid to believe his ears.

"YES! Yes, yes, yes, and yes! We can be together."

His prayers had been answered. She wasn't going to Hollywood. She was coming back to New York. And she'd be a big Broadway star. It was a win/win. How did he get so lucky?

"That's wonderful. I never thought. I mean. The movie and all. I thought you'd never come back," he said, stuttering, emotion choking him, tears burning his eyes.

"Oh, Jake! Did you think I'd leave you?"

He nodded.

"I'd never leave you, babe. Never."

After several deep breaths, he got his voice back. "And I have a surprise for you."

"Goody. I love surprises. Nice surprises."

He got out of bed and rifled around in his suitcase.

"It's time to make you my leading lady, officially, and for a very long run."

He opened a black velvet box and flashed a ten-carat marquis-cut diamond ring. Her eyes doubled in size.

"Oh my God! Jake! I never expected this."

"You will, won't you?"

"Of course! You know I will."

"Good. For a minute there…"

"Hadn't we already done this?"

"Not with the ring. It makes it official. Real. That it's going to happen."

"I love you so much," she said, moving closer.

He slipped the ring on her finger. She stared at it, then kissed him. "It's beautiful!"

"Nothing's too good for my wife. Geez. God, that sounds great." He touched her face.

He ordered champagne and chocolate covered strawberries. They ate and drank in bed. Jake flipped on the television. There was still news about the Nighthawks win.

All of a sudden, the picture switched to the ticker-tape parade. Jake had been busy with his team, waving to fans. He didn't see that the cameras focused on Lucy Albright, hanging all over Nat Owen. Nat had grinned like a ten-year-old locked in a candy store overnight. Then she planted a big one on his lips. In answer to a newswoman's question, Lucy piped up,

"Yeah. Nat Owen and I are dating. Takes a winner to know a winner."

Jake choked on a berry. Kate pounded him on the back.

"Turn up the sound!" he commanded. "That's Nat. Nat Owen! Dating Lucy Albright?"

His cell rang. It was Bobby Hernandez. "Did you see Nat on TV?"

"What the fuck is he doing?" Jake asked.

"Guess you did see it," Bobby chuckled.

"Yeah. What's going on?"

"Nat's stepping up. What a pair, MVP in baseball and MVP in country music," Bobby said.

"I guess he knows what he's doing," Jake replied. "What about Dusty's teammate, Nicki? I thought he had something going with her?"

"Hey, which one would you choose?" Bobby asked.

"Are you kidding? Albright'll eat him alive," Jake replied.

"Gotta go. Skip's on call waiting."

Jake stared at the screen. Kate cocked an eyebrow at him. "Is there a problem?"

"It's my teammate, Nat Owen. Either he's made the biggest match of his life or the biggest mistake." Jake shook his head, his eyebrows knitted.

THE END

About the Author

Jean Joachim is a best-selling romance fiction author, with books hitting the Amazon Top 100 list since 2012. She writes contemporary romance, which includes sports romance and romantic suspense.

Dangerous Love Lost & Found, First Place winner in the 2015 Oklahoma Romance Writers of America, International Digital Award contest. *The Renovated Heart* won Best Novel of the Year from Love Romances Café. *Lovers & Liars* was a RomCon finalist in 2013. And *The Marriage List* tied for third place as Best Contemporary Romance from the Gulf Coast RWA.

To Love or Not to Love tied for second place in the 2014 New England Chapter of Romance Writers of America Reader's Choice contest.

She was chosen Author of the Year in 2012 by the New York City chapter of RWA.

Married and the mother of two sons, Jean lives in New York City. Early in the morning, you'll find her at her computer, writing, with a cup of tea, and a secret stash of black licorice.

Jean has 30+ books, novellas and short stories published.

Sign up for her newsletter, on her website, and be eligible for her private paperback sales. Sign up for her newsletter on her Facebook page: Jean Joachim, Author

Watch for NAT OWEN, First Base – Bottom of the Ninth, book 4 – coming soon!

Made in the USA
Lexington, KY
16 February 2017